Ka_____ _____bestselling, multi___-award
contemporary fiction. Her work has won numerous awards,
including the Indie Excellence Award and Reader's Choice Award.

She lives in Southern California with her family and you can
connect with her on Facebook at Kaira Rouda Books, and on
Twitter, Pinterest and Instagram: @kairarouda.

For more, visit Kaira's website, www.kairarouda.com.

Also by Kaira Rouda

Best Day Ever

Favourite Daughter

Kaira Rouda

ONE PLACE. MANY STORIES

HQ
An imprint of HarperCollins*Publishers* Ltd
1 London Bridge Street
London SE1 9GF

This edition 2019

1
First published in Great Britain by
HQ, an imprint of HarperCollins*Publishers* Ltd 2019

ISBN: 978-1-84845-692-1

To my perfectly imperfect family.

And especially to my favorites: Trace, Avery, Shea and Dylan.

I love you all so much!

Nature, the gentlest mother,
Impatient of no child,
The feeblest or the waywardest—
Her admonition mild

Emily Dickinson, 1893

SUNDAY

FOUR DAYS UNTIL GRADUATION

1

6:30 p.m.

I glance at my creation and smile: behold the dining room table. It is critical to create the proper atmosphere when entertaining, the illusion of perfection. As one of the most important hostesses in The Cove, I can assure you I pull together elegant dinners without a second thought. I know all the key ingredients: arrangements from the best florist in town, tonight white hydrangeas nestled in between succulents, and linens from the exclusive small boutique where everyone must shop to purchase ridiculously expensive tablecloths and napkins, in this case, brushed silk, off-white.

I've outdone myself with this table. This will go down in the record books as a crowning achievement in my life.

I'm kidding, of course. I don't care a smidgen about entertaining. And typically, if I'm going to spend time adorning something, it's going to be myself. Truth be told, the crystal and china pieces on the table were wedding gifts from long-forgotten friends, rarely used. I dug them out from the back of the cupboard. Perhaps I am trying a bit too hard, but tonight is special. It's my coming-out party, so to speak.

After a year of grieving, it's time to step back into my family, or what remains of it, and that's precisely my plan. I'm reclaiming the throne, like a queen who has been in exile but returns with pomp and circumstance. I shake my head as I look around my castle. I used to be so proud of this home, something so expensive and so uppity that my mother would never be comfortable stepping foot inside. Good old Mom. She taught me everything she knew about how to put yourself first in life. She was ruthless, delighting in bringing others down, including her own daughter. But look around: I'm winning, Mom. I touch the diamond-encrusted heart pendant hanging between my surgically enhanced, perfect breasts. All gifts from my husband in happier times.

My husband, David, will be so surprised when he arrives home tonight, and he deserves it. He's been full of surprises this year. In fact, I discovered another little secret when a piece of mail arrived at our house last week. Typically, he has his mail sent to his office, says it's easier to pay bills that way. This particular notice from the bank must have just slipped through the cracks. I'm playing along. For now.

The letter congratulated David on the purchase of a new home. I must admit, the thought of a fresh start made my heart flutter. I know it will be even bigger, more expensive than this home. I mean, this home was fine when the kids were growing up, but now we need something grander. More fitting of our station in life. We deserve it after all we've been through.

Maybe he'll tell me all about it tonight? That would be wonderful. I'm planning our reconnection dinner and he will announce his surprise. I glance at my platinum watch, enjoying the sparkles of the diamond-encrusted face, until my heart thumps at the time. It's getting late and I have so much more to do. I can't believe I've lost a year in my haze of grief. Sure, some of the haze can be blamed on all of the antidepressants the doctors made me take. They were both a relief and a distraction. While I was stuck in bed, at home, my family members have made the most of their time, both so busy, in fact, I've had trouble keeping up.

But not any longer. I'm back, drug-free, and better than ever. I grab the final crystal wineglass from the kitchen counter and walk to the table, glancing out the window as the bright orange sun drops into the deep blue Pacific Ocean. In an instant, the glass topples from my hand and seems to tumble in slow motion as it falls and shatters on the stone floor, sending sound waves echoing through our lifeless house like an earthquake. Shards of glass sprinkle the tops of my bare feet and dot the floor around me while a large chunk of the stem rests under the dining room table, glistening like the blade of a knife.

I fold my arms across my chest for comfort and can't help but admire my ribs poking into my hands, a reminder of how much weight I've lost the last year. Grief is good for the figure. You and I already know thin women get attention, respect in our society. On the few excursions I've made out of the house lately, when I've taken care to dress and apply makeup, I've noticed an uptick in appreciative glances from men. That's nothing new. My whole life I've enjoyed the admiration of the opposite sex.

For months, I've been secretly working out in the garage when David is at work and Betsy at school. Just me and the handsome P90X instructors. My mom would be impressed by my fitness commitment. She never missed a chance to remind me being skinny was the key to our future. And then she'd take my dinner away. She's long gone, died when I was fourteen in a tragic car accident, but she still haunts me. That's the power of the bond between mothers and daughters. It can never be broken, even in death.

But glass can. I stare at my almost-perfect table setting—I even nestled votive candles in crystal holders around the centerpiece and in front of each place setting. Just call me Martha Stewart.

I wonder what I should wear tonight? Here, in the land of expensive designer purses and shoes, most women blend in, their monochromatic coolness anchored by jeans, topped by their perfectly smooth, porcelain faces. I remember my first dinner party at The Cove: me from the South, them from Southern California. I'd worn a yellow silk cocktail dress, my biggest pearls and wrapped a white cashmere pashmina around my shoulders. I was as out of place as a Twinkie at a Weight Watchers meeting. But you know what? All the husbands approved, tired of the sameness they endured in their wives. Back then, David was proud to have me on his arm, proud I stood out like a beautiful flower in a meadow of boring grass. It's ironic, really: I gave up my dreams to move here, to become the perfect Orange County housewife. I could have been so much more.

This ocean view is why we bought this home all those years ago, scraping together every last dime and tapping into David's trust fund to move into The Cove, the best community in Southern California. We were young parents, and so madly in love. The ocean was romantic, beautiful then. Not deadly and dark and cold.

I feel the rush of heat as my hands clench into fists. Anger and loss, did you ever notice how those emotions mix together? It's a toxic combination. I swallow. I need to focus on the table, the first step of my coming-out party. All that's missing from this perfect setting is the fourth wineglass. I have another one, of course. It's almost symbolic. It was Mary's spot at the table, Mary's wineglass that fell to the floor.

Mary who dropped into the sea. I shake my head to quiet the voice.

My therapist, Dr. Rosenthal, assured me at our last session that it would be a step forward to eat together as a family in the dining room. She wants us to reconnect, and I most always do whatever she says. At our next session I'll happily tell the doctor all about tonight. I am committed to reenergizing my life, reconnecting with my family. I tell her what I want her to know, what she wants to hear. Sure, she's the one with the PhD, but I'm the one with life experience. I'm the heart of this family. That's a mom's place.

Perhaps I won't mention the broken glass during our session, although it is emblematic of all that has happened this year since Mary left us. Nothing is right. My husband has thrown his energy into work, he tells me. He's gone all the time these days. Betsy is focused on graduating high school in four short days. I swallow. I push away the silly fear, the nagging sound of my mom's voice telling me Betsy will leave me. It's nonsense. Betsy loves me, would never leave me. I mean, it's not like she's brilliant like Mary was, or smart like Mary was. No, Betsy is average. She'll be dependent on me forever, and that's just fine. And David, well, he's buying us a new home. Everyone is getting in line.

The hair at the back of my neck tingles on alert. Someone is watching me. I look out the window and see the five-year-old cherub next door, his round face pushing through a partially open window, his eyes bright and curious. He's up too high. He must have climbed onto a chair. Where is the nanny? Twenty children under the age of eleven die each year because of falls from windows, and another five thousand are critically injured.

Tragic accidents happen all the time. That's why I watched my daughters every moment of their lives, never letting them out of my sight, one way or another, ever.

They were like extensions of my arms, a hand for each of them. My little mini-mes.

I glance at the boy next door and then to the ground two stories below. There is nothing to break his fall if he topples out, just a thin strip of cement between his house and ours. I shudder at the thought. We pay astronomical prices to live on top of each other at the coast. Proximity and privilege means it's hard to keep secrets here. Turns out it's also hard to keep friends, and family.

The child is waving at me. I try to help him, pointing and mouthing the word *down* like I'm commanding a dog. I know all of the tragic things that can happen to him. Children who land on a hard surface, such as concrete, are twice as likely to suffer head injuries.

I can't witness this tragedy. Glass or no glass, I tiptoe away from the table, waiting for the sharp sensation of a shard slicing through my foot. I'm almost out of the mine-field of glass when I realize I have company.

"What are you doing?" Enter stage right: my handsome husband, David, thick brown hair, blue eyes, dimpled—a model WASP—is in the kitchen and assessing the scene. He could have been an actor, he's perfectly typecast as the successful businessman, 1950s to today.

"I made a mess of things," I say before covering my face with my hands. I can't resist leaving a small space between my fingers to peek at him. His smile fades as he drops his briefcase on the kitchen counter. Poor dear.

"Is that broken glass on the dining room floor?"

"Dropped a glass. An accident." I mumble my response from behind my hands.

"Are you hurt?" He takes a few steps, shoes crunching on glass, and he's beside me.

"I think I'm fine, but can you call the people next door?" I drop my hands from my face and point out the window.

"The Johnsons?"

"Yes, their child is about to die."

I watch David push his thick dark hair off his forehead, a nervous habit he's acquired in the past year. "What? Stop talking like that. It's creepy."

I sort of scare him these days. I'm not sure why exactly. Perhaps it is my seemingly unshakable grief? Is he afraid it will envelop him, too?

He steps closer and looks out the window. I do, too. The child has disappeared, hopefully safe in his nanny's arms. Or he's died from the fall. My mind jumps to terrible conclusions these days, but unfortunately, my mind is often correct. Feminine intuition, you really can't beat it. Mine is superbly tuned.

"There's no one there, Jane."

"I can see that. He *was* there just a minute ago." I hate it when he doesn't believe me and it's been happening more and more these days. I don't like it. That's one of the reasons I stopped taking the pills. I mean, your husband should love you and worship the ground you walk on. He doesn't just now, I know, but he will again. I'm back. He'll see. I take a deep breath. I need to make my husband treasure me again. I will provide him with that opportunity starting tonight. He has been avoiding me. Like I carry a disease. I'm not contagious. Of course, there are other things holding his interest these days. He thinks I don't know about that. Silly man. I force a smile to my lips, blink my eyes.

"Are you hurt?" Now he attempts kindness. What's the old saying: a day late and a dollar short?

"Don't think so." I shrug as he takes my hand. As we touch I wish it was electric like in the long-ago days, but it's not. Of course, all relationships change over time, and we've been married for more than two decades. Back in the early days, that first year together, he would have scooped me into his arms and carried me to a chair. Now that we're a longtime married couple, he escorts me old-lady style to the kitchen and pulls out a bar stool. I slide onto the cold, hard wooden seat.

David checks my feet for glass while I stare at the top of his head. He's blessed with thick dark brown hair, without a streak of gray. Mary had the same glorious mane of hair. In fact, Mary looks a lot like David, despite the fact she was adopted. Isn't that funny? Two daughters, one who looks just like my husband, the other, Betsy, our biological daughter, who looks like a watered-down version of me. Perfect, isn't it?

"You're not cut. I'll sweep up the glass. Why don't you go put socks on? Your feet are freezing."

I slide off the bar stool. "Thanks for coming to my rescue, handsome." I bat my eyes at him and slowly lick my bottom lip. I should win a domestic Golden Globe. Oh, come on. You know as well as I do that men love to be flattered. David's no exception. Tell a man he's handsome, smart, strong or, the doozy, the best you've ever had in bed, and, well, they'll love you at least in that moment. I just need to win him back, make him love me again. And I know I can do it. He loved me once, and deep down, he still does. For now, I'll just kill him with kindness. It's the Southern belle in me. You catch more flies with honey than with vinegar.

See. David flashes a smile, a crack in the armor, pats my shoulder. I used to have him so well trained. Husbands. You let up just a little and they regress. And then he's back to business. "Are you sure you're all right? You're not overdoing it, are you?"

"I love this, this entertaining, you know that." I never did, actually, and I'm not fine. I'm angry, but I smile. I glance at David, my eyes taking in his cool demeanor, his practiced professional air. We speak in a stilted language now, tiptoeing around each other like we're both surrounded by broken glass. This year has been hard on our marriage in so many different ways. I'm committed to fixing things, to getting us back on track. I know this happens in every relationship. We're just in a down cycle. I'm sure you've been there, too. I'm afraid we're running out of time. Betsy will graduate soon. She needs to see us, her parents, in love. All kids want is happy parents. While she's at community college going to class, she should imagine us here, at home, waiting to share dinner together each evening, a model of marital bliss.

I hope we can present a united front for her this week. It's always best to hang on to the one you know, at least until you find something better, that's what my mom told me. And we were so good together, David and I. Meant to be.

"You set the table for four. That's just creepy. Are you trying to upset us?" he asks, his voice thick with emotion. Is it anger, too? I don't know.

"No, I'm trying to have a family dinner. Dr. Rosenthal told me to. I'm sorry, I must have made a mistake. Subconscious. I miss her so much." I look out the window. It's safe now because it's dark outside and the ocean is invisible. All I see is my reflection. Tight, formfitting white T-shirt, sparkling heart. I do look good.

"How do you make that kind of mistake? Really, Jane?" David's shaking his head. I need to woo him, not disappoint him, and I should try to refrain from spooking him.

Focus, Jane.

"I'm sorry. I didn't mean to, darling." I dig my fingernails into the palm of my right hand and smile at my husband. David's watching me admire my reflection. What does he think when he sees me? He can't deny that I'm beautiful, but I know he doesn't see me with the same loving thoughts of the past, that much I know is true. We all change, especially in the face of unimaginable tragedy like we've been through. It's understandable. That's why I'm giving him one last chance. Starting tonight.

I turn to face him and take a step closer. He crosses his arms in front of his chest, tilts his head. His jaw is clenched, eyes dark. He thinks he's a tough guy. I take another step toward him and he backs away. Ha!

I smile and ask, "Let's start over. This is a special night. Darling, do you know when Betsy will be home?

She knows how important tonight is to me." Truth be told, I'm not sure I told her about our dinner. But she's a senior in high school, she still lives in my home. She should be home for family dinner. This is part of my plan to do everything I can to make this graduation week extra special, for both David and Betsy. I hope Betsy knows that even though Mary is gone, we are still a family. None of this is easy, it never has been. I mean, it's hardest for me trying to be so selfless, the perfect wife and the perfect mother. I spoiled the girls, of course. Sometimes when you give them everything, they take you for granted. My mom warned me about that, too.

David bites his lip, another new habit. It's not really a good look for him—it shows doubt, weakness, condescension. I hate that.

David says, "Betsy has art class tonight. It's every Sunday night, has been for a year." He says the words sharply, and with a big exhalation, as if he's had to say them every week to me. As if I'm an idiot. He hasn't. I'm not.

"Right, I forgot." It's hard to keep her schedule straight, especially when time shifts and moves with those pills. Don't worry. I'm not taking them anymore, like I told you, it's just that lately Betsy is acting more like her father. She's hardly ever home, and has one excuse after another. Besides, David should remember that Dr. Rosenthal explained to him that grief, like many other strong emotions, makes it hard to think straight. I've read a lot about the grieving process. I am a textbook case of complicated grief. I know, I've researched it.

Betsy only has ordinary grief, of course. Betsy's grief

has made her tense, angry. She's focused on school, making sure she graduates. She's hired her own tutor, and actually seems to care about grades for the first time in her life. She hasn't even spent much time with her boyfriend, Josh, which is fine with me. He's a bit of a loser, not the kind of boy we'd choose for our little girl, but he's the type Betsy attracts. Poor thing.

Before I can leave the kitchen to retrieve my socks, David says, "Did you actually make dinner? There's nothing cooked. I don't think you even told me you were doing this." His hand sweeps over to the table, to include the broken glass, and captures the stovetop devoid of dishes and meal prep, the counters pristinely clean.

"Oh, darling, of course I told you about tonight. I didn't want to overdo it, so I ordered in, from Salerno's, your favorite. Delivery arrives in half an hour. Pasta Bolognese just for you. Hope you're hungry." I smile. I've thought of everything. I'm back. "If it's just the two of us for dinner it will be so romantic. I hear Italian food is made for lovers." Before I turn away I watch David's face flush, his cheeks a rosy pink. He recognizes the phrase, and the restaurant, of course.

I walk away before he can respond. Perhaps I will slip into a sexy dress for our date, because just maybe, tonight, he'll decide to do the right thing. I know he loves me. We were such a good team. He remembers those days, too. I know he does. We just need a fresh start.

I head toward our bedroom, walking past the front door and glancing out into our courtyard lit with white twinkle lights, the fronds of our twin palm trees rustling in the gentle breeze. I stop and scan the outdoor space. I like to try to be ready for anything now, to be one step ahead and to avoid being startled or surprised. I learned that from my childhood. My mom was full of awful surprises. For a moment I see her standing in the courtyard, a ghost from my distant past. I shake my head. *Stop it. These thoughts aren't productive.* That's Mary's voice, or perhaps it is Dr. Rosenthal's? They sound similar these days. *You're safe. Your mom is gone.*

I hurry to my bedroom, reminding myself it is possible to be scared to death. Not the outcome I'm looking for in life. A scare floods your body with adrenaline, makes your heart pump faster. If you have an underlying heart problem, fright can induce sudden cardiac death. I've become a bit fixated with tragic death, so I apologize in advance. Remember, knowledge is power. I have a lot of tragic knowledge to share.

Mary's tragic death shook us all, of course. My beautiful daughter Mary, how I miss her. I'll never be able to curl her shiny dark hair, laugh with her about the lavish wedding we'd plan together one day, revel in her constant achievements, guide her choices as she prepared for her future. There is no future now, not for her. But I can focus on David and Betsy. I've been watching over them, but not engaging with them. That changes tonight. At dinner.

I'm reenergized. Truth be told, I'm a bit more awake these days than I should be, and that makes me a little on edge, a little temperamental. You understand, of course, after all I've been through. But still, I need to watch it, practice the breathing exercises Dr. Rosenthal taught me.

I take a deep cleansing breath, and exhale some of the tension of the day. I imagine my frustrations flowing from me like a fast-running river, just like Dr. Rosenthal tells me to do. I don't tell her about the dam. I'm sure my flowing river thoughts will return soon, right? I mean, breath work is the key to health, that's what these yoga people keep saying and what Dr. Rosenthal repeats on her relaxation podcasts. They really don't work, but I'm not going to be the one to tell her that.

I trudge into my bathroom and through to the walk-in closet. I look at the section of cocktail dresses, but with the chill in the air I decide to grab warm socks and a cozy gray cashmere sweater. It's brisk here at the beach once the sun sets, even in the middle of summer. Evenings in May, like tonight, always hold an extra special chill.

I glance at the cluster of picture frames on the counter next to my sink. Mary on the day we adopted her, swaddled in a soft pink blanket. Mary at age ten throwing her arms around our new labradoodle puppy, Cash. I pick up the last frame. In the photo taken a year and a half ago, Mary's grinning, so excited to be pledging the sorority of her dreams. She wears a white cocktail dress and holds a huge bouquet of red roses her dad hand-delivered to her— without me since I had to stay home with Betsy—during one of his now-frequent business trips to Los Angeles.

Mary's happiness her freshman year in college was almost too big to contain in a photo, too grand for a picture frame. Boundless potential and limitless opportunity once she left home, left me, for a new life and flowers from her dad. She was so excited to be miles away from me, my rules, my one line in the sand. I shake my head, glance at my reflection in the mirror.

Betsy is different. Although she shows all the outward signs of teenage rebellion, she's really a good, obedient daughter. My new favorite, I suppose. Mary promised me she'd be back after freshman year, of course, but she never really was. It was so hard for me when we moved her into her dorm room and then had to drive away. It was like cutting off my right hand. It was hard for David, too. He was vulnerable, missing his eldest, even though Betsy and I were still here. Are still here.

"I loved you, Mary."

"Who are you talking to?" David materializes behind me. He thinks he sneaked up on me but I heard him coming. I see the judgment in his dark blue eyes as he shakes his head.

"Nobody." We lock eyes. He looks at the photo in my hands and I know he thinks I'm talking to myself. Another "creepy" habit of mine, as he says. I place the photo back where it belongs.

He's changing in the closet. I hear a swish as he tugs off his tie and know he's hanging it neatly next to the rest of his collection. Next he'll open the drawer to find a casual shirt. He reappears in jeans and a white T-shirt, dark brown Gucci loafers. He's brushing his teeth. We make eye contact in the mirror. Sometimes he knows I'm watching him. Most of the time he doesn't. I wonder if he has decided to stay with me for dinner? Perhaps I should have changed into a dress? I still can. I smile. "I'm looking forward to our romantic dinner."

"Did you sleep well last night?" He spits in the sink, ignoring my statement.

I check my face in the mirror and decide I don't look too sleep deprived. I doubt he notices the circles under my eyes. I'm an expert with concealer. Tomorrow, I'll look even better. It's only day one of operation reconnection.

I lie. "Yes. Like a baby."

He tilts his head, slaps his expensive cologne on his neck. How manly, like he's the Old Spice guy or something. "Are you sure you can handle the Celebration of Life ceremony tomorrow?"

No. What a stupid name. I'm sure this is all his assistant's idea. I answer, "Of course. I have to be there. I'm the mom. Star of the show." I meet David's eyes. I am the lead actor in this house, in this family, I'm reminding him. Every mom is. And I will be there tomorrow for the ceremony. It's my duty, it's the beginning of my reemergence, an important aspect of my strategy even though I didn't want this memorial service, and didn't arrange it. Despite all of that, of course I'll be there. She was *my* daughter.

I know he'd like nothing better than to soak up all of the attention, both from the attendees and the event planner. The perfect father. He loves the spotlight, hosting parties, chatting with friends. But he's not going alone. I've been preparing myself for this week. I'm looking forward to reviving my role: his adoring, beautiful wife. I reach over and run my hand along the limestone countertop between our two sinks, the stone cool to the touch. I tap my nails, a slow drumbeat.

"I'm coming to the ceremony," I say and walk to the bedroom, and pause next to our king-size bed. Large enough we don't bump into each other at night. I touch my favorite pillow.

"I can take care of it, host it alone, if you're not up to it." He is behind me. I feel his eyes on the back of my neck.

"I'll be fine." I turn to face him. "Dinner should be here any minute. Tonight will be lovely, and tomorrow night, at the ceremony, I'll be right by your side, David, as you will mine."

I'm back. I smile at his frown. He doesn't like my answer.

His shoulders drop. "I can't stay for dinner. But you eat the pasta. You need to gain some weight. People in The Cove are talking."

"Oh, are they? About my weight? I don't think that's the hottest topic in the neighborhood." I glance at the bed. After he leaves, maybe I'll take a nap? I may be able to fall asleep even though it's barely past seven. It's been so long since I've slept. I've been so busy.

"Maybe it isn't the hottest topic, but it's a concern." David walks toward the bedroom door.

"Stop!" I blurt, my tone sharper than I'd intended. I cover my mouth with my hand, forcing myself not to say more. He can't just walk away from me. It has been surprisingly comforting to have David home this evening. I even allowed myself to imagine him joining me for dinner. I was feeling a little sentimental, a little needy. How stupid. This isn't about love. We already have that, as you can see. This is about control. We will dine together soon, and for as many evenings as I'd like, once I get back in charge. The way I had been, from the moment we met.

Our relationship began slowly like an orchestrated dance number. I was in the lead. David had been dropping into the Santa Monica club where I worked for more than two weeks and we'd been making eye contact and flirting, despite his regular blonde date attached to his arm. Sure, she had a gorgeous body and the air of money that made the space around her sparkle like gold. But I knew I was different than all those sorority girls. *Special beauty*, as my mom would say when she was sober.

I'd worked hard since I'd moved to LA after high school. I'd lost my accent but I hadn't lost my Southern charm. I could tell David was looking for someone like me, someone different, someone more exotic than the cookie-cutter sorority girls, someone with big dreams, a charmed future: a diamond in the land of cubic zirconia. I slipped him my phone number, in the most old-fashioned way, written on a napkin placed under his beer, our fingers brushing as electricity surged between us.

Now, as David stands at the door to our bedroom, he laughs and shakes his head. "You shouldn't yell, Jane. It's not becoming."

I walk to his side, my hands clenched. It's part of our dance these days, this feigned politeness, this lingering something. Is it nostalgia or just an endurance test to the finish line on Thursday? I still believe in us. I put my hand on his chest, imagine I'm touching his heart. "Sorry. Please stay."

Instead of embracing me, he takes my hand from his

chest and squeezes, an awkward gesture that presses my two-carat engagement ring into the knuckle of my middle finger. "I'm going to work out and grab dinner after at the club. Don't wait up."

Once he's gone I sigh, trying to push my frustration aside. In the bathroom I pick up his bottle of cologne. When I unscrew the lid I take a deep inhalation of his favorite scent, the smell of my husband. In our closet I see his silk ties hanging up in a neat little row. He's so tidy. Likes his things under control, orderly. For David, and I suppose most husbands and fathers who are the "sole providers" for their families, their personal spaces at home provide the comfort they don't find at the office. The sense of order, the semblance of routine.

Home is so much more than a place, it's your anchor, your retreat. I know it is especially important to him now that Mary is gone, his favorite daughter. He finds peace in his color-coded closet. David is a cyclone of activity out in the world ever since the accident. He's kept up a frenetic schedule this past year, but he always comes home to me, eventually.

I shake my head, knowing I don't have the energy to straighten up the chaos on my side of the closet. I've learned to embrace my mess. And besides, I have other things to focus on. My husband deserves my thoughtfulness, my presence at the ceremony tomorrow, and I can't wait to surprise him with everything else I have planned.

Each time he walks out our front door he becomes someone different. At home, with me, he's the grieving father of a dead daughter. Out in the world, he's an über-successful businessman with his sculptured chin held high, invincible. Out in the world he doesn't worry about his sad wife. I'm sure of that. Most of the time, it's easier for him if he doesn't think of me at all. But I'm always thinking about him.

For example, who wears cologne and Gucci loafers to the gym? No one. I swallow and try to control my shaking hands by shoving them into the pockets of my jeans. I hurry from the bathroom and climb in bed. I stare at the dark black glass of our huge flat-screen TV. David insisted on having a television in the bedroom, something I opposed. I know myself. I can get sucked into a show, a story, and always ended up staying up too late when the girls were little. I like to lose myself while I watch television, one of the things my mom and I had in common. She had the television on all day and night, making me watch her favorite shows with her when she was in a good mood. She taught me how to critique actresses, and to learn from them.

And I've learned a lot over the years. That's why it was time to pull myself out of my seemingly unshakable depression. After this week, I'm going to begin my career again. I've already lined up a photographer to shoot some head shots. David will be so pleased. He fell in love with me when I was acting in LA. He'll be so surprised when the old me makes a comeback. I'm focusing on the future now.

Instead of dinner tonight, tomorrow's ceremony will be the beginning of my second act. Us women, especially moms, we're resilient. At times life just throws us punches. But I've always been a fighter. Sometimes we have to take a stand for those we love, protect them from bad choices, love them even when they don't think they need it. I know some women who are stuck in their relationships, in their lives, who don't have choices.

I know how lucky I am and I know how to fight to get what I deserve.

So, life, let's get ready to rumble.

2

11:30 p.m.

I stand at the edge of a cliff when suddenly the earth gives way and I'm falling, my hands reach for something to hold on to, something to stop my fall, but it's only air. I'm tumbling, screaming.

I wake with a start and sit up quickly, my heart racing. My regular nightmare, I can't make it stop, bursting into my subconscious. I jolt awake before I hit the water, before I drown like Mary did.

My heart races as I take deep breaths and try to calm down. I'm safe in bed. It's dark outside. David is home, how nice, snoring beside me after his workout and dinner.

Climbing out of bed, I'm desperate for a drink. Of water, or wine, or both. But first, I creep into the bathroom, illuminating my way with the soft light from my phone. And there is David's phone, where he always leaves it, plugged in and resting on the counter next to his sink. My heart thumps as I quickly enter the code and smile with relief when I realize he hasn't changed it. It's our two birthdays, 1420. I open Find My Friends on my phone, a feature I didn't realize we all have until I did a little research. How wonderful. I send David's phone an invite, and accept on his behalf. Now I'll know exactly where he is all the time. I glance out toward the bed, listening for the quiet rumble of his snore. There it is.

I grab his phone again and open the text messages even though I've already read them in real time with my handy parental control app, otherwise known as spyware. These products are versatile. I mean, they sell them so we concerned parents can track our kids, a perfectly legitimate use, am I right? And can you ever be too vigilant, too protective? Of course not. Don't judge—everybody uses these things, not just me.

I simply added one more person to my bundle, my loving husband. Oh, look, there is a new text. From her: smiley, kissy face, red heart. She's so predictable with her childish overuse of emoticons, and her stupid declarations of love. As if Italian food is romantic. It's not. It's fattening. She's ridiculous. David, I'm sure, has realized it, too.

It's not all his fault that he fell into her arms. Men are needy. And I know, I've been rather distant, ignoring him, first adjusting to Mary going away to college and then her tragic death. I've been lost in my complicated grief. So he looked for attention elsewhere. That's finished now. I'm back in the game, large and in charge, as they say. Sure, she'll be sad for a little bit, but she'll move on. She's so young, so good at the game. There are plenty of wealthy, older men for her to latch on to. Tomorrow at the memorial service she'll witness David and me in love, unified. The service will be our recommitment ceremony of sorts. It also will be the end of smiley, emoticon over-user. Time's up.

I replace his phone on the counter, just where he left it, and hurry through the bedroom, down the hall and into the kitchen. I adjust the lights to the dimmest setting and feel my way along the smooth countertop until I reach the sink. I fill a glass with water and chug it, noticing lights are on downstairs in Betsy's room below me. Our home tumbles down the side of the hill. The front door is at street level, but the girls' rooms are downstairs, downhill. Not a basement—we don't call it that here—just a lower level.

This is the best hour to chat. I often surprised the girls during middle school and high school, at night, catching one or the other as she raided the refrigerator after studying. It's best, I find, to get them alone and hungry, to give them food and share my wisdom. But Betsy doesn't join me for kitchen chats anymore, not since Mary left for college. But that's okay. I go to her.

I like to keep track of Betsy, too, but I'll admit, I've been a little lax when it comes to my younger daughter. Sure, I check the app regularly, but she isn't as active on her phone as David or Mary. Likely, it's because Betsy doesn't have many friends. But still, I need to reconnect with her. I pull up Betsy's account, just to check. Yep, nothing there. She needs me, poor Betsy. Such a lonely girl. But I'm here for her, always. Even with all that I have going on, I did call the school counselor last week to find out if Betsy was on track to graduate, and Angelica surprised me.

"Betsy is doing *remarkably well* her senior year considering all that has happened," Angelica had said. Then she proceeded to effuse over Betsy's choice of community college, followed by a transfer to a more prestigious college. Betsy likely won't make it out of community college, but I didn't tell Angelica that. I'd thanked her and hung up.

Angelica was right about one thing: for Betsy, community college will be *fine*. It will keep her close to home, where she belongs. Without Mary to place my biggest hopes and dreams on, I'm left with Betsy. At least she doesn't need to bother with sibling rivalry anymore. Things have shifted between us this year, just normal teenage rebellion, I'm sure. I'll get us back on track. I mean, we were all teenagers once. And I love Betsy. So much.

I pull open the refrigerator and spot the Salerno's to-go order of four, white-boxed pasta dishes. David must have retrieved them from the front door, where I'd asked the driver to leave the food. How nice of him to bring them inside. I consider throwing the food away, but instead I grab my bottle of chardonnay, pouring a generous amount into a coffee mug. It's not like I have an issue, but I don't want to set a bad example for my daughter. You understand. I take a big gulp of wine, and open my junk drawer, every great kitchen has one, and pull out the letter from the bank that arrived in our mailbox last week. I unfold it and stare at the now-familiar words.

Dear Mr. Harris. Congratulations! You have been approved for the mortgage on 1972 Port Chelsea Place, Newport Beach. All of us at First Federal thank you for choosing us...

My heart pounds as I fold the letter into a square, and tuck it away at the back of the drawer. I love that David is surprising me, that he wants a fresh start. I just hope he announces it soon. It's so hard for me to keep this a secret—it must be killing him. This letter is proof he still loves me, loves our family despite the tough year we've had since Mary died. I realize my grief was hard for David to handle. It was a necessary, normal part of what happens when a mom loses a daughter. I know, I've re-searched it, choreographed it. Truth be told, I may have enjoyed the pill haze a little too much. I mean, there isn't a national pill-popping crisis for no reason. These things are addictive.

It's ironic, isn't it? A letter from a big bank snapped me out of it. This is likely the only good thing a big bank has ever done for anybody, ever. I'm looking at you, Wells Fargo.

I take a drink of my wine and feel just a little sorry

I've ruined the surprise he has for me. But, like I said, I'm a professional actress. I was just one role away from getting my SAG card back in the day. When he tells me, which should be any moment now, I'll throw my arms around him and cry tears of joy. I'm already familiar with the new neighborhood. Although it isn't a gated community, it's a fabulous choice. The Port Streets are lovely, quiet and safe, with sidewalks, green spaces galore and a smattering of people out walking their dogs before bed. How exciting it will be to walk through the door of our new home. Even though I'm beyond tempted, I've been so good and haven't driven past it yet, or looked it up online. I know you're impressed.

Maybe David will take me to our new home tomorrow, and then we can step through the front door together. Or, better yet, he'll swoop me into his arms and carry me across the threshold. Okay, no, he won't. The wine is making me a little giddy, combining with the itty-bitty Xanax I took to help with my nap, no doubt. No matter how he tells me the good news, I can't wait.

I rinse the coffee mug in the sink. I'll go downstairs and tell Betsy it's bedtime in a friendly, warm voice. I will reignite our mother-daughter bond. In my mind, Dr. Rosenthal nods and says, *Good idea, you need to take care of your only daughter, be there for Betsy,* her curly salt-and-pepper hair bobbing up and down. She twirls her black-rimmed glasses in her right hand, before placing them in their case for the night.

The doctor is not here. *I know that.* But she would be pleased I am being the mother she wants me to be.

I make my way to the stairs and grasp the handrail tightly, reminding myself that the number one cause of accidental deaths at home is falling. Six thousand people trip and die annually in the US. At the bottom of the stairs I stop to remember the "girls only" phase as if it was yesterday. Mary in fifth grade and Betsy in fourth grade decided their floor would be girls only and taped a sign to the steps to that effect. I was welcome, David wasn't. The way it should be, but it didn't last long.

I dart past Mary's closed bedroom door, stop in front of Betsy's and turn the knob. It's locked, as always. David threatened to have a locksmith make a master key years ago, but we never did. Never will now. I knock on the door.

"What?" Betsy sounds mad. I think she might have a temper. She always was the difficult one.

"It's Mom."

The door opens and Betsy stands in front of me in an oversize USC sweatshirt—Mary's, I presume—with a smirk on her face. "What did I do to deserve this midnight visit? If you're trying to gossip about something— or someone—you can forget it. I'm going to sleep."

Betsy thinks I am a gossip, but I'm not. I share important information, things she needs to know. She should be glad she can rely on me. She's running out of time to learn. "You have a very vivid imagination. I'm not a gossip."

"No, you just share negative things about people, keep us guessing. I'm sure that's not harmful at all." Betsy makes a chuckling sound and steps away from the door.

I wonder if I'm allowed in.

"Don't be rude. I came down to tuck you in. It's bed-time. But never mind. You know I've only ever loved you and tried to make you happy." I pout. I pretend to feel hurt, but I'm used to this treatment since Mary left for college. It's an unfortunate development.

"Fine. Come in." She feels bad. Good. Betsy walks to her bed and flops on her stomach. I follow her inside. The walls of her room are covered with her original art, oil paintings of various sizes, mostly abstract subjects, and phrases such as Manifest Abundance and Nourish Your Higher Self.

A light blue dream catcher dangles from the ceiling above her headboard. This is the bedroom of a busy, creative mind. I agreed a long time ago to let her do whatever she wanted to decorate her room. No one really sees it except the two of us. It's for the best but I don't tell her that, of course. I'm all support, all nurture.

I glance at the name *Mary* tattooed on her right wrist surrounded by tiny pink hearts, and bite my tongue. As far as a tribute to your sister, I could think of many better ideas. But we disagree on that, too.

She catches my smirk and pulls her hands inside the sleeves of her sweatshirt. "Dad said you were passed out for the night."

Charming of David to say such a thing. "Did you two have dinner together?" I hear the questions tumble out of my mouth, the hint of jealousy and judgment in my words.

Betsy rolls onto her back and sits up. If she were a cat, her claws would be out, ready to defend herself. My daughter is intuitive, I'll give her that. She says, "No, we didn't. I guess he was with his friends and I was out with mine. I mean, after art class."

"Of course he was. How was art class?" I'm grateful she doesn't add *too bad you don't have any friends, Mom*, as she's said before. She's watching me as usual. She's learned from the best.

"Oh, great." She smiles. Suddenly I know she's hiding something. But what could it be?

I need to ask her about the email I received from school. "Volunteer Day is Tuesday. Do you want me there?"

Betsy considers me. "Did you go to Mary's Volunteer Day?"

"Yes. I did."

"Okay, sure, why not? I'm in charge of painting the backdrop."

"I can't paint, but I'll try." I can paint as well as Betsy can. I focus on what appears to be a new piece of art hanging on the wall next to where I stand. It looks like a thick, bright red heart. It's dripping a rainbow of colors that pool into a black sea at the bottom of the canvas. I don't enjoy abstract art. I like realism, clarity. Not this interpretive style Betsy has concocted. I should tell her it is good but it's not. Secretly I don't think she has much talent. But a good mom would never say that to her daughter, and I'm a great mom.

"You don't like my new piece?" Betsy challenges me. She tries to stir me up. Don't you just hate it when your teen tries to push your buttons? That's why God made us smarter than them.

"It's nice." I meet her eyes. I smile, sweetly.

She laughs. "Whatever."

"You know what, you're right. It's not my favorite. I just think you could do better. This looks like blood or something. It's just dark."

"Wow. An artist paints what she feels, what she knows. It's subliminal, emotions. You just don't understand." She shakes her head. She hasn't moved from the bed. I don't think she's frightened by me, not like I was with my mom. I've never hurt her physically. That's when it's scary. This little temper of mine, well, it's nothing compared to my mom. She doesn't even know how ugly this could be between us. You've seen the horror show of moms and teen daughters who despise each other? I have, too. I lived it.

Betsy has no idea just how fortunate she has been.

In fact, it's almost as if she pities me. She shouldn't. It's weak. It's an emotion that won't serve her well in this life, certainly not around me. And soon, she's going to need to be strong: she's about to enter the cold, hard real world.

I'm not sure how to respond to her silence, so I stare at her and shrug. "I've had a long day."

"Sure you have." She chuckles again. I know she thinks I do nothing but mope around in our home all day. I guess that is all she sees of me.

I glance at the door across from where I stand. It leads to the back patio. Both girls' rooms have exterior doors and an external stairway leads to the front, outside courtyard. This is how Betsy comes and goes as she pleases. I should have turned the doors into windows before the teenage years. It's too late now.

"Mom, anything else?" She's watching me as I stare at myself in the full-length mirror in the corner of her room. I know she wishes she had my sexy figure, thin build. She has David's big bones, poor girl. I turn my head, check out my backside looking over my right shoulder. Not bad for forty-two years old.

I remember a question I'd been meaning to ask her, my memory finally coming through. "I haven't seen Josh lately. Why don't you invite him over for dinner this week to celebrate graduation?" I haven't seen him at all, come to think of it. Why didn't I keep up with them, invite him to dinner? I know they've been texting this school year and Betsy is very sweet with him. I just haven't seen him. I've been focused on other things, and healing, of course. It's hard to explain to anyone who hasn't been through this how debilitating the loss of a child can be. It makes it so hard to keep track of the other people in your life because you're so consumed with the one who has gone. But I must. I'm the mother. That's why I have my handy app. And Betsy has used the *love* word with him in texts. I need to monitor that kind of language.

"We broke up a couple weeks ago. I meant to tell you." Her eyes focus on a stain on her bedspread. She picks at it with her fingernail.

"What? Really? Oh, I'm sorry, honey." I blink and stare at Betsy. She seems unfazed.

"It's not a big deal. I still love him, as a friend. We've always been more friends than anything." She finally stops picking at the bedspread and smiles at me. "The passion was gone. You know the feeling?"

I don't want to know, no. I swallow. "I always thought you could do better anyway." Josh seemed perpetually barefoot, smelled vaguely of weed and needed a bath. Even when he was wearing tennis clothes he seemed, well, dingy. I care about Betsy, and who she dates. It's a reflection on me, everything she does, everything she will do. "So is there anybody new I should know about?"

She meets my eyes. "No."

"Well, that's good. You should focus on your studies. Spend time with me. And Dad. You'll be graduating so soon."

"Thank God. And I know what you think, Mom." She's staring at the ceiling. Telling herself to be patient with me, perhaps? Her frustration zings through the air, hits me in the gut. Nothing I haven't handled before.

She should watch herself tonight. I've already been so disappointed by her dad this evening.

"I love you." I walk to her bedside, touch her soft, shoulder-length blond hair with my hand. I lean forward and kiss her cheek and try not to react to the diamond stud sparkling from the side of her nose. I can't remember if we shopped for a dress for graduation. Did we?

"What are you wearing for graduation?" The look on her face tells me that I should know the answer. One of the aftereffects of strong emotion is memory loss. My memory also is hazy because of the free-flowing pharmaceuticals prescribed by Dr. Rosenthal. But I stopped most of those. I need to focus. Even without the drugs, I can't seem to hold on to things like before.

"The purple Free People dress. Remember?" Betsy shakes her head.

I don't remember. "Of course. Now I remember. You'll be beautiful."

Betsy smiles, and it's hollow. I don't think she believes me, but maybe she just doesn't care. "I'm wearing the silver one to the ceremony tomorrow." She looks down at her hands, her fingernails bitten to the quick, another result of the tragic accident we'll commemorate tomorrow. She curls her hands into fists, hiding the carnage of her fingernails. "Are you sure it was a good idea to invite the whole world to this funeral celebration thing?"

"I'm not sure. Your dad handled it all."

"Woo-hoo! Come grab a drink. My sister's dead." Betsy hops off her bed, takes a step toward her bathroom and stops. Her hands are in fists but her blue eyes have a glassy sheen, as if she's about to cry. She crosses her arms in front of her chest.

"Oh, honey, you know it's to remember her, not to celebrate her death. Your dad always likes to go over the top where Mary's concerned. He always spoiled her. She was his favorite. They had all those secrets. Those inside jokes. That's why it's you and me against the world." I smile at my pot stirring. I dropped some of my best refrains there.

"Mom." She shakes her head no, but she knows I'm right. "Time for you to go."

I reach out to her, pull her into a hug. She's stiff, but she doesn't push away. I'm glad she trusts me, at least a little. We stand for a moment, locked in a comforting embrace. She's a good girl at heart.

She breaks the hug, but I slip my hand around her wrist. Holding her tight. Just a little reminder of who is boss. Then I notice a new tattoo on the inside of her left wrist, her Mary tattoo is on her right. I smile and grab her left hand, holding it in the air.

"What's that? On your wrist?" My tone is too sharp. I force a smile.

Betsy shakes free, steps back from me, recovering her composure, pulling her sleeve down, covering her hand. "It's an infinity symbol. You know, eternity, empowerment, everlasting love."

"You didn't have my permission to mark yourself again." This is totally unacceptable. The next thing you know, she'll be covered in those awful things.

"It's tiny. I've had it for months and you didn't even know. So chillax." She stares into my eyes until I look away.

Defiant daughters are the worst. "You'll be sorry, later. When you're old and saggy."

She arches her eyebrows. I know she's thinking about adding, "Like you, Mom." But I'm neither. So she smiles instead and says, "FYI, I'm meeting some friends after the lame ceremony tomorrow night. We're planning a few surprises for senior day, and graduation night. I'll be home late." Betsy arches an eyebrow. "No need to stalk me." A challenge.

I meet her eyes and she laughs. She's teasing me, of course, not laughing at me. She's eighteen years old. I can't stop her from doing what she wants and I have other people to stalk right now. "Just be smart."

"I am smart, Mom, even if you don't think so."

"Oh, don't be silly. I love you." I'm a master at dodging her, you see. I try hard not to compare her to Mary, but it's not easy. Mary was brilliant. Beautiful. Oh well. I walk out of the room in silence, pull her door closed behind me and make my way to the stairs. My heart thumps from the tension between us, a tension that only develops when two people love each other deeply. There's no deeper bond than a mother and a daughter. Betsy knows that, too. She's just having a little phase.

Upstairs in the kitchen, I pull the bottle of chardonnay back out from its hiding spot behind the orange juice and vanilla almond milk and pour a full glass. I've limited myself to one glass a night lately, but tonight is a celebration. I'm proud of my self-control. My liver thanks me, too. Right after Mary died—well, for months after—it was a different story. But now we try to move on.

Some of us have.

In the living room I twist the knob and the fireplace bursts to life. I sit on one of the two overstuffed cream couches that face each other framing the fire. I never dreamed I would live anywhere like The Cove, let alone in a multimillion-dollar, beach-chic soft contemporary. But as I look around, that is where I am. It's too bad my mom couldn't see me now, surrounded by all the luxury money can buy. And soon, we'll move to an even grander home, 1972 Port Chelsea Place. A happy address. I wonder if there's an ocean view from the second floor of the new house?

I take a big gulp and finish my wine as I stare at the flames leaping in the fireplace. It was a warm day in May, more than a year ago now, when David and I were driving to Los Angeles to help Mary pack up her dorm room, a task I was dreading. I mean, a kid's dorm room after a full year of college is about the least sanitary place on earth. But there we were, David and I, on a mission together.

"I have a great idea." I had tapped David's arm, as if I'd just come up with the idea. I wanted to understand why he had broken his promise to me and allowed Mary to connect with her birth mother. I thought tequila and sex could help me extract an answer. "Let's go to Cabo for the weekend! Reconnect."

"You think that's what we need? To reconnect?" David answered, eyes hidden behind sunglasses, focused on the 405 North.

"I do." My voice was warm, happy. Inviting. I missed him, us. I missed our family, how it had been. I wanted everyone to be close again. And it started with David.

"And why, exactly, would we go to Cabo now when Mary's coming home from college today?" He turned up the radio. End of discussion. Tears filled my eyes and I blinked them away. But the betrayal, the hurt? You don't just blink that away. Those feelings sit at the bottom of your heart, festering.

Once we'd finally packed up her despicable dorm room, Mary took us on a walk around campus.

"Next year I live in that house. Can you believe it?"

she gushed as we walked down 29th Street, otherwise known as The Row. The impressive Southern-style Kappa Kappa Gamma sorority house, complete with Doric columns and window boxes bursting with red geraniums, was intimidating to me. I couldn't imagine living in one house with all those women.

"It looks nice, but not as nice as home. I can't wait to have you back for the summer." I slid my arm through hers. She stiffened, or was it my imagination?

David wrapped his arm around her shoulders and she leaned into him, leaving me to walk alone on the sidewalk. Typical.

He said, "This sorority thing will cost me an arm and a leg, that's all I know." He pretended to complain but he loved every moment of Mary's joy, of Mary's college life. And living vicariously through her social acceptance. A daughter who is a member of the top USC sorority meant good connections for David's investment business. "Proud of you as always, kiddo."

"Thanks, Dad. I can't wait for next year. But, of course, it will be fun to be home for a couple weeks, too."

"A couple of weeks?" I'd asked. My heart hammered in my chest. She had all summer to be home with us.

"I got a killer internship here. So I'll come home for a bit and then head back up to LA. My friend has a place I can crash. It's all worked out perfectly."

This was new. "You said you'd be home. That you'd work, save up." My old-fashioned, came-from-nothing work ethic was shining through.

Mary leaned against me. "I know, Mom. But I'm premed. Dad agrees it is a great idea and it is an amazing opportunity with a hospital. I'll be working with patients and I've been offered a research position. It's important for my résumé, for med school."

"It's with her? Elizabeth James? Isn't it?" They were teaming up against me, again. Tears stung my eyes. Mary had found her birth mother, a woman who was now a leading plastic surgeon in LA. She had agreed to work with her, spend all summer with her.

"Just drop it, Jane. This is a great opportunity for Mary," David had commanded. The liar. The cheater.

Looking back now, I realize what I had done wrong. I allowed Mary to go away to college, to leave my orbit, and she went awry. Stupid amateur mistake, but she was my first child, so I didn't realize the pull of college life. I never had the desire for more school, for that fake sorority experience, for the liberal arts degree that leads you nowhere. At her age, I had a career to launch, a future to secure.

And no money. There was that, too. So, sue me. I slipped and let Mary go to USC. A huge mistake.

Once Mary was away, David strayed. It was all because of Mary's choices. She disobeyed me, disrespected me and caused chaos in our family. I won't make that mistake again. I'll keep Betsy close to me, one way or another. I've learned my lesson.

That day, in the car, I did as David commanded and dropped it. I didn't say another word, not on the entire drive back home. I was so furious I don't remember where we had lunch. The effects of betrayal are deep, and lasting, especially when you are harmed by the people you love the most. I know you've been betrayed by someone you loved, haven't you? See, you don't forget it. You say you're over it, but you still remember it, feel the weight of it deep down in your heart. I'm just like you. That day I was in shock, consumed by anger. It's understandable, don't you agree?

I force the memories away and stare into the fireplace. I am looking forward to my little coffee date with Elizabeth James tomorrow. It's step one in the Jane back in control plan. I need her out of our lives completely so I can reconnect with David and Betsy. She's a malignant tumor I need to extract.

We haven't seen each other for more than a year. She'd been wary to meet me, for good reason, but I pleaded with her, one mother to another. It's just coffee, I'd promised.

I stand up feeling a little dizzy from the wine, but it's nice. I should be able to go back to sleep now. I turn off the fire, flip off the lights in the kitchen and living room, and walk to our bedroom, following the sound of David's snores. I slide into bed, praying for sleep. Tomorrow is a big day.

As I try to fall asleep I remember my first ladies' luncheon at The Cove. I'd taken extra time to curl my hair, to wear my most expensive, best-fitting tennis dress. The girls were home with the babysitter. All heads turned as I walked into the room, the new, hot young mom. We've all been there. You think you're queen of the castle until a new princess arrives on the scene. A silence washed over the four white-tablecloth-draped tables.

"Hello, are you Jane?" A woman with a big smile, huge fake boobs (not done as expertly as mine) and an impossibly large diamond extended her hand. "I'm Sarah. Welcome to the neighborhood." She broke the ice. Deemed me worthy of their acceptance. I should thank her someday, I suppose.

As Sarah escorted me to the seat next to her at table three, the idle conversation started up around me. I knew I was the topic. Once seated, all of my tablemates introduced themselves. I was invited to a Mommy and Me playgroup on Tuesdays, another woman asked me to be her tennis partner in the upcoming mixer. Another asked me to join her book club. Bunco was every Thursday night. I accepted every invitation.

I had arrived. It's hard to crack into a group of women like this, let me tell you. Have you tried it? My palms were sweating the entire lunch. But they liked me. I was a great girlfriend. I was.

I think the trouble with me and all of them began when I started winning at everything. Tennis, Bunco, even on my snack day at Mommy and Me. Jealousy is a powerful emotion. Slowly, over the years, invitations stopped arriving. And the moms all started looking older, too. Bedraggled, sunburned, sleep deprived. But I never compromised my looks for my kids. I took care of myself. While they all started sagging, I looked even better. It happens. It wasn't my fault their husbands would give me approving winks.

It hurts. I was invisible to them during the last few years before Mary died and I'm incommunicado now.

I always had my kids and my husband to focus on. But what now? What is a housewife to do when her kids leave home? That's the million-dollar question. Well, actually, I believe our net worth is much more than that, I can assure you. My eyes pop open again and I stare at the ceiling. Grief has given me time to think, to strategize. When everyone ignores you, and tiptoes around you, you have space.

David's rumbling snores aren't the worst part about trying to sleep at night. It's what I see when I close my eyes. Sometimes I wonder if it would have been better if she were never found. Then I would never have viewed her face. I wouldn't be haunted by the nightmare of the half-eaten shoe still laced onto her half-eaten foot. That's the other nightmare. It's falling or the foot.

When those images zoom into my head, I open my eyes and I focus on other things, like random accidental deaths. Did you know hippos kill almost three thousand people a year? I know, I didn't either. See, you're distracted just thinking about it.

I don't tell anyone about these two nightmares. I know they'll fade away in time, like the memories of my mom getting fainter every day. No, it's best they all think I am fine. Sure, Betsy and David have caught on to some of my routine. Betsy doesn't join me in the kitchen for late-night chats these days, and David wasn't wooed by tonight's impressive table setting. But no one really knows another person, not fully. And I have so many more loving tricks up my sleeve.

Elizabeth James, for example. She will not come near

the ceremony tomorrow, even though I'm certain she has been invited. She isn't wanted or needed by anyone there. David and Betsy won't even notice her absence, but they will notice the new and improved, sweet-as-molasses Jane.

The three of us will link arms, walk to the front of the service together, our little family. And then, after the ceremony, David will tell me about our new house and I'll wrap my arms around his neck as he scoops me into an embrace. The crowd will be so happy that we've made it through our loss, that we have found happiness together again. It will be smiles all around, like a dream come true. Even Betsy will be happy, her nose ring sparkling as she nods in approval.

But seriously, I'm going to win them over. Surprise both of them. You'll see.

MONDAY

THREE DAYS UNTIL GRADUATION

3

6:30 a.m.

My foghorn alarm blares and jars me out of bed. I scamper to the bathroom to turn it off. Shaking fingers jab at my phone. This routine happens every morning. Normal people have a soothing alarm, not this blaring foghorn. But I'm not normal. I'm special. Even though the sound scares me to death every morning. It works, though. I'm awake.

I grab my toothbrush and turn on the water, quickly dampen it before turning the water off again. I'm not worried about California's perpetual drought. After what happened last year, I've developed a fear of water, especially the vast, deep ocean surrounding us. Did you know water covers 71 percent of the surface of the earth? Oceans hold

96.5 percent of the earth's water. The Pacific Ocean, my view, is the deepest ocean, reaching more than six and one-half miles deep. The California Current moves south along the west coast of North America. I shudder as I tap my toothbrush on the edge of the sink. I learned from the coroner's office that if you drop something into the ocean north of here, it always drifts this way, even a body.

From the bathroom I glance at David's empty, cold side of the bed. He's left for work extra early this morning. But that's fine. Today's our coming-out party and he probably has to knock out some things before he can focus all of his attention on me, and Betsy and our remembrance for Mary.

I study my reflection in the mirror above my sink. Not bad. I'm sort of like an actress who's been on sabbatical and is offered a part: she reluctantly takes it and wins an Oscar. There is work to be done but I can see the beautiful me in there. I slept in yesterday's makeup. It's mostly faded away, rubbed off on my pillow, most likely. Dark smudges hang under my eyes from worn-away mascara, but what's new and a little alarming is the deepening web of wrinkles beside each of my eyes. Botox will get rid of those in an instant.

In the closet, I slip off my T-shirt and stare approvingly at my own body in the full-length mirror. I look a little thin, but you can never be too rich or too skinny. Mom loved to repeat that one. My stomach is flat, a feature that only departed from my physique about three months into my pregnancy with Betsy, and returned shortly after her delivery. And of course, my surgically enhanced breasts are exactly right, a little larger than necessary, but hey, go big or go home. If David and I were to go on one of those island vacations he loves, I could rock a bikini for old times' sake. I try to imagine it, us, on vacation again. Me in a floppy hat, white bikini, skin warm from the sun, and David unable to keep his longing eyes off my body. He grabs me as we walk into our casita, whispering "gorgeous" in my ear as he pulls me to the bed. Yes, we'll do that again, soon, perhaps in the new house.

I check the time. I need to hurry to be ready for my coffee date with Elizabeth. Once I'm showered, I enjoy putting on full makeup for the first time in a while. I take my time, and I'm pleased with the results. I pull on jeans—they're baggy, but they'll do for this morning's activities—and a flattering white blouse.

I wait for Betsy in the kitchen, hoping for more mother-daughter time like we had last night. Sometimes I'm lucky and I catch her in the morning when she's hungry or needs a water bottle to take to school. Most days, though, she exits through her bedroom door and rushes through the courtyard to her car before I even realize she's gone, like her dad, the other mouse running from momma cat.

I can't blame her. She doesn't think about me, or my needs. I remember acting the same way with my own mother when I was ten. It's a selfish phase most girls go through, and Betsy and I are enjoying an extra long, extra trying phase. It balances the fact Mary and I never had one. Sure, we had our disagreements, but not the ongoing war of disappointment and misunderstanding that Betsy and I seem to be locked in.

Last week, David walked into a huge fight between my daughter and me. It was after 11:00 p.m., far too late for Betsy to be out on a school night. I waited for her in a chair, outside in the dark, sacrificing my own comfort. I care about her and her curfews. When Betsy had finally walked into the courtyard, I had confronted her before she could sneak downstairs via the outdoor steps.

"Stop right there." I stood up. I scared her and that made me smile.

"Oh my God," Betsy yelled. "You would be out here like a freak. Leave me alone."

"You smell like smoke. Where have you been?"

"I told Dad I had a bonfire tonight. You can't keep treating me like I'm a child. I'm eighteen. Besides, if you had taken the time to have an actual conversation with Dad, he could have told you where I was." Betsy backed away, heading toward the outside stairs, trying to escape to her room to get away from me, her mother: the person who gave birth to her, the person who gave her life.

"Who were you with? I want to know your friends." The fact was Betsy never brought her friends home. I knew all of Mary's high school friends, for years, and they all seemed to like me. Some of the boys liked talking to me more than they did Mary. But with Betsy, I only knew Amy, from middle school. After Amy moved away, Betsy didn't bring anyone else home, no matter how often I pushed to meet her "group."

Mary had told me when she was a senior, and Betsy was a junior, that Betsy was in a totally different crowd. *Mom, we don't overlap friends, not at all. I can't really tell you more.* That's why I had to surprise her in the courtyard. I have to catch her when I can. She's sneaky, my Betsy.

Last week in the courtyard, Betsy wasn't just sneaky, she was mean. Her voice was cold, firm. "Your snooping is freaking me out. You need to cool it. I'm going to bed—don't follow me."

"Don't you dare walk away from me, young lady!" I had yelled. Too loud. We're all too close together here at The Cove. I can't believe I raised my voice.

David stepped through the door from the garage at that moment. Mortified by my outburst.

"Jane, honestly. I heard you from inside the garage. What will the neighbors think?" He was mad at me, not worried about what Betsy had said or done. David still cares about the neighbors, still has friends in the neighborhood. Clients, too.

Betsy saw her chance for an exit. "Welcome home, Dad. Good night." She smiled as he walked to her side.

"Good night, honey." They hugged and she was gone.

I am very tired of this treatment. Instead of backing me up, supporting my good parenting, David had walked past me into the house, leaving me alone in the courtyard staring up at the stars piercing through the night sky like laser beams. Just then one of the palm trees in our courtyard shed its hull, something that happens at least once a year. The heavy wooden canoe-shaped beast landed with a bang a foot away from where I'd been sitting. I could have died.

But I'm a survivor. And I always win. Something Elizabeth will discover in ten minutes, the palm trees later this morning.

4

Elizabeth is late but I'm fine with it. Gave me time to settle in, grab the corner table at Starbucks, order a small black coffee. Why can I never remember what I'm supposed to say for small? And why can't I just say small? As I sip my coffee I watch the line of well-dressed women and men, and wonder which one of them is happy. Who is cheating on their spouse? Who is living a lie?

Have any of them given up a child for adoption and then pushed their way back into that child's life? I mean, after the adoptive mother gave up everything and raised the girl as her own, cared for her, made her the woman she was, and then you swoop in for the easy part? For the glory? Who does that?

Elizabeth does. And there she is now, pushing through the glass door with an air of importance, her long dark hair cascading down her shoulders. She's wearing a white lab coat to enhance her doctor status and high heels. Sexy doctor status. Nice try, but you still have nothing on me. She spots me in the corner and I watch her lips purse. Is she nervous? I mean, when I visited her clinic in LA last year I didn't *really* threaten her, although she seems to have taken it that way. Silly restraining orders. They don't really do anything, do they?

I should have taken one out on her. She is the one who didn't listen, she's the one who never backed off. She lured Mary to her with an internship. Unforgivable.

She pulls the chair out across the table and sits, crossing her arms in front of her.

"Don't you want anything to drink?" I ask. I'm not getting her anything, and the line is ten deep, but I'm being pleasant. I tuck my blond hair behind my ear, making sure my huge diamond studs sparkle in the sunlight streaming in over my shoulder.

"No. What do you want, Jane?" She folds her hands together on the table. Pity she's never found a man. Maybe she isn't interested in them, not that I care.

"I want you to get in your car and drive back to LA. You aren't welcome here."

Elizabeth smiles. "That's funny. Mr. and Mrs. Harris invited me personally. You know I used to work for them. I'm part of the family in more ways than one."

"This ceremony is for me, her mother, and David, her father, to say goodbye to Mary in front of our friends. Not for you, some servant, a housekeeper who had random sex and didn't want the results. You act like you're family but you're just the help. I'm family, do you understand? I was nice, before, when Mary found you. I had to be. I didn't want to upset Mary. But now Mary is gone. You have no hold over me, nothing."

Elizabeth smiles, her face flushes. Good, she should be embarrassed, the slut. "You've never been nice to me, or to your daughter, from what I can tell. And you don't even know what you're talking about."

"Oh, really? I know David allowed our daughter Mary to contact you, and unfortunately, you responded even though you promised to never have contact with the baby you gave up." I take a sip of my coffee but I continue to stare at my nemesis.

"You're still mad about that, aren't you? As you know, Mary contacted me first. I did nothing wrong, and neither did Mary. It's all just so small-minded of you." She shakes her head at me like I'm a toddler about to be put in time-out.

I'd like to wipe that smirk off her face, or throw my coffee at her. But I won't. "No, I'm not mad. Just disappointed."

"You liked pretending Mary belonged only to you. But she was mine, too. I loved her. I just didn't have the means to provide for her, not like David does." Elizabeth sits back, takes a deep breath.

My mind is pinging, facts merging together, swirling

around like the time does these days. But there's something. "You mean like David and I do. He is my husband."

"Yes, and Mary's father, her biological father." Elizabeth smiles.

The thing about the truth is you can see it when it's revealed. Even if it's been in front of you all along, even if you never, ever, wanted to see it. Oh my God.

"You didn't." I lean forward as she scoots her chair back.

"I'm not the one who was married. I didn't do anything wrong. But I do feel a little bad for you, I mean, it was during your first year of marriage. Isn't that supposed to be the golden year?" Elizabeth stands up. "Don't worry. Mary didn't know David was her real dad. We never told her. To protect her. And I suppose, to protect you."

What? This is nonsense. She's lying, she must be. This cannot be true. My head is swirling, heart pounding. I want to throw my coffee at her. I want to force her to stop talking. Force her to go away for good. I take a breath. "You're lying."

"Why would I? Mary's gone now. I don't care about you, or your petty jealousy. Mary was going to be a brilliant doctor, just like me. Her mom."

I want to grab her by the neck and squeeze. I want her to stop talking. David was with her? Our first year of marriage? He has cheated on me before? And with her? A servant? I can barely breathe. I manage, "David wouldn't do that to me. We were in love then."

Elizabeth leans forward. "He was already regretting

his choice. I really can't blame him. You have control and boundary issues, Jane."

"Oh, do I?" I hiss. I stand up, hands clenched in fists.

"You do. And besides, Mr. and Mrs. Harris were in love with the idea of a grandchild. You should have seen the way they pampered me, feeding me exquisite meals, buying maternity clothes for me. David was married, they couldn't understand the delay, and meanwhile, I was pregnant. It all worked out."

I take a step forward and I'm standing next to Elizabeth now. The air between us is toxic. "I didn't want to get pregnant then. If I wanted to I would have."

"Well, something made him turn to me." She takes a step back. She's leaving. But then she stops and says, "Look, Jane. It didn't mean anything. It was a one-night stand. I was house-sitting for his parents. It was a mistake. Except it gave us Mary. All of us were blessed to know her, to have her in our lives."

I'm shaking all over. If she comes to the ceremony I won't be able to control my rage. I cannot have her there today. I won't. It's my new start. "Do not come to the ceremony. Do not or you will be sorry."

She shakes her head and laughs. "You are a piece of work, threatening me again. This isn't about you. It's about Mary, and David and his parents, too. They asked me to be here, to mourn Mary. She's my daughter, too."

As she walks away I pick up my phone. My hands shake as I punch David's number, and the call rolls to voice mail. "We need to talk. Now. Call me or come home."

I sit down, trying to breathe. I will not allow this to

ruin things, not now. No, I will get David back, and then we'll discuss his further betrayal. For now, I will keep the peace, play my role. Once we've moved into our new house, he will pay for this.

5

10:00 a.m.

Tree service companies are so responsive, especially if you're calling from The Cove and willing to pay double the typical fee because it's an emergency. I called last week after my near-death experience and today here they are. The crew and I already had assessed the situation and they'd explained their strategy by the time David bursts into the courtyard, red faced and frantic.

He got my message, apparently. I've been ignoring his return phone calls, forcing him to come home. I won't confront him about what I've learned from Elizabeth James. Not now. But still, he came home to me. That's a good sign. He must be reminded of my power.

I give David a little wave and notice the shock on his face when he finally spots the guys, one climbing up each of the two trees. "What is going on here, Jane? What are you doing to our magnificent palms? What's the emergency?"

"I'm getting rid of them. They're a menace." I put my hands on my hips and take a sip of my coffee. He grabs my shoulder. I shake his hand off.

He says, "They're one of the primary assets of our home. We can't replace them. They're grandfathered in. They represent our two girls." David talks to me as if I were a child. As if I care about what he is saying. As if I hadn't already spent a half hour plotting the demise of his precious trees with the guys implementing the plan.

Above our heads I notice the men are listening to David instead of me. They stop climbing.

"Oh no you don't. Keep climbing. I signed the papers. Cut them down now. I've already paid, signed on the dotted line. Do it," I command. It feels good to hear the chain saws rev up.

"You're destroying our home, the value," David yells. I can tell he wants to say more but he shakes his head. It is loud, with the chain saws, hard to talk. I watch as he walks into the house and slams the door. Poor, pouting David. He doesn't realize, even after twenty years, that I know what's best for our family. Palm trees are killers. They have to go. Period. And I'm not the one destroying our home, dear.

I hurry inside the house, per the men's directions, and listen as the chunks of palm tree crash to the ground in the courtyard. It's satisfying knowing they are dying, knowing I won. I destroyed them first, before they could get me. That's what winners, survivors do.

Back inside, I try to find my husband. I fight the urge to ask David about Elizabeth's accusation. Maybe I'll just ask him for a hug, for some reassurance about the ceremony this afternoon. I'll demand that he make sure Elizabeth James does not attend. That's the first step.

"David, we need to talk. The ceremony tonight has me all out of sorts. Let's hug." I stand near the front door and hold my arms out to him.

"You are unbelievable," he says as he walks past me and out the door.

"Wait, we need to talk," I scream after him, but he can't hear me over the chain saws. It's fine. If he had stopped, hugged me, I might have asked him if he is actually Mary's biological father. I'm certain it isn't true. What kind of man would cheat as a newlywed? Not David, not my David. As I watch chunks of palm tree drop to the ground, my stomach turns.

Of course it's true.

I take a cleansing breath and walk to the kitchen. It's fine that he ran out the door. He's angry right now and he wouldn't be fun to talk to about this newly realized betrayal. I will stick to my plan, reunite our family. And then we will have the important chat, once we're settled in our new home.

I wonder if Betsy is home. If she passes through the kitchen, I'm ready to smother her with love. I walk to my desk and glance above my laptop at the invitation pinned to the corkboard:

JOIN US FOR A CELEBRATION OF THE LIFE OF MARY HARRIS
BELOVED DAUGHTER OF DAVID AND JANE HARRIS
BELOVED SISTER OF BETSY HARRIS
BELOVED GRANDDAUGHTER OF DAVID AND ROSEMARY HARRIS
5:00 P.M. AT THE COVE PRIVATE BEACH
PLEASE DRESS IN THE COLORS OF THE SUNSET
MONDAY, MAY 20TH
RSVP: KYLIE DORN

Most of the details of today's event were handled by David's assistant, Kylie Dorn, a spunky, sunny young woman with full, pouty lips and a waist to breast ratio like Barbie's. I know she's mostly man-made, but the guys don't seem to mind. She draws the appreciation of all men she comes into contact with, much like I do. We have a lot in common.

I briefly wonder if she'll be in attendance this evening, full lips pouting even more, breasts wrapped in the tight black fabric of feigned mourning. Oh, scratch that. The invitation directs us to wear the colors of the sunset. How cute. Of course she'll be there.

Stupid Elizabeth is likely on her way back to LA by now. She's afraid of me, and she should be. Good riddance.

I hear footsteps in the hall. Betsy walks into the kitchen wearing black jeans, a black T-shirt and a frown. Her nose piercing taunts me, sparkles, challenging me to say something about it.

I swallow. "Good morning. Can I get you breakfast?"

Betsy's face scrunches together with disgust as if she's having an alien encounter. She wasn't expecting me to be here. I enjoy surprising my daughters. It keeps them off balance.

She says, "No. I don't eat breakfast. I thought you knew that by now."

She's so surly. Perhaps I should give her something to think about at school today, a little tidbit of juicy information for her to ponder during art class. "Did you know your father is Mary's biological dad?" I ask.

Betsy's disdain face has been replaced by something else. Her mouth drops open. She didn't know.

"What are you talking about? Have you been drinking? Popping pills?" She throws her hands on her hips, ready to argue with me.

"No, of course not. I had coffee with Mary's birth mother, you remember Elizabeth? Mary told you all about her."

"So, that's old news. You always told Mary she was adopted. I still don't know why you made such a big deal about her wanting to meet her birth mom." Betsy shakes her head.

She's trying to act like this revelation doesn't matter, that it isn't true, but I can see the stress in her clenched jaw, her rigid posture.

"It is a big deal. All of it." I know my voice is cold, hard.

Betsy takes a step back. "You're lying about Dad, aren't you?"

I fight a surprise burst of emotion threatening to choke my voice. "No, I'm not. We were married when he, well..." I cover my face with my hands, push tears from my eyes.

Betsy leans against the counter, deciding what to think.

I mumble, "I'm devastated."

"Did Dad tell you this is true?" she asks.

"No." I sob. "Haven't talked to him yet. But it's true. Your dad is a liar. I'm sorry." I've needed a little leverage, something to force a space between them. I've found it.

"I have to go to school. I need to get out of here. It's all screwed up, everything. I mean, when are you going to get rid of Cash's dog bowl?" She points at the white porcelain bowl tucked under the kitchen island. The words—*Love. Eat. Play. Cash.*—are glazed in black block lettering on the side of the bowl.

Obvious change of subject, darling daughter, but fine, I'll play. "Oh, does it bother you?"

"Kinda, yeah. He died six months ago." Betsy yanks open the refrigerator, hiding her tears.

As if I didn't know when he died. But I need to be patient and kind with her. It's a hard day, the anniversary of Mary's death. Learning your dad has cheated, fathered a baby who became your sister. It's a lot. I remind myself I need to smother her with warmth and cheer and support. Besides, she'll love the new house and we'll just put all this nastiness behind us.

I say, "I can put the bowl away if it bothers you." I flash

her a big, fake beaming smile. My jeans are sagging and I yank them up on my waist.

Betsy closes the refrigerator. She holds a container of pomegranate seeds, a healthy choice. I'm proud. I always worry about her weight ballooning up. "You know what? It does. It bothers me. And that's not the only thing wrong. I cannot believe I have to go celebrate Mary's death today, like I don't think about her, miss her, every single minute."

I try to catch her arm but she darts past me, stopping at the door to the kitchen, watching me.

Tears fill my eyes, running down my cheeks. "I miss Mary every minute, too. That's why I care about you so much. You're my only focus now. We'll sit together at the ceremony, I'll be there for you, Betsy. You can lean on me."

My tears match Betsy's. Poor girl. I'm the only parent she needs. I hope she confronts David for me. That would be much more satisfying. He'd be crushed by the disappointment. It's so important to him to be the hero, Betsy's perfect dad. Not anymore. Not ever again, it seems.

She wipes her face with her sleeve. "I can't cry anymore. I can't do this. I can't listen to you and your lies. I have to go." She's gone, out the door before I can remind her to be home in time for the ceremony. I know she heard me, though. She heard the truth about her philandering father.

A text pops up on my phone: I'm here.

I glance at the time and can't believe it's already 10:45 a.m. Such a busy morning. I grab my purse and hustle through the almost tree-free courtyard and out to the street. Sam, my driver of sorts, jumps out of the front seat and opens the passenger door behind the driver's seat.

His hair is brown and unruly. Always. As if he doesn't own a comb. "Hey, Mrs. H."

"Hi, Sam. I took your suggestion and finally did something nice for myself. I had a manicurist come by the house. What do you think?" I flutter the fingers of my right hand.

"Glad you did something nice for you for a change, instead of just taking care of everybody else like you tell me you do. You know, when you're not sad."

I slide into the back seat. He closes the door behind me and hurries to the driver's seat. When he gets in I say, "Yes, motherhood is trying sometimes. Sorry to keep you waiting. I was just finishing up the breakfast dishes. Betsy and I had a lovely meal together. She's such a wonderful young woman, so sweet."

He meets my eyes in the rearview mirror. His eyes are dark, widely spaced, caring. "Glad you two are getting along. I know today is a hard day."

I may complain to Sam too much about Betsy. I'll change that, perhaps. But I'll start tomorrow. It's so easy to talk to Sam, unlike my family members. And he's always on my side. I allow him to see me open my purse, reach for tissues. My facade of cheer crumbles. The ceremony is tonight. "It's such a hard day. One year since Mary died. And can I confide in you, Sam?"

"Of course, Mrs. H."

"Betsy isn't really nice to me. She's mean."

"You've told me that. I'm sorry. Maybe she's sad."

I shrug. "That could be it. Or maybe it's something else? Guilt?"

Sam meets my eyes in the mirror. "Guilt? For being mean to you?"

No. It's so hard to get people to see things sometimes. "No, for fighting with her sister, at the park, on the day Mary died. Never mind. It's not important. I'm saying too much."

"It's okay, Mrs. H., you can tell me anything." Sam and I have been together now since a month after Mary's funeral. I don't drive much anymore, or so I tell him. It fits with my grief and I like being chauffeured by a person who listens to my every command. Sam takes me most of the places I need to go. He still drives for Lyft, but he blocks out our schedule: doctor's visits, grocery store trips. And Friday morning, whatever errands I need to run, if I can get myself up and out of the house and away from my addicting computer.

Some errands I handle on my own, but he doesn't know that. "Well, let's see. I don't think I have to worry about Mary's birth mother showing up and ruining things this evening, so that's good." I love being able to confide in Sam. He is so loyal. Like a friend. I smile at the thought.

Sam says, "You don't like Elizabeth, that much I know. But how do you know she won't be there?"

"I made it clear she isn't welcome. We had coffee this morning." Oops, I sound a bit mean. I soften my voice. "I hope she listened. I asked her to see things from my point of view. I've lost so much." I dab at my eye with a tissue. Sam looks concerned. He's watching in the rear-view mirror.

"Do you have a dress for tonight?" he asks.

I haven't given my attire much thought. Funny, I've been imagining my coming-out party, but not my dress. Sure, I could wear the orange silk one I'd expected to wear last night, still hanging up with the expensive price tag dangling under the arm. But no, Sam's right. Why not splurge? I need to look good. Focus on the future. David owes me some retail therapy.

Sam turns into the parking lot of the office building and into a reserved space.

I say, "I suppose I do need to find a sunset color dress. That's what the invitation says. Any ideas?"

"I'll make a couple calls, Mrs. H. What is the name of the store you like?"

"The Boutique. It's pricey but fabulous."

"On it." Sam does whatever I ask. Why can't everyone in my life be like this? My husband couldn't even be faithful in our marriage during our first year together. My daughter can't share a meal with me. But Sam, he listens. He cares.

He hops out and opens my door for me. I walk into the now-familiar lobby of the sleek twelve-story office building. Dr. Rosenthal's office is on the first floor, discreetly located around the corner from the elevator bank. I keep my sunglasses on and scurry inside. I've never run into someone I know here. I suppose if I did, no one would be that shocked to discover I'm visiting a shrink.

Dr. Rosenthal was highly recommended by Detective

Alan Branson, who was the lead investigator on Mary's case. He told me it would be helpful to talk to someone, to help me sort through my devastating loss. Part of me thinks he was tired of being the one I talked to, but I'm pretty sure he had a crush on me and handed me off to Dr. Rosenthal so he wouldn't be tempted. He's an honorable man. There aren't many of those around these days, I've discovered. #MeToo.

I don't know if the detective still talks with the doctor, about me, or Mary, and of course, everything is confidential with her. But as far as Detective Branson was concerned, if he needed to, I would let him read the notes of our sessions. He'd fall in love with me even more. I tried to do everything he told me to do, and I listened carefully to everything he said. It's always a good idea to have the police on your side, crush or no crush.

The bored receptionist meets my eyes and nods as I take a seat in the waiting room. She and I know each other now, but we never speak. There is nothing pleasant to say, nothing fun about being here. It's just an important part of what I do now. At least she understands I don't want to talk to her. Most people don't.

"Hello, Jane. Please come in." Dr. Rosenthal opens her door and welcomes me.

I do as she says, and once inside her office, I settle into my regular spot: a light blue velour La-Z-Boy. Of the other choices, a wooden rocking chair, a saggy forest green couch or the La-Z-Boy, I was drawn early on to the soft velour.

Dr. Rosenthal takes her seat behind her thick wooden

desk, folds her hands together. "You look good, Jane. I know today's the day she was found. I'm so sorry. The first anniversary of a tragic death is very difficult."

"That's why we're having the memorial, I guess." David's stupid idea.

Dr. Rosenthal stares at me. "I know it's hard but the ceremony is happening, so let's try to do a little work to get you prepared."

"Sure. Of course." I meet Dr. Rosenthal's eyes. I'm preparing for the future, stepping back into the spotlight. I'll be fine. I suppose she doesn't realize that.

"Jane, today's ceremony will be hard. Guests will say the wrong things but they don't mean to upset you. I need you to practice your meditation. Your breathing." The doctor is a big believer in meditation. She's given me CDs to listen to, her voice attempts to calm me in between sessions. Dr. Rosenthal is staring at me. I must have drifted off.

I'm not sure what to say. I nod.

"People will say insensitive things, like Mary's in a better place or everything happens for a reason, or you're lucky to have another daughter. They will blurt hurtful things because they're uncomfortable."

"I know. I'm their worst nightmare." I try to feel guilty about that, but I don't. I blow my nose. The sound makes Dr. Rosenthal cringe every time. I rather enjoy the reaction.

"It's frightening for most of us to imagine what you have lived through. How are you and David?" She pulls off her reader glasses, twirls them in her hand.

"He's very busy, at work." He's also a liar, and a serial cheater.

"Hmm." Dr. Rosenthal says a lot without words sometimes. She stares at me. I am supposed to fill the air again.

Fine. "We're focused on Betsy. We had a beautiful family dinner in the dining room Sunday night, even though I accidentally set four places. Habit, I guess."

"Oh, Jane." She covers her mouth with her hand. I surprised her with that one.

"I know. It was a mistake. Everything is just so hard. I'm trying. Dinner together was a good start. It's complicated."

Dr. Rosenthal nods. "Grief is complicated."

I nod. "Some days I don't want to get out of bed." That isn't true, but it's what she wants to hear. Recently, I can't sleep. I'm agitated, restless since I stopped taking all the sedating drugs she prescribed.

This new information about David, and his inability to be faithful, his lies, well, all of that makes me want to kick a hole in a wall or light a fire in his closet. I see his shirts smoldering, his perfect row of ties light up in a blaze. I stare at Dr. Rosenthal, milling over my revenge fantasies while she analyzes my grief.

"You should be moving through the acute stage of grief by now, but I fear it may be more severe. From what you've told me, you may have what researchers are calling complicated grief." She pauses. "Not many people have heard about the diagnosis."

I have. I'm smart. I smile. "I am complicated." My attempt at humor falls flat. But my acting skills are superb.

My research also pointed to complicated grief. I've read all about it online. Hand me the golden statue.

Dr. Rosenthal isn't smiling, so I suppress my grin.

She tilts her head, makes a note in my file. "Anyway, women are more vulnerable to complicated grief than men. It often results from a difficult loss, like the loss of a child. It's a pathological condition. Do you think we should put you back on the pills?"

Oh good, the diagnosis I was shooting for, and an offer of more pharmaceuticals. Does the diagnosis cover a cheating husband and a disrespectful surviving daughter, too? As you surmised by now, there is too much going on for me to numb myself into oblivion for days on end, as tempting as that sounds. Been there, done that. It isn't a productive state. Things and people slip away from you if you're not paying attention.

"No, I don't think more pills are necessary." True. I could knock out an entire herd of cattle with what is in my medicine cabinet presently.

"All right, well, we'll stay on top of it. Grief isn't as simple as the five stages." Dr. Rosenthal pulls out her box of Cheez-Its and offers me a handful. I decline as always. It's our pattern, codependent patient/doctor thing. It feels familiar, and weird. I know she's trying to deepen our connection. But I think we've got a good thing going here.

She pops a few overly orange crackers in her mouth and talks while chewing. "Grief is stressful, so it's common to alternate between acknowledging the emotional pain of your loss, and setting it aside. Grief comes in waves, like the ocean."

The cold, dark ocean. I look at my freshly painted nails. The color is called deep ocean dreams. Yes. Makes sense for grief and death to come in waves. It may take up to four minutes to die from drowning, but drowning people can only struggle on the surface for sixty seconds before submersion occurs: a truly horrible way to die. Poor Mary. I blink and look up at Dr. Rosenthal.

"Jane, do you have any unusual fixations these days?" She stares at me, her dark eyes trying to pierce through me, see inside my mind, see the truth.

"No, not really." I wonder if she knows more than three thousand people die in the US because they choked on their food?

Death by Cheez-Its? Possible but unlikely.

It's time for her to think I'm getting better. After today's memorial service, of course. Next week, she should tell anyone who asks that I am suffering from complicated grief but I am improving. So, no, I won't share my tragedy obsession, or my fear of the ocean. Or the nightmares. Or the bubbling rage I feel toward my husband at this moment.

She's still waiting for me to speak, to elaborate. Her eyebrows smash together on her forehead, she twirls her pen in her right hand.

"No fixations, not really, unless you count getting Betsy through high school graduation. I mean, that's typical mom stuff, right? It takes all of my attention. I'm volunteering in her school, shopping for the perfect graduation dress. We've been looking at colleges online, swapping stories about all of her friends' futures. It's wonderful. I'm just a typical mom in most respects. Preparing family dinners, making sure Betsy does her homework. Baking cookies. Wow, I must be getting better if I'm complaining about typical housework." I smile. I am so normal it hurts.

I'm the perfect vision of a happy homemaker. I always set the perfect table, remember?

"Well, that all sounds good. How is Betsy?" Dr. Rosenthal notes. "She could benefit from counseling. I know she feels extremely guilty about her sister's death."

This I know is true. Betsy was there, fighting with Mary at the park. She feels responsible deep down. I've been mining her guilt, too, feeding it, fueling it like a fast-moving wildfire. I say, "I hope she hasn't convinced herself it was her fault. I hope she didn't have anything to do with it."

"Of course she didn't. It's just that the mind is powerful. She should come to me so we can be sure she's processing all of this correctly. Grief is confusing, as you know. At the beginning, it's really intense, all consuming. It cancels out everything else, all the people and activities that are important to us. But over time, it settles down, makes a space in our hearts, our lives. It's not healthy for Betsy to believe any of this is her fault. I know you're re-inforcing that."

I shift in my La-Z-Boy, wiggle my toes. She is correct. I am reinforcing things. "Don't worry. Betsy's fine. She is my daughter, strong like I am. I'm so proud of her. I'm getting better and so is she. I'm her role model. We all turn into our mothers eventually, right?" I smile. Betsy is my legacy.

"Are you like your mother, Jane?" Dr. Rosenthal's face is frozen, a poignant look, as if this is an important question. She still doesn't realize I don't discuss my mother. Ever. She doesn't realize I'm in control of these sessions, not her. Sorry, Doc. For the record, I'm not like my mother. Gayle Lambert was a monster.

Dr. Rosenthal is so easy to manipulate, as you can tell. I pivot: "You've said all along that grief is the most painful form of love. Betsy loved Mary very much, even though they were opposites and they fought a lot, too much. Betsy has that bad temper, you know. Must be from David's side. Poor Betsy, I don't want to imagine her hurting anyone." I shake my head. I'm a gentle, simple housewife worried about her daughter's explosive anger. Meanwhile, I'm the one seething, but we won't discuss that right now.

"Rage can be a sign of underlying issues. Tell her to come in. It's important." Dr. Rosenthal is leaning forward on the desk.

Really? "It will have to be after she graduates on Thursday. She's too busy right now." I smile. I have no idea what she does, but she is busy. I'm the best mother.

"Mmm. Let's get back to you." Dr. Rosenthal takes another handful of crackers, pops them in her mouth and slides the box out of sight. Orange crumbs dust her black sweater.

I am my favorite topic. "Yes?"

"Are you still isolating yourself in your home?"

"No, of course not. I'm on the graduation party vol-

unteer committee. Such an honor." It's not really a committee. Everyone is included. But I will look like a good
mom for being there, and Dr. Rosenthal seems pleased.
Good job, Jane. So far this session is going well. She's
concerned about Betsy's rage and guilt, so my work here
is done. By next week I'll be relaunching my acting career
and too busy to be bothered with coming to these sessions.

Dr. Rosenthal glances up above my head at the clock
mounted over the door. "Let's focus on the memorial this
afternoon with our remaining time."

I thought our time was up. I shift in my lounger. "There
were seventy RSVPs for the memorial service. And a lot
of donations to the charity in Mary's name." I report the
facts as if this is a birthday party, a happy event. David
must have picked the charity, something about kids. I
guess Mary would have supported that. We always agreed
in our parenting of Mary, of course. David was hands-
off. I was in charge. Our relationship was built on one
simple pact: no contact, ever, with the birth mother. That
isn't unreasonable.

"How are you feeling, though, about this afternoon,
Jane?" She blinks and looks as if she is about to cry. She
didn't even know Mary. Imagine how hard it is for me, all
of this. I won't cry, not here, not now. I like my makeup
job today, and I'm shopping next.

I drop my head, look at my hands folded in my lap. "I
am trying really hard to move on, for Betsy and David.
I'll always have a hole in my heart. You never get over a
huge loss like this, as you know. Tonight is the first step

of reconnecting our family. David needs me by his side tonight and I'll be there." Watching his every move.

Dr. Rosenthal stands, indicating our time is up. "Are you writing in your grief diary? Going to group? Listening to the breath-work podcasts?" Dr. Rosenthal walks me to the door. I feel her hand on my shoulder. "I can tell you are improving. Good job, Jane."

"Thanks." I don't tell her that I don't do anything she tells me to do, that she doesn't understand anything. I know who I am, Dr. Rosenthal. I walk out of the office door and avoid eye contact with the old man sitting in the corner waiting for his appointment to begin.

My mind flashes to David, to what he'll be like as an old man. I wonder if we'll still be married all those years from now, sitting in our home, holding hands on the couch. We might be, if he straightens up. Atones for his sins, both current and past.

This is his last chance. We'll move to our new home, try to start again. But if he makes one more mistake, I'll ruin him.

6

On the drive back from Dr. Rosenthal's office, Sam tells me he talked to the owner at The Boutique, and he has the "perfect" dress for the memorial service. "You deserve it, Mrs. H."

I laugh. It feels good. "I'm not sure what I deserve, but you could use a wardrobe update." I glance at his baggy jeans, muscle shirt. It works for him, though.

"Hey, I like my style." He parks in front of the store, glances at me in the rearview mirror.

"Oh, I do, too, Sam. It's just those jeans. Well, I don't understand your generation, that's for sure." Or do I?

Sam hops out of the driver's seat, ending our little conversation. I wonder if he enjoys our time together as much as I do. I like to think so. On the way to Dr. Rosenthal's office I sit behind him. On the way back, I sit behind the empty passenger's seat: always away from the ocean side of the car. I'm waiting for someone to notice this, to mention it, but no one has. It's a unique and compelling symbol of complicated grief. Her daughter drowned therefore she is afraid of water. Textbook.

Sam opens my door. "Should we pick up a dress for Betsy, too?"

What? No. This is me-time. "She is fine. Has a dress."

Twenty minutes later and we're back on the road, after I dropped five hundred dollars on a long-sleeved cream dress. Mary would have liked it. Oh, Mary. Why did you disobey me?

Mary was home for only two weeks before she planned to leave us again for her internship. The night before she died, Mary appeared in the living room, where David and I were sitting. David said, "Wow, honey, you look beautiful. What's the special occasion?"

Mary did, in fact, look gorgeous in the red floral silk cocktail dress. But there was a problem. "That's my dress. How many times have I told you just ask? Don't take."

Mary's dark brown eyes narrowed, hands jumped to her hips. "You have so many clothes. I just wanted to look good, for Brad. Tonight is special. We're talking again. We missed each other this year. You need to learn how to share. Everything. You come from a place of scarcity and it's driving us all crazy."

David grabbed my hand and pulled me back down to

the couch. "She does look spectacular in the dress, Jane. Let it go."

"Great. Take it. And why are you going out with Brad? You told me he was a loser. So high school. I guess you just lied about that, too." I stood up and stomped off into the kitchen. I needed to get a grip. Resume control of the situation. Fighting about a dress wasn't smart. And it wasn't about the dress. Truth be told, I was more mad at myself than Mary in that moment.

As I stood in the kitchen I heard Mary hurrying out the door, high heels clacking on the stone floor, as her father called after her, "You know what it's really about. She's jealous. That's all. Have fun. Love you."

His good cheer fueled my rage. I stepped around the corner. "You promised not to ever let this happen. How could you?"

"It's just a dress."

"It's not about the dress," I hissed, my hands clenched in fists.

"Mary finding her birth mom, that's normal. She's an adult. She can make her own choices, and she has. If you keep trying to control her like this, try to keep them apart, you'll lose her. You're being ridiculous, acting like a child. Elizabeth is a good role model, a doctor."

"I forbid it. All of it," I had said, but it was too late to stop them. They'd been scheming since they connected. Elizabeth James was going to steal my daughter.

Rage boils in my veins again, right now, just remembering how I'd been deceived. My hands clench, my jaw aches with tension. It was the one thing I demanded: the one thing he promised when motherhood was thrust onto me, when I agreed to the choice that ended my career. And now I know there was even more to the story. My husband had sex with Elizabeth James. A one-night stand at his parents' house.

My husband is Mary's father. I'm not sure I can take this. I realize I'm crushing the dress in my lap, balling it up in anger. I stop, smooth the creamy silk across the back seat. I take a deep breath as Sam pulls into my drive-way. I paste on a smile and meet Sam's eyes in the mirror.

"See you tomorrow, Mrs. H.?" Sam opens my door and helps me out. I must look confused because he adds, "The graduation committee? You volunteered, remember?"

"Busy week." I nod.

"Betsy wants you there, right?" Sam closes the passenger door but doesn't move. "Good mother-daughter mojo."

Betsy doesn't care if I help with graduation. We don't have any mojo.

"Okay. Fine. I'll text you if I change my mind. Or she does. Thanks, Sam."

I unlock the gate to the courtyard, hurry to the front door and inside. When Cash was alive he'd greet me at the gate, tail wagging, searching behind me for Mary or Betsy. Instead there is only silence.

In the kitchen, I flip on the local news. Good background noise while I force myself to try to eat something. I glance at Cash's empty bowl. For Betsy, I open the cabinet under the microwave and tuck it in beside my beach picnic plasticware. Another relic of happy times before: beach picnics with friends and the kids, sunsets enjoyed while sipping rosé and planning the future. S'mores made, laughter shared. Standing guard at the edge of the sea while the kids, skilled at swimming in the ocean but still your responsibility, frolic in the cold water. Standing at the edge of the sea, on kid duty, enjoying all the eyes staring at my perfect bikini body. Ah, the good old days.

I close the cabinet, forcing the end of the memories. I can always pull the bowl back out if I need to remind them of Cash, that he's gone, too. That accidents happen. That life is short, that loyalty is rewarded.

I open the refrigerator and pull out a plastic tub of left-over salad. Something David brought home late, a few nights ago. I recognize the to-go box from one of his new favorite places. Always sniff before you take a big bite of something you didn't cook. Contaminated food kills five thousand people each year in the US. Appetizing, right? I am hungry, though, so I decide to risk it.

I push on the corners of the tub and the seal breaks, launching the lid into the air like a rocket. It falls, landing on the kitchen floor with a clatter. Never have a stone floor in your kitchen. Everything breaks when it lands on it, no matter what. Sort of a given, just like when you fall two hundred feet from a cliff you die. When you fall two hundred feet from a cliff into the ocean you also die. The surface of water isn't soft. It's like hitting a brick wall, a stone floor.

I pick up the lid and dump the old salad into a bowl. I sit down at the beautifully decorated table and take a bite.

My mind taunts me. If you've fallen from a cliff and no one is there, do you make a sound?

7

I look good. My new dress is elegant, suitable for the mother of the deceased, I guess. My makeup is perfect, and waterproof. I slip on a pair of sand-friendly flats. I'm ready but David is late. We haven't spoken, not since the little scene in the courtyard. He's enveloped himself in a cloak of rage over palm tree removal and sends my calls straight to voice mail. Maybe he won't pick me up at all?

I believe I have a more valid reason to be furious than he does. I pace up and down the entry hall, wondering if Betsy will come home before the ceremony, or simply appear at the beach, like a stranger, one of the invitees as opposed to one of the family.

No matter how we all arrive at the memorial service, David and I will be a united front starting tonight. Betsy will join us. We will all three sit together, up front, grieving but harmonious, loving. This is my plan. For now, for tonight, I will keep quiet about the new information that Elizabeth James revealed. As hard as it is to bite my tongue, I will. Revenge is best served cold, as you know.

As for the actual ceremony, I don't really care what goes on, I just want it to be over. Only David and Kylie seem to look forward to it. All week she has copied us both on email updates filled with perky hashtags and exclamation points. David effuses back with thanks. I delete them all.

This evening will be perfect!! #sunset #meaningful, Kylie wrote in her latest missive this afternoon. Please find me when you arrive and I'll show you to your seat. #frontrow. There will be a brief presentation by the pastor and a song, and then just mingling and remembering. See you in three hours!

David answers, Thank you for all of your hard work!!!

What should I say? She doesn't work for me!!! We barely know each other beyond a hello at company functions!!!! Get away from my husband!!!!!!!! When is the last time I have been invited to a company function? Not since Mary left for college, I realize with a start. I'll need to ask David about this. There are so many things I should be asking David about. And I will.

I hear a honk. That couldn't possibly be for me?

I check my phone. I've missed a text from David. Out front.

Another honk. Seriously?

You are honking at your wife!! #rude

I hurry out the door, through the courtyard and out the front gate as David honks again.

I yank open the door to his silver Tesla and lean in. "Really? Honking?"

David puts his finger to his lips, shushing me. He's on the phone. A man's voice booms over the car's speakers. "Again. Great job, David. I'll see you in Cabo and we'll celebrate. Bye for now."

I roll my eyes and climb in. We've sunk to a new low. He cannot actually believe I'd put up with them taking a Cabo trip, does he? After he told me no last year? After all of his lies?

"Sorry. Just wrapping up a business call." David drives off. It's three minutes to the beach from our house by golf cart, one minute by car.

"When are we going to Cabo?" I smile. I will draw the line at beach trips with others.

David looks confused for a moment but realizes I overheard the end of his conversation. "Oh, well, I'm not going. It's to celebrate the big deal closing. I was just humoring him. And why are we talking about Cabo, today of all days? We're driving to a memorial for our daughter. Your wires are all crossed, Jane." He shakes his head but I note the flush in his cheeks.

He slipped not finishing the call before I slid into the passenger seat. He knows I've caught him. I'm sure he's dreaming of that trip to Cabo—I know my husband. I want to challenge him further, but it isn't the right time.

What else has he hidden from me these last twenty years? In silence we pass by the community clubhouse, the tennis courts, the park and zip through the tunnel underneath Coast Highway. Oh crap. I feel a panic attack coming on, a real one. I realize I'm holding my breath. I feel dizzy, it's hard to breathe. I open my purse and press my face into it, breathing slowly.

"Should I pull over?" David exhales at the question. Frustration? Embarrassment? Who knows? "Take you back home?"

"No." I tell myself to breathe in, breathe out, breathe in, breathe out. I focus not on the ocean, but the green wooden benches lining the edge of the sand. I know the cause of this attack. It's not the memorial service for Mary. It's the man sitting next to me. His lies never stop. I wish I'd taken a pill, just one, to dull all of this nonsense, to avoid looking at him. Too late.

At the south end of the beach a sign informs us the area is reserved for a private event. I almost wonder who is getting married, and then I realize, it's our event. Dr. Rosenthal agreed to this idea, David's idea, because the funeral had been small. I'd told him I couldn't handle a big service, not after the days of hope, not after all I'd been through. So this is our gift to the community, to help with the healing, David explained as Dr. Rosenthal nodded. Closure. It was the last time he came to a session. I guess he got what he wanted. Permission to throw a party with Kylie.

David parks the car in the only "reserved" spot. I turn and look at him, chiseled chin, thick dark hair. He looks about the same, but he's not the man I married twenty-two years ago. Nor, of course, am I the same woman. Well, actually, that's not true. I am exactly the same. I've just been hiding until now. I guess I really should have tried harder to make it in Hollywood. I'm a natural, they all told me that back in Arkansas. Next week, head shots. I repeat that in my mind like a mantra, calming myself.

David's jaw clenches and he turns toward me, noticing my stare and my awkward breathing. I look at my lap. I'm imagining what I will do if Elizabeth dares to show up. She had better not appear. She's not welcome here.

She never was.

I take a deep breath. I must be calm, in control. Later, I will confront my husband, the man sitting next to me, the father of our adopted daughter.

"Hello, Jane? Have you settled down?" David stares at me like I'm a toddler who's having a fit over nothing.

I swallow. "I'm fine, dear."

"Good. Let's just get through this ceremony together, as Mary's parents. Don't embarrass yourself this evening. Or Betsy. It's important for people to see you are fine, sort of returning to normal. My parents will be here, too, of course. Please, let's just all get along. For Mary's sake, please." David opens his door and gets out of the car without hearing my answer.

That's probably for the best. I won't repeat it here.

I wait for David to open my door, to hustle around like Sam does, but he has forgotten me already and is swarmed by our guests. I push my door open and stand up next to the car. From here I take in the rows of white folding chairs, all facing the ocean. Some are occupied, some empty. I look down, remind myself to focus on the soft sand, the green grass, anything but the cold, deep, blue ocean, the same ocean Mary floated in for three days until she washed ashore. A chill runs down my spine and I wrap my arms across my chest.

I jump when a hand grasps my elbow and an arm slips through mine. Sarah, my first friend all those years ago at the ladies' luncheon at The Cove, speaks softly in my ear. "Let's get you to your seat, shall we? Just this way."

Sarah still has her same short blond hair, and a beach volleyball player's thin, muscular physique. Sarah's daughter, Liz, was Mary's best friend. Inseparable. Well, I guess that's not entirely correct. Liz went off to an Ivy League college, so they were separated. My mind is racing. I take a deep breath.

"Hello," I manage to say with enthusiasm. I hope. She was a moderately consistent friend back in the day. I glance at her as she takes me across the sand and realize it would be good to have someone like Sarah on my side these days. It seems she's forgiven me for the little gossip I spread about her and her gardener. I mean, I was just having some fun, knocking her down a peg or two on the women's social ladder, and it was years ago now. It's a dog-eat-dog world, so we all have to play to our strengths.

As for my strengths, in addition to my captivating beauty, it's my perfect little family, David and Betsy. I realize I've allowed them to team up against me, to believe they are stronger than I am during my period of complicated grief. It's two against one. Just like I felt toward the end with Mary and Betsy. Back then, both girls were the problem, the way they'd hide things from me, work together against me. Now Betsy is the only problem daughter.

Sometimes I wonder if she received all of her genetic material from David's side, I mean, just look at his awful, conniving parents.

I spot them sitting in the second row of chairs, on the aisle: Pompous (him), rigid (her), self-righteous (both of them). They want everyone to think they're so perfect, except for this tragedy that befell their granddaughter. But they aren't perfect. For example, they'd be mortified if I told everyone about the Harris family secrets. Let's start with crazy Aunt Emma everyone is terrified of being around. What if Betsy is just like her? Is that what's happening to their only living granddaughter? I mean, she has a nose piercing, tattoos, she smokes weed. She was with Mary the day she died, at the park. What has she done? And if that's not enough to really get their old hearts racing, perhaps I should announce to everyone here tonight that their beloved only son screwed a servant of theirs, knocked her up, all while he was a newlywed. Oh, and then talked his wife into adopting his love child? That would turn some heads. I wonder if I should bring all this up to Sarah?

No, not now. I need to focus on the memorial. Sarah leads me around the side of the chairs, far enough so no one bothers us as we trudge through the thick soft sand. Sarah says, "They've seated family up front, of course.

I see David's parents are already seated. Is Mary's birth mother coming?"

What? I stop walking as a wall of rage crashes on my shoulders, tenses my neck. How dare she ask me this? I turn to Sarah. "Of course not. We don't even know who she is. I am Mary's mother." My heart is racing. No one is to know about Elizabeth. Mary must have told Liz and Sarah about her birth mother. Mary is a complete traitor. My whole family: turncoats. Sarah must sense my anger, probably because my arm has gone rigid in hers, my pulse beats in my temples.

She stutters, "Oh, I guess I'm mistaken. Mary had mentioned something about meeting her, how wonderful she is. A doctor? Anyway, where's Betsy off to when she graduates?"

I turn to her, my sunglasses so dark Sarah's face is shadowed, silhouetted to its basic parts. Small nose. Pointy chin. Patrician. "Saddleback Community College."

"Good for her." The way she says it makes me think Sarah worried Betsy wouldn't be off to college anywhere, our lost daughter. Another lost daughter. But mostly my mind is buzzing with Sarah's knowledge of Elizabeth James. Before I can delve further into my anger, Betsy catches up to us.

Through my dark sunglasses, I see she's wearing a dress of some sort, presumably the one we ordered from Free People online, but I cannot be sure. Her stomach is bare, as if a piece of fabric is missing, but it must be the style. I've fallen behind on young adult trends. I'm assuming she is fashionable. David gives her the allowance to be able to afford it.

"Mom? Hello?" Betsy stares at me, waves a hand in front of my face.

"Hello, honey. You look beautiful. Are those army boots hard to walk in on the sand?" A caring, nonjudgmental question. I'm proud of myself.

"Really?" Betsy shakes her head. "Hi, Mrs. Murphy. Thanks for babysitting my mom."

"Good to see you, dear. Your mom told me your college news. Saddleback is wonderful and everyone transfers to impressive schools from there." Sarah keeps speaking even though I wish she wouldn't.

I just want to sit down. Did Mary have a big party and tell every single person she knew about Elizabeth James? How could she humiliate me like this? Betray me? I need to think. I should be one step ahead of developments in my family, not perpetually behind. This is all David's fault. And Betsy's.

"Thanks, Mrs. Murphy. I'm stoked."

What? She is?

"I'll take it from here," Betsy says.

Did she just call me "it"?

Betsy leans in and says, "I asked Dad if it was true. If he was Mary's real dad. He looked like he was going to have a heart attack."

"Yes, that's what happens to liars. Cheaters. And did he admit it?"

"He wants to talk tomorrow. So yes. It's official. You're right. So weird," Betsy whispers as she slips her arm into mine and gives me a little nudge. "This way. I'll take care of you today, Mom."

Validation helps my neck and shoulders relax. Betsy is being nice to me. I whisper to Betsy, "Thank you. But you don't seem mad at your father." I unhook my arm from Sarah's as she drifts away mumbling something about Liz wanting to say hello and catch up.

"I don't feel much of anything these days, to tell you the truth. I just want to get this service over with, get this week over with. Come on, Mom." Betsy escorts me to the front row of chairs. David is seated on the aisle and he's reading something on his phone. I take the empty seat next to him. Betsy's place is next to me, but instead of sitting down, she waves at David's parents and literally goes behind my back to greet them. I'm sure they're hugging. I don't turn around. We aren't close, but for this, for David's showy memorial for his daughter, we will all go along with the act. I bring my hands to my face, breathe in, breathe out. I focus on the deep sand covering my right shoe, the pink radiance of the setting sun glowing on my silk dress.

And then my mind clears. I drop my hands from my face and turn to look at the man seated to my left.

The bright light of a text catches my attention and I see CLOSED ESCROW!!! ☺ before he quickly flips his phone over, trying to hide the screen from me.

Has he told someone else about our secret house? Confused, I grab my phone, open my app and see the full extent of his betrayal. The full measure of what he has done. He's texting with Kylie, just before the ceremony for his dead daughter.

Kylie: Is it ours yet? ♥ ♥

I swallow. Glance to my left. He isn't watching me, of course.

David: Yes!!

Kylie: CLOSED ESCROW!!! ☺

My neck tenses and I fight the urge to punch my husband in the face.

Beside me, David types on his phone, and I read it on mine. A new beginning just the two of us. Love you.

Kylie: ♥

I stare at my husband as my heart thuds in my chest. How could he? I cannot believe the audacity of this man. This is the final straw. This changes everything, reconciliation to ruin in the blink of text.

I'm finding it hard to breathe. My hands shake as I grab the edges of the seat. Betsy slips into place next to me and she pats my leg. I know I'm being watched by all of the crowd. Normally I like the attention. But tonight, just now, I fight the urge to run. I lean forward in my seat, about to stand up, to get out of here, when David grips my wrist.

"Calm down, Jane," he says in a firm whisper. "The program is starting."

I look up and see the pastor step to the podium. He nods in our general direction and begins. "Welcome, friends and family. We are here to celebrate the life of Mary Anderson Harris. A beautiful young woman. A…"

I sit back in my chair and David releases my wrist. Fine, I will sit here, but I don't need to hear about my daughter. I spin my wedding ring around on my finger. It's looser by the month. Beside me, Betsy cries softly into her tissue. I look past her down the row, expecting to see Josh, forgetting they broke up. Poor Betsy, all alone. I touch her knee, patting it softly. I look over my right shoulder and I'm surprised to see Sam, my driver, standing behind the last row of chairs. His presence calms me. I take a deep breath. How nice of him to be here for me. I nod at him and he smiles.

I feel a shift next to me and watch in disbelief as David stands and walks to the front. I didn't know we have speaking parts. I'm not prepared. I haven't rehearsed any lines. I could tell them all about Mary, about how she was the daughter everyone would want to have, until she picked a different mother. I could tell them about my heartbreak, my anger, my sadness. I loved Mary. I pull a tissue out of my purse. I could explain to them all that I'm not like my own horrible mother. That I was a good mom, the best mom: the only mother Mary needed. I could tell them all how much I miss her, every day.

But I'm not the one at the podium. I look up, and there's David, backlit by the setting sun, the crashing waves.

He pulls a piece of paper from his pocket and reads: "'Thank you all for coming this evening. On behalf of the rest of Mary's family, Betsy, Jane and my parents, David and Rosemary, we want you to know we couldn't have made it through this last year without you.'"

I flip open the program and realize David will be speaking for all of us. I'm not on the agenda, even though I would have had the best delivery, the best performance. Fine. I take a breath and relax. My mind drifts to a house on a tree-lined street, the next community over. I thought it was for us, to start over. Instead, it's for *new beginnings*. I look up to the podium and David has tears running down his face.

"'She was my pride and joy. Along with her sister, the girls made my life happy and worthwhile.'" David pauses, wipes under his eyes. "'I'll never get over Mary's loss, but because of all of you, I can go on. Please, stay and join us for a sunset cocktail in Mary's memory. Come and tell me your favorite story about my daughter. She'll be alive in all of our hearts, forever.'"

"Amen," the pastor says and leads the way to the open bar, followed closely behind by David.

Bravo, David. You stole the show. No part for me, Mary's mother. But I will deal with him appropriately. He has gone too far now. There cannot be a simple reboot to our relationship, not anymore. Things have gotten out of hand with Kylie but it turns out he has been out of control almost since the day we married. Silly David. I thought he knew me better than that. He thinks I'm a fool, that I don't see him for all that he is. But he's wrong. I do.

I hear sniffles behind me even though I've tried to tune out everything. The menacing ocean. The other guests. But it's the sniffling that gets me. I turn around. It's David's mother. My sunglasses hide the evil-eye glance I shoot her way. She and her husband stand and begin shuffling out of their aisle away from me. They are complicit in all of this, of that I'm sure. Good riddance, folks.

With the Harrises out of the way I'm staring directly at Elizabeth James still seated, tears marring her perfect makeup. She came here despite my warnings. Well, she was already on my list, of course, but she's bumped herself up in the rankings. Way to go, Elizabeth!!! Thanks for the exclamation points, Kylie!!! Game on, David!! You cannot even begin to understand the rage I feel.

"You're here." I point at my nemesis. I don't care who is watching.

"I needed to attend Mary's memorial. Tonight is important to me. For closure." Diminutive, brilliant Dr. Elizabeth James, plastic surgeon to the stars in LA, meets my blue eyes with her brown ones. Her lips, Mary's lips, part and she begins to talk again.

You slept with my husband? You stole Mary from me.

I don't hear anything she says. I stand up, dizzy. If I knew how to throw a punch, I would, but I don't, so I throw the memorial program at her. "How dare you?"

I watch as Elizabeth scampers down the row of chairs, making it to the aisle to stand by my in-laws.

"Jane, get a grip." My dear, sweet mother-in-law steps between us and says, in a hushed tone, "This poor woman came to say her final goodbyes to her daughter. What is wrong with you?"

I'm shaking with anger. I could explode. I point my finger at her, at the three of them, complicit in this plot to ruin my life. I keep my voice low, calm, my words angry, final. "You are not Mary's mother. You gave her up. You promised to never be part of her life. You two promised this would be our little secret." I point at my in-laws and they both step back, two rats shuffling in the sand trap.

Elizabeth steps in front of them. She's wearing a stupid navy dress. That isn't a color of the sunset. She wears glasses like a professor and her eyes are rimmed in red. I can see all of this, all of her, even though the light is almost gone from the beach.

"Look, Jane. I know you never wanted me in Mary's life. I held up my end of the bargain. As you know, she found me. I've done nothing wrong. Could we just stop this? We need to remember Mary." Elizabeth finishes her speech and Mrs. Harris slides her arm around her.

My dear mother-in-law. Did she arrange the playdate for her son and this woman? Did she mastermind all of this for a grandchild? For control? To get rid of me by breaking up our marriage? My heart pounds in my chest as I realize I've underestimated my mother-in-law, too.

Just look at her, comforting Elizabeth. Oh. My. God. That's more kindness than she has shown me in twenty years. I take a step closer, lower my voice. "No, Elizabeth, we cannot just stop this. I told you to stay away when I visited your office last year. And again when we had coffee this morning. Have you no shame? You slept with my husband, you slut."

"I know. And I'm sorry about that. I didn't know about you." Elizabeth swallows. "But I do now. You're ruthless, selfish and jealous. But, Jane, you're not in control of me."

She's wrong about that. I know I scared her when I visited her in LA last year. It was the point of my trip. Clearly I didn't go far enough, though. She called Mary and told on me and then Mary and I had a big fight, and then Mary went to the park with Betsy. And then she died. This is all Elizabeth's fault. I'm shaking all over.

I point my finger at my enemy. "Jealous of you? Don't be ridiculous. Look at me, I have it all. It's your fault Mary is dead. I hope you can live with that. With what you've done."

"Jane, that is enough," my father-in-law says as he takes his wife's hand, and together they surround Elizabeth like geriatric guards and walk away through the sand toward the reception. I watch them go, filled with fury. Does David still want to screw her? Was it really just a one-night stand? Are they together now?

No. I happen to know David is otherwise engaged and that Elizabeth is single. So she's pathetic. Mary was her only chance at happiness, and she gave her away.

My hands clench into fists. Mary only had one mother. And it was me.

I drop into my chair, shaking from the encounter. I really can't believe the moxie of that woman, showing up here, despite my threats and warnings. She underestimates me. They all do.

A hand on my shoulder startles me. It's Sam. "I'm sorry for your loss, Mrs. H." He must have heard the whole argument with stupid Elizabeth.

My driver is my only friend, it seems. "Thank you. Nice of you to be here."

He nods and walks away.

"Mrs. Harris." I turn and look up. Standing in front of me is Brad, Mary's high school boyfriend. A nice boy. A local guy. Captain of the football team, and went on to one of the state schools. Long Beach, maybe? Mary broke up with him before they headed off to college. I don't know if they saw each other after the night Mary wore my red dress. That night was the second-to-last night of her life.

I just never imagined he would be her last boyfriend. I thought he was just a start, as unimportant as a bicycle once you buy your first car.

"It's good to see you." I try to stand, falter, and Brad steadies me. I need to move away from the front row. I'm too close to the water, too close to Dr. E., as her patients call her. "Could we go over there? Do you mind?"

"Of course." Brad slips his arm through mine and escorts me to the back of the ceremony setup, behind all of the chairs and far away from the bar where everyone is gathered. We sit next to each other on one of the green benches at the edge of the sand. It is nice to have grass beneath my feet. I'm still fuming from the Elizabeth encounter, among other things. I wonder what time it is. I wonder when I can get away from here.

Brad clears his throat. "I miss her every day. It's just

so hard. That's why I've gone away. I can't be here, in The Cove, without Mary."

Sweet boy. "I know. It is so hard." I pull off my sunglasses. It's almost dark out now. Laughter floats our way from the cluster of mourners by the stand-up bar nestled in the sand. David is holding court, with his parents and Kylie, his "assistant." He has a rapt audience, that husband of mine.

A few guests are leaving, nodding to Brad and me on our bench, unsure whether to approach me, and my armor of grief, and deciding against it. I see Josh, Betsy's former boyfriend, with a parent escorting him on each side. The parents don't notice me but Josh looks in my direction as they pass by. I manage a wave. And he nods. But to most people, David is the host. The popular one. The friendly one. I am the suffering mom. The embodiment of their worst nightmares. I'm also "that bitch" if you ask my former tennis team.

"Have you seen Betsy?" Brad doesn't seem to be a fan of my youngest daughter but I need to be sure.

"She was with Mr. Harris, over at the bar. But no, I don't see her now. I didn't see her friends here, either." He crosses his arms. The wind has picked up, the usual chill begins to descend on us like a damp invisible curtain.

"I wouldn't recognize Betsy's friends." I surprise myself with that admission to this boy, an almost stranger who loved Mary.

I watch Brad's face and catch a wave of tension, a decision made. Something not said. He looks around, nervous. "That's too bad."

"I hear it's a different crowd, not the popular one that you and Mary were a part of," I say. I'm a mom, the heart of the family. I pick up on some clues, even those my family tries to hide.

"When she goes to college next year, that will be good. A fresh start."

"Brad, did you meet Elizabeth, Mary's birth mom? Did Mary tell you about her?"

"Ah, yes, well, she is great, but Mary told me it was awkward with you two. I, um, you know, um, I've got to go. I'm flying back to Spain tomorrow. It's where I go to school now." Brad stops abruptly and stands. "Good seeing you, Mrs. Harris. Just want you to know I loved Mary. I wanted to marry her."

That would never have happened, poor boy. But I can leave him with that dream. "Of course you did, dear." He bends to give me a hug as I sit on the bench. It's formal. Quick. And then he's gone, jogging away in his suit, disappearing in the parking lot.

I reach for my purse, but it's not here on the bench. I've left it on my chair on the beach, thrown off by my encounter with Elizabeth. The last place I want to go in the almost dark is toward the ocean. The group of people near the bar has dwindled to a dozen or so. David's parents and Elizabeth have left, thank goodness. If I can make it over there to the bar, perhaps David, the serial cheater, will show some sympathy and grab my purse for me.

I stand slowly while holding the back of the bench, like an old woman testing a walker, not certain if her legs will hold. Goose bumps dot my legs. I feel something crawling on me and swat an ant away. The little buggers kill fifty people a year, if I remember correctly. Accidental death by ants sounds gruesome and I try not to imagine it. But I do, and shudder at the thought.

The remaining mourners, celebrators, whatever you're called a year later, are a cheerful, drunk bunch, including my husband. I see the woman reporter from the local television news, remember her impassioned pleas for information, her somber reporting of the facts. Day one: Missing. Day two: Still missing, meet the parents. Day three: Horror washes ashore.

And there's Kylie, Saran-wrapped in a light pink dress that matched the sand an hour or so ago, presumably why I haven't spotted her until now. The fact she blended in is impressive. Intuitively, she knows to stay out of my path. She ducks behind David, trying to become one with the bar. The bartender, for one, seems happy to claim her.

"There you are, Jane," David slurs. Is he drunk?

"Here I am. It's time to go, don't you think? I left my purse on the chair out there." I point but don't look toward the ocean. "Would you mind grabbing it?"

"I'll get it for you!!" Kylie leaps into action, a shrink-wrapped superwoman hopping through the now-cool sand. David watches her go as I watch him. She's so happy, almost like she's celebrating something as opposed to attending the memorial of a dead girl.

"Here." David hands me a glass of white wine. "You okay?"

I smile. Take a sip. It's good wine. Of course, the Harris family would serve nothing but the best for all of us missing Mary, or all of us who pretend to, like Kylie.

"Fine. Nice ceremony except for the appearance of Elizabeth James. By the way, did you consider asking me to address the crowd? I should have stood up there with you." I stare at David as he picks up his drink and sips.

"No, not really. I figured I could speak on behalf of our family since I'm the one who wanted the ceremony. As for Elizabeth attending, my parents invited her. Not me." He squints at me.

"Funny that you're comfortable having her here, given the fact you broke your promise to me and helped Mary find her. There's more to the story, isn't there, David?"

David smirks, clearly unsure what to do with that. "It's not the right time or place to discuss this. But I didn't mean to hurt you, Jane. It was a mistake."

At this moment, I hate him. More than words can express. Did you know crimes of passion are based on insecurity? People are struggling to trust their significant other. With 73 percent of marriages in wealthy coastal communities ending in divorce, that's a lot of insecurity. But I'm not insecure. I'm certain. Only 5 percent of men are killed by their significant other, and at this moment, I could easily join the 5 percent.

Unfortunately, my husband is not one of the victims. Yet.

He holds up his hands. Surrender style. "Let's talk about this at home. Betsy told me you were fixated on this."

"Me? Fixated?" I glare at David. I know he can feel

my rage before I speak. I watch as he leans back on his heels in the sand, stumbles against the bar. I whisper, "No, you told me Mary was MY baby, that she always would be, only mine. It was our one deal, the line in the sand. You promised. You're a liar. And so are your parents." We lock eyes.

Beside me I smell a bouquet of flowers, and Kylie's overly enthusiastic voice arrives. "Here you go, Jane! Just where you left it!"

She hands me my purse and I manage, "So nice of you to plan the ceremony. You didn't even know Mary, did you?" Sure, you were lurking around for a while. You came into our lives just as Mary was slipping out of them. Mary's off to college, our home is unsettled, and there you are, ready to provide emotional support and constant understanding. Flattery and companionship! Oh, and exclamation points galore. Yes, you were there. You saw an entry point. I hope, soon, you'll enjoy the exit wound.

Kylie's face is flushed and her eyes wide. I watch as David turns to Kylie and shakes his head slightly, almost imperceptibly. But I saw it. Gotcha. She did meet Mary. How many liars must I suffer?

Kylie beams a big smile and says, "I love party planning!! But no, unfortunately, I didn't meet her at the office. I joined the firm after Mary left for college. But I've heard all about her from David." Her lipstick perfectly matches her dress. Her eyelids are the same shade, too, with sparkles. I don't know how she did that but I can't help but be impressed. She's what you call perfectly put together. Like I am, only she's younger, and not very smart.

"So you met Mary outside the office?" I ask with a kind tone and a smile.

"Yep!" Kylie answers without thinking. Oops.

She's an idiot. I look at David and say, "We should go, dear."

"We need to wait until the guests leave." David waves his hand in the general direction of the five people still standing at the bar. These people are drunks, not mourners, at this point. He doesn't want to go home with me. He'd rather spend the night on the cold sand, with Kylie!! I know the feeling, the urge toward avoidance. And the other: the search for something better. I share it, believe me. But still. Pretense is pretense.

I shrug and point to my bench. "I'll be over there. Hurry, I'm getting cold." I walk away and give him a chance to say goodbye to his guests, and Kylie. I think I hear David mumble something in my wake. The waves are building, crashing to shore, so I could be imagining things. The bench is cold and damp with dew. I sit anyway, knowing I may be ruining my new silk dress.

I open my purse, feel around for my phone. Something pokes my hand. I pull out an envelope, The Cove's signature stationery. Dark green The Cove logo in the top left corner, crisp thick white paper stock.

I saw guests placing letters and cards in the basket by the podium. We'd asked for donations to some charity or another. Someone must have noticed my purse and tucked the donation letter beside it. Kylie no doubt put it inside.

I tear open the envelope and pull out the letter. When I unfold it, I'm worried I won't be able to read what it says, or that I'll drop an enclosed check on the ground. I shouldn't have worried. There is no check. The words are clearly legible even in the dim light.

MARY'S DEATH WAS NOT AN ACCIDENT. JUST ASK BETSY.

My hands shake and I'm having trouble holding the note. I gulp for air. I scan the beach. No one is watching me. A shiver runs down my spine and I notice David walking toward me with Kylie. I watch as he slips his arm around her waist for a moment—their heads lean together as he whispers in her ear, before they break apart again. If you weren't watching closely you would have missed it. They aren't holding hands, but they might as well be.

I slide the letter inside its envelope, and slip it into my purse. My heart races as I watch them part, reluctantly, Kylie waving to me before walking away to her car. I stand on shaking legs. The dark weight of all of this is becoming too much to bear.

David joins me at the bench and we walk to his car in silence. He opens my door for me, and I slip inside. Who would write such a thing and leave it for me, here, now, of all times? Everyone knows Mary drowned in the ocean after falling from the cliff. All those months when we searched for answers and never discovered a clue to explain how Mary fell from that cliff? Perhaps now someone has the answer? Someone saw something? Is someone on my side?

Ask Betsy what? I've told you I have my theory about what happened, a clear line of questioning the police didn't explore. Who was the last person to see Mary alive? There's your answer. Now it seems someone else agrees. I'm not saying Betsy did it, of course. I'm just not certain she didn't. Does someone know the truth?

Or maybe someone wants to push me over the line, that blurry place between sanity and insanity, maybe it's David's parents, or David himself? I told you, I've stopped taking all those pills. I'm in control, but others might not see it that way. Maybe, like my husband, most people don't really see me at all anymore. There are so many ways to look at it. One person's crazy is another's brilliance.

After the one-minute drive, David pulls slowly into the garage, drunk and extra careful. He gets out of the car and stumbles through the courtyard and into the house in front of me. No lights are on. Betsy isn't home, I'm sure of it. Is she hiding from me, keeping more secrets from me?

"I'm going to bed." David waves and heads down the dark hallway.

I watch him walk away, the master of conflict avoidance, and shake my head. Talking to him any more tonight would be a waste of time, anyway.

I'm too wired for sleep. I'll wait for Betsy in the kitchen. When she comes home, I'll confront her with this note. She always was jealous of her older, more attractive sister. Jealousy is such a powerful emotion. It makes you do crazy things sometimes but I'll talk to her, get her to tell me the truth.

I pour a glass of wine and walk with my laptop and the note to the kitchen table. Many people believe I'm crazy with grief. *Complicated grief,* as Dr. Rosenthal calls it. Betsy and David are convinced I'll never get over the tragic accident. I see it in their eyes, the way they look at me. They think I'm someone to be pitied. Ignored. Out in public, they tiptoe around me, hoping I don't draw attention, hoping people will think we're all just fine.

But at home, behind closed doors, I'm simply someone to run from, to hide from, to leave.

They are both wrong. I'm so much more.

TUESDAY

TWO DAYS UNTIL GRADUATION

8

2:30 a.m.

Shoot. I squint my eyes and check the clock. I've fallen asleep at the kitchen table. My neck is stiff, my mouth is sour and dried drool cracks at the corner of my lip. I'm not sure how long I've been here, but I know it's long past time for bed. My computer's screen saver swirls colors and shapes at me, nonthreatening and comforting. I vaguely recall researching the meaning of dreams, something I've done often since Mary's death. While I have been able to take control of most parts of my life during the day, it's the recurring nightmares that terrify me. I can't seem to make them stop.

I touch the keypad and my computer reveals Analysis of Falling Dreams. It looks to be a clinical paper, something Dr. Rosenthal would read and enjoy. I must have nodded off while reading it.

The article reads: *Many patients dream of falling from a mountain cliff. Of the many locations to fall from, mountain cliffs seem to be a favorite. Patients usually wake up before they land.* I take a deep breath. I shouldn't read this. I should just go to sleep again, a hopefully dreamless sleep, in my own bed. But I'm a moth to the flame with my computer. I can't help it. I read the last part of the paragraph: *"Living on the edge" is not just symbolic. The dream actually could be warning the patient of a real and imminent threat.*

Hmm. I wonder if David and Betsy dream of falling? Like most things these days, dreams—or nightmares—are not something we discuss. If they don't dream of free-falling, they should. So should Elizabeth James.

I push away from the table, stand up and check my surroundings. Kitchens are dangerous places. For example, a woman died after she slipped in her kitchen and landed on knives sticking upright in the utensil holder of a dishwasher. Always point your knife blades down. I'm not making this stuff up.

Nobody ever expects to die in her own home in a tragic accident, but a kitchen grease fire can happen in the blink of an eye. Look around your house. Killers lurk everywhere. A slip in the tub, a fall into the sharp corner of your coffee table, a pot of boiling water spills on you, well, tragedy. I could go on. But it's bedtime.

At the kitchen window I look down, wondering if Betsy's light is on. But everything is dark. We'll have our visit in the morning. I make my way toward my bedroom, turning off lights as I go. My heart thumps in my chest but I breathe deeply and calm myself. I'm aware of the danger in my life.

In the bedroom, David snores. That sound is really getting on my nerves.

9

9:00 a.m.

Brilliant sunshine floods my bed, the entire bedroom. The shades are wide open but my eyes squeeze shut, trying to block the spotlight.

The good news is I slept a thick, dreamless sleep. The bad news is I slept too long. I hurry to the bathroom and brush my teeth. I hustle into my closet, pull out my most recent online purchases: yoga pants, a tight cotton T-shirt with a smiling Buddha face on it and finish the look with a bright blue, fitted and zippered hoodie. I look almost normal for a mom around here. Mindful. Meditative. Wholesome. I'm a poster child for healthy living.

I wash my face and comb my hair, pulling it into a low ponytail. Apply just the right amount of makeup for my daytime appearance.

I smile at my reflection. I'll be seeing all of the moms at Volunteer Day. I don't want Betsy to be embarrassed by me. She won't be now. I look, dare I say it, young and hot. Anyone would be proud to have me as her mom. Betsy should consider herself lucky.

ASK BETSY.

I will. But I already know the answer.

I trot out to the kitchen to make a cup of coffee and, like a mirage, David and Betsy are at the table, eating together.

They both stop chewing and watch me walk into the room.

"Good morning!" What a wonderful development. I can't wait to talk to them about my secret pen pal.

They look at me and then each other. They're silent as I make myself a cup of coffee. What have they been talking about? David's infidelity, perhaps? Or did they stick to their favorite topic: Crazy Jane? What did I do to upset them this time, I wonder? It doesn't take much, not with either of them these days.

"Good morning. You look good, like you slept for once. No more vampire hours?" David's voice is gravelly. He is no doubt hungover. But there's something more. An edge.

Betsy nods. "Morning. You do look different."

"Thanks, I guess." I don't know what different means, but I suppose it's a devious daughter compliment. At least she notices things have changed. I'm back.

I join them at the table, slip into the chair across from David.

"Mom, where did you get this?" Betsy holds up the note, my note, from my purse.

"That's mine." I grab the paper and hold it close to my chest. "What are you doing with my note?" I don't want them seeing this. I need to find out who wrote it first, and why. I am in control now. This note is now part of my plan.

"Calm down. You left it here, on the table." David exhales for added drama. Since when did he become a daytime soap opera star? The looks, the sighs, the attitude? Annoying.

I take a breath. I suppose I did leave it out by mistake but it's mine.

"Mom, where did you get this?" Betsy locks eyes with me. A challenge.

"Someone left it in my purse last night. I don't know who."

David puts his chin on his hand and turns to the camera for his close-up. The effort to speak to me must exhaust him. "Perhaps we should talk to Dr. Rosenthal, get you back on some of those meds you were taking? This is crazy stuff. Anonymous notes. Really, Jane? Did you write this last night? Do I need to call the doctor?"

"What? No. I feel good today, I look good today. I know you noticed." I wink at him and he breaks eye contact. I take a sip of coffee. I love being in command.

I turn my attention to my daughter. "I don't know what theory you've concocted while I slept, but here are the facts. Someone left a note in my purse during the memorial service last night. And that note writer wants me to ask you something, Betsy." I have the chills, do you? It would be such a shame if David lost both of his daughters. One murdered. One in prison. David has been a very bad person. He deserves to lose everything. "Darling daughter, what do you know about Mary's death?"

Betsy shakes her head. "You're losing your mind. You're telling us someone slipped a big envelope—"

"Business-sized envelope," David adds helpfully.

"Business-sized envelope into your purse and you didn't notice?" Betsy asks, vying for a job as the newest member of Orange County's detective squad. It's good for her to practice. She should get comfortable around police.

"Correct. I left my purse on the chair."

"How convenient," Detective Betsy notes.

"No, it wasn't. I needed tissues. I noticed it was gone. Kylie, helpful as always, retrieved it for me!!"

"True. That happened." David's eyes light up at the mention of her name but he looks down to conceal it. I see you, David.

Betsy says, "Mom, Mary's death was an accident. There's nothing else to it. Nothing to ask me about. Someone is messing with you." She stands and carries her plate to the sink. I thought she said she never ate breakfast. Another lie.

I say to David, "I'm going to call Detective Branson. I'm going to tell him someone thinks there is more to Mary's death. It's a gift. A new witness, perhaps? I wish you two would believe me, believe this person."

David rolls his eyes. I watch Betsy rinsing her dishes in the sink.

"Betsy, do you have anything new to tell the detective?" I shake the letter in the air.

David sighs. "I'm sorry, Jane. It's just cruel, whoever did this. Macabre. And poor Betsy has been through enough. We all have." David pushes away from the table and carries his cereal bowl to the kitchen sink. "Someone is trying to confuse you and you're already in such a vulnerable state. It's the last thing you need. Mary fell from that cliff. End of story."

"What? No. This person is trying to help. He or she knows something." I look at David and then at Betsy. I stare at Betsy until she flushes. So much guilt there. "Betsy was the last one to see Mary alive. Maybe someone saw them together."

"Jane, stop it!" David hurries to Betsy's side. Wraps his arm around her shoulders. "Two more days, kiddo. Hang in there."

Betsy leans her head on David's shoulder. "You're right. Two days." Then she looks at me, with a scrunched-face look that can only be construed as hate. "I can't believe you're my mother. You really think I had something to do with Mary's death? Don't come to Volunteer Day!"

"Of course I'll be there," I call after my retreating daughter. To David I add, "I'll visit Detective Branson. Tell him he should reopen the investigation. He needs to find this witness." I pound my fist on the table for emphasis and he jumps.

I know what you're thinking. Why would I want to

stir this all up again? Mary is dead and nothing will ever bring her back. Trust me, I have my reasons.

"No. Don't do it. He'll think you're crazy." David narrows his eyes. His phone vibrates with a text message and he can't resist. I watch as he checks his phone, covering the screen with his hand so I can't see it. He types his response, smiles and types again before shoving the phone in his pocket.

He doesn't realize it's futile to hide the screen from me, silly man. I'll read his texts as soon as he leaves. "Is something important happening at the office?"

"Yes, yes, that's it. And I've got to get going." David grabs his briefcase, pours the rest of his coffee into a to-go cup.

"Dear, what's all this *two days* stuff between you and Betsy? What happens in two days besides the graduation?"

"See ya!" my husband answers with a wave and walks out the door.

That's fine. Who needs them? Perhaps they both have plans after we make it through the next two days. But so do I. And I have plenty to do between now and then. I need to convince Detective Alan Branson to reopen the case. He will sigh, too, be reluctant at first. But I will corner him. And he'll enjoy that. Trust me. I know men. I finally have the evidence I need.

I learned two things last night. One was about David. I realize now his multimillion-dollar plan for the future doesn't include me. I may have been clinging on to a dream, a vision of our future together that could never come true. Denial is such a powerful thing.

Still, nothing breaks through that denial like proof. I open my phone and read his texts, the ones he had with "the office" just before he walked out the door.

Kylie: I'm here at the house!!! Waiting!!

David: Be there in 10.

Kylie: I want to go inside!!

David: Don't you dare go in without me ☺

Charming, I know. I drop my phone on the kitchen counter, punch my left palm with my right fist. My heart thumps with rage. Pain shoots through my jaw. I've been played. I want to throw something. But I won't. Not now.

On the plus side, I have an unexpected ally in the note writer. I take a deep breath and force myself to settle down.

Don't you just love it when the plot thickens?

10

I check the dashboard and confirm I'm driving fast. It's because David has a head start on me. I know exactly where he's going. But I can't afford to be stopped, so I ease off the accelerator a bit. Slow and steady wins the race.

Even though I know I'm fooling myself, my heart hopes David is heading to the new house alone. Or just maybe I'm reading things wrong. Perhaps his assistant, Kylie, is meeting him there, but that's only to help with the key transfer, finish up all the paperwork, that sort of thing. She's helping him keep the new home a surprise for me, and Betsy. She's excited for our new, fresh start. That's why she's anxious to see inside. Could that be the case? The truth?

I realize I'm holding on to threads. It's as if the tapestry of our marriage has unraveled, and this new home is the only thing that can mend it.

Marriage is hard for everyone. If you tell me you haven't had a few bumps in your wedded road, then you're lying. We've had more bumps than I care to admit, and clearly for longer than I even knew. A bad taste floats into my mouth as I think of Elizabeth James. It's the taste your mouth has before the dentist shoots you with novocaine, the acid that floods your taste buds just before you realize you're going to throw up.

At the moment, Elizabeth isn't my biggest issue, though. I take a right onto Port Chelsea Place. I love the mature trees, the blissful suburban perfection of this street. All of the homes have been redone in a shingled cottage style, but they aren't cottage sized. I take a deep breath and pull to the curb behind a bright yellow carpet cleaning van, its color scheme sure to draw more attention than another black Audi on this street.

I hurry out of my car, careful to stay shielded behind the carpet cleaning van. Two doors down, across the street, David's car is parked in the driveway of the beautiful Cape Cod–inspired $3.85-million-dollar, 4,227-square-foot residence. From the real-estate listing page I have saved on my computer—oh, come on, you didn't believe me when I said I hadn't looked online, did you?—I already knew about the "open and airy floor plan," the casual elegance that will make entertaining "simply a delight." The large great room with sliding, invisible doors opening to the meticulously landscaped yard. The home boasts six bedrooms and six baths, including a spa-like master suite with a vaulted and beamed ceiling. "It's move-in ready, professionally staged, and all furniture is available for purchase with the home." What a deal!!

I tip my head down into the collar of my black rain jacket and hurry down the sidewalk, stopping behind the huge eucalyptus tree between the street and the sidewalk, directly across the street from David's Tesla.

And there they are. Kylie and David, standing side by side near the front door. A woman wearing a bright pink top hugs Kylie and then David before walking to her car, a typical Realtor luxury Mercedes in beige, and driving away. It's just the three of us now. I hope for David's sake that Kylie, too, will walk away, jump back inside her brand-new white Audi and drive back to the office. She's facilitated the transaction and now it's time for her to go. She can keep the car. I'll keep the rest.

A pain shoots through my right temple and my stomach flips as I watch David bend and scoop Kylie into his arms, slip the key into the light blue front door and carry her inside. As the door closes behind them I feel the fire in my belly ignite. That's it. It's war.

As I hurry back to my car, I do have to give Kylie credit. She works fast. That's the younger generation for you. And David turns out to be an easy mark. David has a type: women like Kylie and me who are not quite what they seem to be. And for some reason, women like us can sense that about him. It must be in his pheromones. Easily conned.

But I'm no longer fooling myself.

Was I a fool? No, I am just a devoted wife who was willing to give him another chance.

And now? Now I'm a formerly devoted wife who is over him. But don't think I'll just leave them to their new little life. I think by now you know me better than that.

11

I pull into the garage at the same time Sam's text lights up my phone: I'm here.

I push the garage door button and welcome the darkness as the door rolls down.

I want to text back: Go away. But not because of Sam. I need to think, reflect. I need to find the note writer, and I need to set everything in motion. David may have carried Kylie over the threshold but he has pushed me over the edge.

I also need to make a showing for Betsy, because this is one of our last times to be together in public. It's important for the other moms to see me, for them to think I'm just like them, showing my love for my daughter by wearing on-trend athletic attire and by being overly involved in every facet of her daily life. To be the helicopter mom they all are, that they expect me to be. That's the mom Betsy hates, or does she hate the housebound mom I've become? I'm not sure. Maybe she hates them both?

For some reason, though, she wants me to be at Volunteer Day or she wouldn't have mentioned it this morning. Does she have a surprise for me? I doubt it. She doesn't think that way. She's simple, her father's daughter. Perhaps she just needs help painting and she doesn't have any friends.

I text Sam: Coming.

Driving to the high school, I sit behind Sam. It's the same direction on Coast Highway, south, as driving to Dr. Rosenthal's office. He keeps glancing at me in the rearview mirror.

"Were you just coming home from someplace, Mrs. H.?" Sam asks, his eyes meeting mine in the rearview mirror.

"No. I don't go anywhere, not without you, Sam." I smile. He couldn't have seen me pull in the garage. He's not that observant.

"Oh, I thought it was you, your car, pulling into the garage just now. I guess not. Anyway, while I was waiting for you I saw a dog walk by that looked just like your dog, Cash. Maybe a brother or sister? Made me miss him and I didn't even know him that well." Sam is staring at me. We are at a stoplight, but still, eyes on the road.

"Eyes on the road, Sam." He drops his eyes. I add, "It's quiet without him around. No barking, no growling. Poor animal changed after Mary died. Wasn't fun to be around. Who knew dogs have emotions?"

"Of course they do. I love dogs." Sam won't drop the dog subject for some reason. Cash is dead. End of dog story.

"Everybody loves dogs." Time for a pivot. "Thanks for coming to the ceremony. That was nice of you." I smile.

"Sure. You looked nice. You look good today, too. Like something has changed." Sam is politely appraising me. I enjoy his flirting. It's not his fault. He has never seen me even try to look pretty before. I've probably shocked him a little.

I smile at him in the mirror. Take off my sunglasses so he can enjoy the full effect. Something has changed, you're right, Sam. "Thank you. Last night's ceremony was just something to get through, but thank you for your help with the dress. It's important for the mom to look good. And now that the year of mourning is over, I'm making an effort to get back to life."

"Well, I'd say you nailed it. Today, too." Sam looks back at the street.

Surprisingly, I feel a little stirring, deep down in my core. I've missed this: a gentle, light flirtation; the promise of something more. Of course, there will never be more with Sam—he's a twentysomething Lyft driver. I'm just lonely, and this is practice.

Back in the day, back when David dropped me off after

our first date in Malibu, hoping I'd ask him in, my attraction to him was so strong I almost blew it.

"Can I come in?" He leaned over, his hand sliding behind my seat. I could feel the current running between us, the stirring between my legs. I couldn't invite him in even if I'd wanted to, of course. I didn't live there, in the Brentwood condo where I'd had him pick me up. And I did want to, I did want him, more than anything and anyone I'd ever met. He'd told me everything about his wealthy parents, his lonely upbringing as an only child, his desire for a big, happy family. He was handsome, and lonely, and looking for a life partner, something I wanted just as much. I'd told him we had so much in common, when of course we didn't.

"I wish you could come in but I have an early call tomorrow. A television commercial for a hamburger chain." I paused, waiting for him to be impressed.

"You're going to be a star." He smiled. "I still think you should let me come in."

"I will be a star. And, as I told you, I have a rule about taking it slow." I blinked at him with my movie-star look. The convertible top was down and the sky was filled with stars. The only ones around, truth be told. I had begun to worry a bit that I was never going to make it in Hollywood. All of my supposed beauty pageant contacts had dried up or didn't return my calls. I was broke and desperate. The gig in the morning wasn't real, but not much is in la-la land. David and his trust fund weren't my only option, of course, but he was by far the most attractive. That's why I took it slow. I remember checking my watch.

It was already past one in the morning. We couldn't linger out here on "my street" much longer. I knew that from previous experience. Stupid nosy neighbors had busted me before.

I turned to him, licked my lip. "Can I see you again?"

"Yes. Although there's still so much more of tonight." He was persistent. He leaned forward and kissed my lips, gently at first and then with urgency, pushing his tongue inside me, tasting me, moaning. I felt his hand on my shoulder, the other on my knee. As hard as it was for me to pull away, I had to break the kiss.

"Yes. Tomorrow? Please." I panted, turning him on even more. I had already told him at dinner I was a virgin. The kiss just sealed his fate.

"Oh, man. Tomorrow, when?"

I opened the door and hopped out before he could help me. I couldn't let him walk me to the door, of course. I whispered, "Thank you for the best date of my life. I'll see you tomorrow night? Could you pick me up at the club? I have to work until eight."

"Of course. See you there. I had a great time." He started to get out of the car. David was a gentleman when I met him. He was about to open the door when I held up my hand.

"Shh, stop. No need to walk me to the door. Mrs. Kravitz is really cranky when I come home late. But I'll see you tomorrow night." I'd opened the gate to the yard, I'd made sure there wasn't a lock earlier during my scouting missions. This wasn't the first time I'd used "my" Brentwood home. I just had to hope none of the actual residents inside the complex would wake up and call the police. That happened once. I couldn't let it happen again. Two months later, we were engaged. Newly funded, I'd had the staying power I needed to break through in Hollywood.

Until everything changed.

I feel Sam's eyes on me. "It's nice to see you smiling, Mrs. H."

"Thank you. Sam, I'm sorry. I don't mean to be rude but I need to make a call." I pull out my phone to search my contacts. There he is.

"Want me to pull over? Do you need privacy?" Sam asks.

Why isn't everyone in the world like Sam? "No, it's fine. I don't mind if you hear. Just apologies for not giving you my full attention."

"I drive for Lyft, Mrs. H. Most people forget I'm up here."

I punch the contact number for Detective Branson. Shockingly, he answers on the second ring. I bet he didn't check caller ID.

"Branson here."

"Hello, Alan, it's Jane Harris. Mary's mother. How are you?"

Soft sigh. "Fine, ma'am. And you? I know you had the memorial service last night. We meant to make it by, but we got a call. My apologies."

I don't believe him, but I need him. "No problem. It was lovely. And, actually, enlightening."

Big sigh. "How so, ma'am?"

"I got a clue. A letter. I need to show it to you. Proof Mary was murdered, killed. And Betsy knows something." I know what you're thinking. I'm overstating my case a tad. But you have to understand what I've been through with all of this, all of them.

"Someone admitted to murdering your daughter?"

I have his attention. "Yes. In a way." In another way, not really, but it does say Mary's death wasn't an accident.

"I need to see that letter, ma'am. Should I swing by?" I hear him cuff his hand over the mouthpiece. I imagine him pulling out his thick day planner, slotting me in. "I can be over around noon."

I take a deep breath. He believes me. "I'll see you then. And, Alan, Detective, thank you for taking my call."

"Of course, Mrs. Harris. You know I'm here to help. I'll be anxious to see your proof."

Sam's eyes are big, and watching me.

"What?" I smile at him.

"You think your daughter was murdered? You have proof? You think Betsy knows something?"

"Yes. I am sure of it. You know, Sam, I've always thought poor Betsy knew more than she's told us. I mean, she was the last person to see her sister alive, but she's never really talked about it." Sort of. I look out the window and realize we're stopped in front of the high school. I take a deep breath. I try not to come here. Memories, vivid, happy, proud memories of Mary and her achievements crowd every corner of this place. My stature was elevated by her achievements. With Betsy, my stature is diminished, but I love my artsy, fringe daughter. I'm here, aren't I? It's so interesting how children can be so different. Same upbringing, same opportunity. Totally different manifestations.

Sam opens my door. The street sign above his head says No Stopping At Any Time. The sign at the cliffs reads: Danger. Area Closed. People Have Fallen to Their Death from This Point. Stay Out. Both very clear, but look: we're stopped right here even though we aren't supposed to be. We're all like Mary. We push boundaries, break rules, disobey the ones we love.

Just six months ago, up the coast a few hundred miles from here, a young woman fell over a cliff as she celebrated a marriage proposal from her boyfriend. She jumped up and down in excitement, and fell, dying of her injuries. In another spot, a young couple fell to their deaths while taking a selfie at cliff's edge. Their children, ages five and six, witnessed the tragic accident. A seventeen-year-old boy hiking with his family along another stretch of the beautiful California coastline ran ahead to see the beautiful vista. He did not feel safe standing and sat down, but as he positioned himself for that better look, the ground gave way and he slipped, falling four hundred feet, landing near the edge of the ocean, dying of his injuries. Accidents happen all the time, sure. But what if, in each of these cases, the story was different? What if the young man found out his about-to-be fiancée had cheated on him the night before? What if the couple taking a selfie had a suicide pact? What if the teenage boy didn't really slip? What if somebody pushed Mary off the cliff? What if it was someone she knew?

"Mrs. H.?"

I blink. I must have drifted for a moment. "Oh, sorry. Sam. Thank you. I'll be ready for a pickup in an hour." I didn't notice we had company. It's Angelica, Betsy's counselor. Mary's, too. "Angelica. Nice to see you."

"Good to see you, too, Mrs. Harris. Actually, the Volunteer Day activities will last until noon. Will that work with your schedule? Can you stay? We'd love to have you."

I need to be home at noon. "Sam, does 11:45 work?"

"Whatever you need, Mrs. H. See you then."

Without warning, the headline pops into my mind unwanted: **Local Woman Dies from Tragic Cliff Fall; Body Washed Ashore Today.** Chills spread through my body and I shiver. Angelica notices.

"Jane, let me show you where we're meeting." Angelica is giving me that sympathy stare, the one I despise. The one that says, *Watch out for the grieving mom. She may be contagious.* "I'm just so sorry for your loss. I can't imagine."

No, you can't imagine what I'm going through. I change the subject. "Are you excited for the end of the school year?"

"I am. It's been a long one. It's good to have the summer off. And you should know, Betsy is doing remarkably well, considering. The AP art teacher is impressed with her work this semester. I just wish she'd shown this effort a little sooner, a year ago, for the colleges. But she'll be just fine." Angelica holds the door to the office open for me and I walk inside.

I follow Angelica around the front desk where I used to sign the girls in and out for doctors, and dentists, for early dismissal sports, for pretend and real illnesses. Loretta is still there, still answering phones. Still pretending to believe excuses that parents concoct on behalf of their kids. I'm sure she's heard every lie imaginable.

"Hey, Mrs. Harris. Good to see you." Loretta waves before taking another call.

"I don't know how she does it," Angelica says.

Is she referring to me, or Loretta? The lies or the telephone calls? I don't respond. We push through the door of the gym and enter a hive of senior kid and senior parent activity. I take a step back, but feel the pressure of Angelica's hand in the small of my back, propelling me forward.

This is the last place in the world I want to be.

Betsy spots me. The feeling appears to be mutual.

"You came." Betsy appears by my side. She knows Angelica is watching us, so she reluctantly smiles. "Hope you don't mind getting paint on your new yoga outfit."

I absorb the feigned display of affection, the offhanded compliment on the new and improved Jane, and give her a quick hug in return. "Of course I did. I wouldn't miss this time with you." We're standing in front of what feels like the whole school and every mom associated with it. I'd say we're giving a commanding performance.

Angelica beams. "You two have so much fun." And then she's gone.

"So we're painting the backdrop, where kids take party photos. It's kind of retro, a soda shop. Like 1950s. Don't ask me, I didn't decide the theme," Betsy says as she leads us through the crowd, head down. She isn't waving or talking or smiling to any of the other kids. I know she's embarrassed I'm here, but she'd get questions galore if I was a no-show. It's better this way.

I'm just like the others, supporting my only surviving daughter, I mean graduating senior. Some of the moms spot me, and the murmur of sympathy, the hint of danger, the undercurrent works its way through the gym. Or maybe they're jealous of my thin body, my tight-fitting yoga clothes. Sarah stands a few tables away. She waves. I wave in return. I hope she doesn't force me to "catch up" with her daughter, Liz.

Betsy stops at a long cafeteria table. Paint tubs and brushes are lined up like a linear vision of the color wheel. "We're a subcommittee of two, at least for now." There are hundreds of kids and parents swarmed around at least twenty tables. Ours is the only one without a crowd.

I reach for Betsy's hand and squeeze. She's such a loser. "This will be great. It doesn't matter if you don't have any friends to help. All we need is each other. You should always remember that. I'm all you need."

I smile as Betsy tries very hard not to roll her eyes and pulls her hand away.

"Although, now that I look at it, can we find anyone to help? That's a big mural for the two of us." I'm calm, no-pressure mom. Just asking a simple question. Without Josh in the picture, the text messages coming in for her have been few and far between. It's odd, for a teenager. But my spyware picks up all social media accounts and text messages. Betsy must just be a loner. Poor thing.

"We'll be fine. Everyone is busy." Betsy hands me a paintbrush. "Start over there with the stool. Black seat. Silver stand. I'll handle the ice cream sodas."

As I paint, my intuition is zinging. Pinging. A dormant maternal instinct aroused. Betsy is a better actress than I realized. Just now, if somebody glanced our way—and believe me, they are—they would think Betsy is glad I'm here at Volunteer Day, happy we're working together side by side. But I know she despises me. She pitied me this morning in the kitchen. Both she and David made fun of me and the anonymous note. I watch her. She is my daughter. Her eyes focus for a moment on the work, and then she's scanning the crowd. Who is she looking for?

"What?" Betsy stares at me.

"Oh, nothing. Just so glad to be here." I shove my brush into the thick black paint and blob it onto the outline of one of the soda stools.

"Sure you are." Betsy isn't looking at me, though. She's smiling at a guy with long blond hair who is working his way toward us, cutting through the crowded gym. The hairs stand up on the back of my neck as my radar senses a connection.

"Hey, Betsy. Is this your mom?" Blond surfer dude has reached our table. He smiles at me, pulls his hair behind his back. He looks too old to be in high school.

"Hi, I'm Jane Harris." I extend my hand even though there's black paint on my pinkie.

"Bo. Good to meet you. I'm a substitute teacher here

and I tutor after school. Betsy's one of my favorite students." He shakes the tips of my fingers quickly. It's weird, it's almost as if he's trying to keep me from seeing something. But then I see it, the proof. His infinity tattoo matches Betsy's. My jaw tightens. Once again, I've been played by my own family member. This is unacceptable. I turn to question Betsy.

Bo says to Betsy, "Can I borrow you for a moment?"

"Sure. Be right back, Mom."

I watch them weave through the gym, lost in each other, not talking to any of the other kids at the other tables. And then they're out of sight. Betsy acted cool, nonchalant, and that likely means they are an item. That's crazy, though. He's too old for her, of course. She couldn't possibly be dating that inappropriate man? But they have matching tattoos. Could Betsy be keeping more secrets from me than I realize?

Someone touches my shoulder and I jump.

"Sorry to startle you." It's Sarah, omnipresent Sarah.

"No worries. Thank you for coming last night." I manage to have manners but I want to think about my devious daughter.

"It was a lovely memorial service." Sarah looks around, scanning the crowd. "Where's Betsy?"

"Oh, well, she just stepped away for a minute. A guy named Bo came to talk to her." I see a look cross Sarah's face. She bites her lip. "What is it?"

"Nothing. I mean, just rumors. Gossip. I'm sure it's nothing. He's also the assistant manager at the hardware store on Beach Boulevard. Probably dropping off supplies or something." Sarah steps back. "I need to get back over to my project table."

"Wait. What is it? What do you know?" I grab her wrist. "Please."

"Hey, Mom. Mrs. Murphy. What's going on?" Betsy is back.

Sarah shakes her wrist free. "Just saying hello, that's all. Get back to work, you two. Have fun."

Betsy hands me my paintbrush and starts back in on a white square of the red-and-white soda shop.

"And who was that?"

"Who? Bo?"

"Yes."

"Stop. He's a sub—and a great tutor. He's just super amazing." She looks up quickly. "We're just friends. He also manages the hardware store, where I get my art supplies."

Two things rankle me. I didn't know Betsy had a super amazing, handsome tutor. And teachers and students aren't supposed to be "friends." I could make a huge fuss about this inappropriate something here. But I have other fish to fry, so to speak. Still, it's bothersome. Surely they must have communicated by phone or text at some point, if only even to change the time of a tutoring session?

I say, "Hmm. Okay. I just didn't know about him. You've never mentioned his name." They must not communicate outside of school, because I'd know. Wouldn't I? Do they use smoke signals? Morse code? I've been missing something. It reminds me of the time Mary discovered the listening device in her bedroom. She was so smart, so mad at me. I swore it was for her own protection as I watched her smash it with a hammer. I don't have a bug in Betsy's room, not after that fiasco. But still, I should know about Bo.

"You don't know anything about me, Mom." Betsy slaps red paint onto the paper.

Clearly. "Want to tell me about you two?"

"Not really."

"You realize he could get in big trouble for hanging out with you, don't you? I mean, if someone were to file a complaint about it." I like swirling the black paint on the paper, thick, dark.

"We aren't hanging out. He's a tutor." Betsy stops painting and stares at me.

"Are you threatening me?"

"Of course not, dear. It's just that I care so much about you. I just want the very best for you." And that wouldn't include the assistant manager of a hardware store. Forget the fact he's a teacher. None of it will matter in a couple of days, anyway, not if everything goes as it should.

"Right. Well, what I want to do is finish this stupid backdrop. And I'd like your word that you won't say anything to anyone about Bo, because there's nothing to talk about. He's my tutor. End of story. Okay?" Betsy holds the paintbrush dripping in red paint. It reminds me of the new painting hanging in her room, the bleeding heart.

"Sure, honey, of course." I will be agreeable now. I need to process this new and important information. To change the subject I say, "I'm meeting with Detective Branson at noon." I grab a different paintbrush and dip it into the silver paint. This is sort of fun, cathartic. "I plan to get Mary's case reopened."

Betsy smacks her hands down on the table, shaking the paint canisters, flipping my black-paint-coated paintbrush onto the table, barely missing the backdrop. The kids and moms at the nearest table to ours, a group that seems to be stuffing paper bags with party favors, turn and stare at our table. It's my turn to blush.

Betsy leans toward me and whispers, "Are you accusing me of hurting Mary?"

I scoot over beside her, my paintbrush dripping black paint on the backdrop. I whisper, "Oh, dear, why would I think that? I mean, all I know is you two had a big fight, went on a hike in Point Park together. You came home and Mary never did."

True. They were fighting about something. Mary was having a lot of conflicts that last day of her life. Anger isn't healthy, we all know that. Holding things inside, secrets, they can eat you up. Anger plus secrets is bad for you: your heart rate increases, your breathing becomes shallow, your muscles tense up and you feel shaky. Your mind may take you back to other times when you've felt this angry.

Like just this morning, for example, on Port Chelsea Place. Anger also triggers acting-out urges, the urge to yell, to scream, to throw or hit someone, to lash out in verbally harmful ways. Right now, I'm calm. I'm in charge here. It's Betsy's turn to feel the burn.

Betsy steps back. I sense a lot of eyes on us, watching, waiting for something. An explosion or something, who knows?

My daughter's face is pale, her lips pursed. "Mary was alive when I left her, you know that. This is why people hate you. Accusing your own daughter of something horrible, of knowing some sort of secret. I don't know what you're up to but I desperately want to be normal again, to feel normal again. It's hard enough to not have Mary. She was my best friend. If you try to open this all up again, we'll lose the little bit of respect we have around here. I can't take it, the stares, the pity. Not again. If you try to open Mary's case, Dad and I will tell everyone you're insane, a monster."

Oh, really? Before I answer her, I look up. There are too many eyes on us, watching us. I don't want them to hear our conversation, to interfere with me and my plans. I need to get out of here. A panic attack would be good right about now. I pretend to try to catch my breath, tears spring to my eyes. "I am not a monster. I love you."

Betsy grabs my arm. I need to get us out of here.

"Mom. Stop. Breathe. Oh my God. Don't make a scene." Betsy pulls me toward the doors, past too many moms, too many kids, too many stares.

I pretend to gasp for air. I keep my head down and cover my face with my hand. Before I know it, we're outside, around the corner from the gym. We sit on the grass. I pull my knees to my chest, cover my face with my hands.

I'm angry. Very angry. I breathe in, breathe out. There

is nothing more to do or say. My daughter called me a monster. Betsy has threatened me, and I her.

I don't know how long we sit there in the grass but Sam arrives.

Sam says, "Hey, Betsy. Got here as fast as I could."

I don't like the way Sam is looking at my devious daughter. He's my knight, not hers. "Thank goodness you're here," I say so he'll focus on me.

Betsy touches his arm. "Thanks again for getting here so fast. Sorry you had to come retrieve her. Take her home, okay? No visitors. She's a mess."

"No problem," Sam says. I feel the air shift beside me as Betsy walks away.

Sam looks down at me in the wake of Betsy's departure. "You okay, Mrs. H.?"

I see the kindness in his eyes. Feel his solid presence. I hope she didn't tell him any lies about me. He wouldn't believe her. Nobody believes teenagers. "Now I am. Now that you're here. Betsy's furious with me, as usual."

"Moms and daughters, they say it's tough." Sam helps me stand and we walk to the Prius. He opens the back passenger-side door. "Straight home, then?"

Mom and daughter relationships are more than tough, Sam. Especially when daughters don't obey. Betsy will be brought under control, one way or another. I slide in, and before he can close the door I say, "No, drive me to the police station, please."

12

11:15 a.m.

Detective Alan Branson hasn't changed much in the past year.

We're sitting across from each other in his tiny office. I'm glad he hadn't left yet to drive to my house even though I bet he'd rather have meetings anywhere but this dingy place. I sit across the beat-up cheap wood desk and smile, waiting as he reads my evidence.

His wrinkled brow is locked in a frown, his thinning hair glued to his head with gel. His green eyes tilt down at the sides, as if his cheeks no longer bother to hold up their end of the deal. He's seen too much, I guess, to ever smile. He slides my letter across the desk in my direction. I beam with excitement.

"What do you want me to do with this, Mrs. Harris?" He speaks slowly, like I'm a child.

I swallow. Undeterred. "I want you to investigate, Alan. That is what you do." I speak slowly, too. "This makes me think there is a witness you haven't talked to. A witness who doesn't think Mary was alone up there."

"It only says Mary's death was not an accident, and to ask Betsy. Mrs. Harris, what exactly do you want me to investigate?" Droopy green eyes droop even more, if that's possible.

"The note, of course."

Detective Branson stands, placing his hands on his grimy desk. He's a stereotype, perfectly typecast. "I'm sorry. There isn't enough here to investigate. Mary's death *was* a tragic accident. Case closed. We've interviewed Betsy, as you know. And everyone else we could find. A letter saying it wasn't an accident from an anonymous rich person doesn't change that."

I ignore The Cove dig. He's set on his story of how things happened, that much I know by now. His reputation is on the line. If he had to admit he got it wrong, well, does he get a demotion? No. My heart is thumping. But not with panic. With anger. And with something else. I feel alive.

I stand up, reach for the doorknob. I need to get out of his tiny stupid office. I pull. Before I walk out I say, "You're wrong. I'll find this person without your help and then we'll both be back here. I'll look forward to seeing you then, Alan." I wink at him.

Branson smiles and shakes his head. He remains standing as I leave but he doesn't say a word. I can feel him checking out my curves as I walk out the door. These yoga pants are a man magnet. He can't help himself.

Sam is where I left him in the parking lot. He seems surprised I've returned so soon, and shoves a book under the front seat before hurrying to help me.

"That was fast," he says.

"Yes." Despite the fact I'll need more to convince Alan to question Betsy, I feel good about things. My revised plan is still in place and this letter was just an extra gift. I'm in control. I'm one step ahead. Sam climbs into the driver's seat. "Home please."

"Gotcha, Mrs. H. What did the detective have to say about your note?"

"He didn't understand the importance of it. But he will. What are you working on? What did you put away?" It's none of my business, but I should know something about my only friend. My paid friend, my servant, really.

"Oh, I'm getting my bachelor's degree. Slowly. Online." His eyes smile in the rearview mirror.

"Good for you. What subject?"

"Psychology." He looks me in the eye through the mirror when he answers. "Just one more semester to go."

"Good for you," I say, although I have no idea how a degree in psychology is going to get him out from behind the wheel of his car. But it's good to dream. I don't ask more because I want him to focus on the road. Car crashes are the number one cause of accidental death, just ask my mom. Well, you can't, she's dead, but if you could she would tell you to check your brakes when the light comes on. I can't imagine the fear she must have felt as she kept stomping on the brakes but the car kept picking up speed. Terrifying.

Sam is doing well, hands on three o'clock and nine o'clock.

I lean back against the seat, close my eyes.

I'll make everyone see the truth I want them to see, soon.

"Did you say something, Mrs. H.?"

I hope not. "Nothing, Sam. Nothing."

Outside, it's another beautiful day in May. And I am on a mission. I look out the window as we drive past the store where I used to buy Cash's dog food, his treats, his bed. I still think about him, even though he turned into a very bad dog. The vet said he was having a nervous breakdown because he'd seen Mary fall. We put him on antidepressants, but he wouldn't come out of his bed. He wouldn't eat.

He wouldn't let me near him.

Perhaps we both were just too sad. And then, one morning, he just didn't wake up. Poor dog, his time was up. Betsy found his cold and lifeless body. Another tragedy for her, and all of us. I didn't even realize how attached David had been to the dog, until he was gone.

I had Cash cremated. David and Betsy weren't happy about it, but I told them the kind vet handled everything and insisted it was for the best. We still had the sympathy of the entire town back then, even from a small-town veterinarian who flirted with me over my dead dog's body. True story.

Betsy and David sprinkled his ashes in the ocean. They returned with tear-soaked faces, another deep sadness swept over our little family.

I couldn't bear to go to the ocean with them, of course, so I stayed home.

I had my own private goodbye with Cash.

13

4:00 p.m.

I'm home and on my phone using my spying app.

It's just the perfect tool for helicopter moms and wives like me. It's for my peace of mind. I know you use one, too. It's important for moms to be vigilant. I mean, that's why my other favorite app, Find My Friends, comes already loaded on your phone, for heaven's sake.

They didn't find Mary for three long days. Even though I had activated the Find My Friends app on her phone, Point Park has terrible service. Rescuers searched Point Park, and the surrounding area, because that was where her sister left her, but the cell phone was no help. And, of course, more people than just Betsy had seen Mary and Cash at the park that day, including some high school kids. Betsy's official story was that she and her sister had a fight during their hike and that Mary had jogged off alone, with Cash, heading up to the top of the point. Betsy felt terrible, but didn't know anything else.

Or did she? What about that Bo creature, her tutor? Could he have been involved in this somehow? And how has she kept him from me until now? They couldn't be a couple, not without me knowing about it. The tattoos must be a coincidence, that's all. Or perhaps Betsy simply has a teenage crush. It happens all the time. They aren't close enough to be confidants, that's for sure.

I walk into the living room and assess the situation. I smile at my reflection. I look good. I am back in the world as planned, both in the day and the night. I have waited patiently to bring everything to fruition, and some things cannot be accomplished in the dark of night. I have now confirmed David is playing house with Kylie. Betsy is only focused on graduating, so we shall see what she comes up with after that. I feel good, a step ahead of them all.

I mean, if I impressed Sam with my hair and makeup done and a new outfit, and he's just a twentysomething Lyft driver, imagine what the rest of the world will think. But I need to take it slowly. Thoughtfully. I realize a woman, a mom, doesn't just shake off grief like an old blanket on a hot summer day. She emerges slowly, gracefully, a butterfly from a cocoon of her own making. Beautiful and ready to take flight.

My phone rings, a sound I hardly hear anymore. Caller ID tells me it's someone from The Cove office. Interesting.

"Jane. Hey, it's Hoffman, how are you?" The community's recreation director is one of the most patient people I know. Kids love him, no matter the age. He organizes events for adults, too. I haven't been to anything for over a year, of course, but I know Betsy has. Hoffman helps me keep tabs on her. He also handles the women's tennis teams and all that drama, poor man.

"Hoffman. It's nice to hear from you."

"I didn't get to speak to you last night at the ceremony. But it was beautiful. Mary will always be remembered by all of us."

"Thank you. Can I help you with something?"

He pauses, an awkward silence. Finally, "Could I come by? Are you home?"

"I am. Sure. I'd love to see you." I think of his friendly freckled face, sandy blond hair. He has the look of perpetual youth, although he must be in his late thirties. "Can you tell me what this is about?"

"I'd rather tell you in person. See you in a couple minutes."

Probably he's going to let me know my tennis partner, Melissa, has replaced me permanently. It's my fault, of course. I've been busy, and preoccupied, and truth be told, she and I just weren't having fun together anymore. She told me I'm caustic, the bitch. I mean, I was simply defending the call I made.

The ball was definitely out.

I can still see Melissa shake her head and say to our opponents, "It was in. Your point."

We lost the match because of *her*. She was wrong and she has yet to apologize. Come to think of it, I didn't see her or her husband at Mary's memorial. Fine. Who needs her, or tennis? It's a stupid game for vapid people anyway. That's a hornet's nest I'm glad to be rid of. My "partner" and I haven't spoken since I quit. My story. Or was replaced by another tennis-playing Stepford Wife. Their story. Who do you believe and what is it with partners? In life, in tennis, in love. They just let you down.

As I wait for Hoffman to drive a golf cart up the hill from his office near the tennis courts in the canyon, I think about all the wonderful summers my girls spent here at The Cove. They had such a charmed upbringing, so very different than my own. Learning to swim, surf lessons, volleyball and tennis lessons. Hoffman was an important part of their childhood. He joined the staff the same year we moved into The Cove.

He's like family, sort of. More like a distant cousin we now see once a year. The doorbell rings and I cross the courtyard and open the gate. I reach my hand down to hold Cash's collar, but he's not there, of course. It's just reflex, like the way I still wait for Mary to come home sometimes, momentarily forgetting that she never will. Hoffman is wearing a white polo with The Cove logo stitched on the sleeve. He gives me a bright smile, a quick hug and follows me inside.

I haven't entertained a guest in ages. "Can I get you anything? Water? Iced tea?"

"No, I'm fine. Thanks. Are we alone?" he asks as we sit down at the kitchen table. He's nervous, eyes darting. I've never seen him act this way.

"Did you leave me the letter?" I watch his face.

He blinks. "What letter?"

"Someone left me a letter, on The Cove stationery. Someone trying to help me." I watch his face. It's a blank, lightly freckled slate.

"Hmm. Well, it wasn't me." He folds his arms across his chest.

He didn't ask me what it said. Is he being polite, or does he already know the contents? We lock eyes. And then I bat mine.

He shifts in his chair. He isn't flirting, but I might be. "Look, I came here because I think you should know something about Betsy."

"What are you talking about?"

"I've known the girls since they were little. I've watched them grow up to become beautiful, talented young women, like their mom." He takes an awkward pause.

"I know. Thank you." I sit up straight, tilting my head to present my best side. I'm camera ready and now I'm on set. I reach for a strand of my hair and twirl it around my finger. I'm glad I have new yoga pants on. I cross my legs under the table.

"I'm worried about Betsy." Hoffman stops and looks at me.

I shrug. "I don't understand. She's fine, actually got

into community college, and she's graduating with her class Thursday. All's good."

"Have you noticed anything? I mean, I know it must be so hard, with Mary gone, and now this. I didn't want to bother you, but I just think you should know. I mean, some of the rumors about her aren't good." Hoffman exhales. He's talking fast, his forehead is shiny with sweat.

"Are you sure you don't want a glass of water?" Poor man. I have him in a tizzy. I lick my lips.

"Maybe I should talk to David? I don't want to upset you." He wipes his forehead with his hand.

"No, you should talk to me. I am her mother." If I haven't noticed anything, I guarantee Mr.-not-ever-home hasn't, either. "Betsy is a lot different than Mary. Always has been. That's all. She's more creative, more of a loner. She hangs out with the artists, the theater kids. The ones without any athletic skills." I almost say Betsy is darker, but that doesn't seem right. I shouldn't say that to Hoffman. Besides, I think I already know what he's trying to spit out. And it must have something to do with Bo.

"There's more to it. Maybe ask Betsy directly? Ask her if she has a boyfriend? An older boyfriend. I got a call, from another mom. She saw the two of them together at Volunteer Day and felt like something was going on. It may be nothing, just gossip." Hoffman stands and shoves his hands into the pockets of his khaki shorts. He starts walking to the door and I have to hurry to keep up.

"Hoffman, wait. I don't understand. What are you trying to tell me?" I'm sure it's clear to everyone that Betsy is flirting with Bo, the teacher. Not that it's okay, but I did it. There isn't anything horrible about it, not in the long run. It won't even matter in two days. Everything will change. It's funny, all this year I thought she was dating Josh. I'm surprised she is so tricky. I'm on to you now, Betsy dear.

Hoffman is sweating and he really wants to leave. I block the front door so he can't.

Hoffman adds, "I'm sure this mom has blown it all out of proportion."

"I'll speak to Betsy. As far as I know, she's focused on graduation, and she should be. It's a struggle for her, school is. Not like Mary."

I open the door and follow Hoffman through the courtyard and he stops with his hand on the gate. He turns and smiles. "And, Jane, you look good. I hope Mr. Harris realizes what a lucky guy he is."

I touch his chest quickly with my finger, a test, a tease. "Why, thank you." My face flushes. This is a role I was born to play.

Hoffman takes a deep breath and nods, pulls open the gate and hurries down the stairs to his golf cart. He yells, "You and David should come to the tennis mixer this weekend. We miss seeing you."

Was that a cover for eavesdropping neighbors? I scan the street and I don't see anyone watching us, but I know they are. Unlike me, those tennis team women are ruthless and always jealous if Hoff pays more attention to one over the other. They watch him like a hawk. That's why Hoffman pretended he was simply dropping by to talk about tennis at the house of grief and loss, that's all.

I force a smile. I try to sound bubbly. Mary would be pleased. "We'll try to be there. Thanks, Hoff!"

He grins back, relieved by my lie, waves and drives off.

I'm left alone trying to imagine David and me on the tennis court as partners again.

It's hard to picture.

I close the gate and grin. Hoffman was putty in my hands. I've so missed playing the role of femme fatale. It's fun to be back. But I can't afford distractions, not now. I need to spend more time watching Betsy. Just when I thought my youngest daughter was simply depressed, focused on school, dating loser Josh, I learn the opposite.

Betsy's been playing me. Who knew she was clever underneath all of that anger and despondence? She'll face the consequences soon enough. If she's been deceiving me, hiding things from me, it will be much worse for her. Much worse.

I grab a river rock from the bottom of the fountain gurgling in the courtyard. It's cold and slippery. I hurl it at the glass lantern on the ground by the outside fireplace and feel the relief as it shatters from the blow. It's funny, I'm able to keep myself contained, calm, even with all the betrayal going on around me. Every once in a while, though, I just have to throw something. You understand, don't you?

It is a release I needed. The cleaning service will be here tomorrow. They'll take care of the little mess I made.

Now back to work.

14

4:55 p.m.

It's check-in time, again.

I pull out my phone, open Find My Friends, and there they are. David is still at the office, or at least his phone is. That doesn't mean much, of course. As for Betsy, let's see, she is in a car, driving north along Pacific Coast Highway. It's long past school hours, so where is she heading? Who is she with? Is her art class Plein Air painting, I wonder? Or is it her official tutoring spot, a class for one, led by a certain substitute teacher named Bo? I'm not exactly sure where she's going. So I watch her dot.

I expand the map in my hand and watch as her dot turns

into the entrance to Point Park. My God. Is she just try-ing to look guilty? I take a screenshot.

Personally, I could never go to that park again. I mean, just a few yards away, her sister fell to her death. Well, actually, according to the coroner, she was alive when she hit the water and was still breathing when she went under. There was water in her lungs. So she was likely uncon-scious and drowned. Chilling to think about, I know, and also seemingly impossible given the height of the cliff she fell from that she would survive the fall.

The experts—the coroner and others—tell me she hit her head on something on her way down, perhaps on the rock outcropping visible from the top. And that's com-forting, they tell me. She would have been unconscious when she fell into the deep, cold Pacific. She would have died underwater. Dead by the time something took a nib-ble of her foot. It gives me the chills, too.

Cold ocean water is a preservative of sorts. She still looked beautiful when she was found. My beautiful, per-fect daughter.

A shudder runs down my spine when I think about that cold room, when we had to identify her body. I glanced at her pretty face before I shut my eyes, and let David handle it. I shake my head, push those images away. I can control them during the daytime at least. When I think about her death, I try to focus on the beauty at the top of Point Park.

From the photos I've seen online, Point Park in May is spectacular. This point is where migrating whales scrape their barnacles off as they swim past. It's the place where the ocean seems to stretch out forever. This point, once you climb to the top of it, is magical and unique and deadly all at the same time, or so I've heard. It's off-limits, so no one is allowed to go there. Mary knew that, but she went there anyway.

It's Betsy's fault. Betsy lured Mary to the park for a hike for some reason. And she is hanging out there today. That's creepy. I look down and Betsy's dot has disappeared.

My tracker app buzzes. David is on the move. For almost a year now, it's been my game to guess which of the three regular spots he'll drive to. Where's Waldo?, in husband form. There's the romantic restaurant nestled in the heart of the village in Laguna Beach, Salerno's, famous for "romantic" Italian food. Most people won't recognize him there, though the hostess most certainly does by now, as he's a regular. When I placed my delivery order Sunday night, the waiter on the phone was excited for my first to-go order, but couldn't wait to see me again in person. I've never been to Salerno's. How cute of Kylie to be playing Mrs. Harris. My jaw tenses.

Focus, Jane.

We're playing our Where's David Dining Tonight? game. If he's tired and confident, he'll opt for his backup spot, closer to home, but still welcoming. A stand-alone Mexican restaurant with a huge bar scene full of older women—my age—and divorced men who don't want anything to do with a woman their own age. It's a frustrating scene I can't imagine choosing to be a part of, but my husband, the new David, is a regular. What a guy.

Oh, but no, according to his dot on my app tonight

he's chosen the quiet restaurant with the ocean view near Heisler Park. It was our favorite when we first moved here, before we knew the "locals" never go there, only the tourists. Las Brisas was where I saved Mary when she inhaled a piece of shrimp. You'd think he'd remember that, honor that memory.

And because it's primarily tourists, David can blend in there, or so he thinks. The oceanfront, sculpture-filled Heisler Park is lovely this time of evening. It's a Laguna Beach treasure.

I haven't been to the park in a while. It's such a nice evening. And I look good, barely recognizable from the grieving mother I was just a day before. Why not take a stroll?

I really have a special gift, this ability to transform myself. Most actors have it, and it's a natural talent. I smile as I drive out of The Cove and head toward town. Others would be envious of my ability to hide in plain sight, my natural capacity to watch and follow, and then to be seen when I'm ready.

Soon, people will know my name. That's my next step. After I resolve the central conflict of my life at the moment, once my plan has been implemented. I'll move back to LA, live in a far better, more luxurious area than where pathetic Elizabeth James lives and give acting a go again. Who needs another house here in sleepy Orange County? Not me, and I'm surprised I allowed myself to dream of it. I'm meant to be in LA.

A new beat. Cue the applause. It's almost time for me to step out of the darkness, and into the spotlight.

After I spy on my husband and his date, from behind a tree in the park. Again. The sight of him carrying her across the threshold of their new home flashes through my mind, as do the words CLOSED ESCROW!!! ☺

Oh, here they are, popping onto my phone through the app:

David: You are the love of my life. Only two more days and I'm free.

Kylie: Can't wait!! You're the best!!! See you at dinner!!! xo

How dare he? I am the love of his life. The mother of his child.

Focus, Jane.

Yes, I'll head back to Hollywood, soon.

First, I need to talk some things out with my loved ones. I find a parking spot easily, which is surprising this time of year, this close to the beach. The restaurant is a short block away, a short stroll through the ocean-front park. I hide my blond hair under a trucker hat and have extra-large sunglasses covering half of my face. I stick to the sidewalk, but most visitors are drawn to the oceanfront path. I myself am drawn to something else.

One last, in-person glimpse of David and Kylie together will seal their fate. It will be the final confirmation that they deserve everything that's coming their way. Yes, I've finally accepted she has won for the moment, but like a moth to the flame I can't resist one more piece of evidence. I reach the restaurant and take the path between the restaurant and the sea. Huge glass windows provide diners with a commanding view of the coastline, especially gorgeous at sunset. The windows also provide a crystal clear view of the people enjoying dinner.

And there they sit at a romantic table for two. Holding hands, across the table, talking about the future. I take a photo with my phone, to capture the moment, to fuel my rage. But I'm certain I won't need it. When you've been married to someone for twenty years, when you've shared love and loss, and been there for him, well, this kind of betrayal leaves you with two options. I could fall apart, continue to pop pills and live in a blur of grief until David walks out, which appears to be soon given his texts. Or I can get revenge, find a place to use my talents and a way to vent this anger he's stoked in my heart.

I open my phone and expand the picture of the two of them together. I zoom in on David, his lying face. This is another image burned into my memory forever. I know too many of us women have suffered these types of betrayal from our spouses. It's unacceptable. I gave up my career, my life, to be the perfect mother, the perfect wife. And it has gotten me here: I'm married to a cheater.

It's clear he doesn't love me anymore. I shove my phone into my back pocket and make my way back to my car. It's fine. I'm getting used to the idea. If he doesn't love me, I don't love him. I will move on soon.

But first, I'll make sure the life he's planning for himself, for them, will turn into the nightmare he deserves.

15

11:30 p.m.

I'm back home.

Alone.

I've been waiting for hours to confront Betsy with what Hoffman has told me, and to get David's help. I know where David is, of course. I have plenty of photos of him from my little park adventure. But I have no idea where Betsy is. It's as if she knows I'm tracking her and she has figured out some way to get around me. Or she has another secret texting channel or something. And just as often, she turns off her phone and I don't receive a signal at all. Her dot on my app has disappeared tonight.

That's my girl. She's smarter than I realized.

With nothing to do but wait, I pull out an old photo album and have a fun walk down memory lane. Well, not fun, really. After my mom died in the *tragic automobile accident* I became an orphan. It was better than living another day with her, trust me. But I didn't have anybody. No one could find my so-called father. I wouldn't have wanted to live with him anyway. I needed a plan B or I'd be a ward of the state.

I flip the page and smile at the photo of the redbrick two-story home, two smiling teenagers standing on the step. Nobody wants to adopt a fourteen-year-old kid, even a rather beautiful one. I stare at my teenage self, trace the lines of my face. Lucky for me, my friend Sally's family felt sorry for me. They gave me a bedroom, and a semblance of family. And Sally's mom helped me through my first wave of panic attacks. She sewed the sequins on my pageant dresses and drove me to competitions. It's too bad I never really fit in with my adopted family. Maybe things could have turned out differently. As it was, I know we all felt a big sense of relief when I told them I was off to Hollywood. Nothing terrible happened—no, it was more of a visceral distaste. They were there when I needed them, a means to an end.

David used to smile adoringly and add, "Her real name is Delilah Jane. Isn't that adorable?"

No, it's not. But it was a fact I had to reveal when we applied for our marriage license and needed our social security cards. Sally and I had a big falling-out when she came to visit me in LA, against her parents' wishes, a few months before I met David. She made the mistake of calling me Delilah Jane in front of my date du jour. His face froze in disgust.

"You really are a little Southern hick, aren't you?" he'd said as my face flushed and Sally mouthed, "Sorry."

I never spoke to Sally again but I'm not mad at her anymore. Anger is so bad for your health: your own and your target's. Ha. I've discovered it's good to let the little things go.

Sally would have liked David, but they never met. David came along shortly after and it was love at first sight, on that romantic date that could be made into a movie. Starring me. I know it doesn't seem that way now, with the way we are together since the accident, but we were magic together at first. Just ask his parents. They loved me when we met, said I was a breath of fresh air compared to his shy, boring dates. They expected a normal courtship, a relationship they could control like they had controlled everything their only son had done his entire life.

Nobody can stand in the way of true love, though. Not even the in-laws.

"We just can't wait," David said as we sat in their grand living room. He squeezed my hand and kissed me on the cheek, sending a chill down my spine. It was like a dream come true. My heart thudded with excitement and happiness. Meanwhile, his mother, Rosemary, cried in her tissue and his father paced the room, pleading for him to take his time. I squeezed David's hand back, and beamed at my husband-to-be. Winning. My beautiful engagement ring sparkled in the sunlight.

David stood then and pulled me into his arms. "I hope you guys will come around and bless this marriage. I'm in love. And I'm certain. She is the one. Forever. Jane completes me. Come on, honey."

"You're making a big mistake, son," David Sr. had said, hands on hips, watching us leave the room. "You'll be sorry. You're moving too fast. Love that lasts can wait for an appropriate engagement, a proper wedding. We haven't met her parents."

"I'm an orphan, Mr. Harris," I had said. "I love your son, very much. I will make him happy."

"David, no. Please." Rosemary was really crying by then. She barely got the words out of her little tiny pinched face.

"I love you both, but this is my life," my David had said. He wrapped his arm around my waist and we walked out the door into our future. We married three months later. They never got over the speed of our courtship, even though David was so certain, so in love. Even though we've been married for more than twenty years now, I recognize the look I see in their eyes when I catch them watching me. As if they know they shouldn't trust me, but can't put a finger on why. We are cordial, for the girls. They do love to spoil their granddaughters.

Granddaughter.

And now I suspect they were responsible for pushing our move to Orange County, for making me give up my acting dream. For planting the seed in David that he had to procreate immediately to be successful. Did they also arrange for his one-night stand during our first year of marriage when I just couldn't seem to get pregnant? No, likely even they wouldn't go that far. David's just a serial cheater.

David thought we were trying to get pregnant. I didn't tell him about the birth control. Trying was the fun part. And I could keep auditioning, keep my figure. Sex is a great calorie burner. Of course I wanted children, just not right away. But things didn't turn out the way I'd hoped.

Suddenly, David was handing me a bouquet of pink flowers and talking me into taking a stranger's child. It's all so dirty, don't you think? David and his parents told me the birth mother was a member of their staff, an indoor gardener, who would be grateful, discreet. The adoption would be private, outside normal channels. No one would ever need to know. And David and I would be parents, no stretch marks required.

"She's gorgeous and the baby will be, too. It's not the right time for her to raise a child," David chirped back then. "But it is for us. Honey, we're going to be parents! It's a gift."

A gift I never wanted: someone else's baby to raise. And all along, David was the father. It's all just sick. And I fell for it all. The baby shower, the diamond bracelet from David.

Find a rich man, Delilah Jane. Have his babies. You are set for life. Great thinking, Mom.

I guess I should have suspected something, but why

would I? David and I were newlyweds, happy and blessed with a lifestyle most people could never afford. Sure, Mary had his same thick dark head of hair. The same shape lips. But that was a coincidence, I told myself. I was a busy new mom, and then, all of a sudden, pregnant with Betsy when I forgot my birth control. That was my mistake, Betsy was my little accident. I don't have many of those. The other was believing the adoption records were sealed. I know now some fancy lawyer hired by my father-in-law drew up the adoption documents promising me the birth mother would disappear and never be revealed. What lies.

In fact, Elizabeth James met Mary. Talked to Mary. Had begun a relationship with my daughter. Against everything everyone had promised. And then the ultimate disrespect: How dare she come to the memorial service and try to insert herself as Mary's mother? The memorial ceremony was the time for the community to extend their love to the family. Me, her mother. Not her. She shouldn't have come. But now that she did, there is nothing left for me to do but to destroy her. And I will. She's the next one on my list, after I finish up here.

David and Rosemary Harris need to learn a lesson, too. They invited her to the memorial ceremony. I have a hunch they paid for the whole ceremony, too. I'm not sure yet, but it felt like them, smelled like them. After twenty-two years, I can pick up their trail. Good old David Sr. and Rosemary Harris. Mary's namesake, Rosemary, a condition of her purchase, so to speak. Here you go. We bought you a baby. It's a girl. Name her Rosemary. Oh, and our son screwed our servant to get the baby for you. You're welcome.

But I digress. I loved Mary, more than any mother ever loved a daughter. You have to understand how stressful that time was. Now, looking back on it, I wouldn't change a thing. I know you've had things in the past you regret, decisions you've made in the heat of the moment that weren't well thought out, right? Adopting Mary isn't a regret, of course not. She was my golden child.

I hear the garage door opening. That means David is home first because Betsy parks on the street.

I hurry to dump the rest of my wine in the sink, rinse the coffee cup I was using as a wineglass and slide it into the dishwasher, glancing at the knives, blades facing down. I pop a Life Savers mint in my mouth—the hole prevents choking. I won't become a tragic statistic. I should remind David that Mary choked on a piece of shrimp when she was a toddler in the same restaurant where he just sat, laughing, holding hands.

I grabbed her out of the high chair, did the Heimlich maneuver and saved her life. Does David even remember? It's frustrating, I'm sure you understand. It's like you've done everything right, raised your girl the best you can, cared for her, played by all the rules, and then suddenly, bam, she's gone. My knees go out and I drop onto the living room couch, momentarily exhausted by the flood of memories. You care for your husband, you are his helpmate, but then he turns to someone else. When I see David walking through the door, a surge of adrenaline hits.

I scoot to the edge of the couch, gripping the fabric so

tight in both hands I feel as if I could rip chunks out of it. I'm leaning forward, a lioness in her lair. African lions kill about seventy humans a year in Tanzania alone, and about two hundred fifty people total. Tragic.

"We need to talk." I watch as my voice hits him like a brick.

He jumps. "God, Jane. Why are you sitting there in the dark? You scared me."

Good. "We need to talk. About Betsy first."

His tie is in his hand, his suit coat is draped over his arm. I notice a familiar, threatening scent, something that smells of orange blossoms, someone else's perfume. I know her smell by now, of course. I know everything about her by now. I'm a quick study.

As I breathe him in, he seems relieved at my topic of choice. Betsy. Not us. And the more he relaxes, the more I would like to confront him. But I won't. Not yet. We must focus on our child first.

David says, "I need to change. And there's something I want to show you. Give me a minute."

"Of course." I don't follow him to the bedroom. I know he'll return after he showers, emerging clean and, he'll rationalize, free of sin. We will discuss all of that soon, but not now. I do understand everyone deals with loss in different ways. Children go off to college. It's hard. Some children go off to college, come home and die in a tragic accident. That's even worse.

It's horrible, really. It's hard to find a way through it all. Some coping methods are socially acceptable. Some are not. I smile, stroke the handle of the knife hidden so close to me. Sometimes it's the smallest things that can be the most deadly. Mosquitoes kill two million people a year. Tragic deaths, if you think about it. Something so small, so easily killed by a human, but yet a menace. The African Cape buffalo, on the other hand, will actively stalk and attack the hunter who wounded it. Because of this revenge motive, this drive to hurt those who hurt it, the buffalo kills more people in Africa than any other predator. I've always liked buffalo.

It's taking forever for David to return. I fight the urge to sneak some more wine. I need to be in control of this situation just as I've been in charge of the family all of these years. It's a skill, running a household, pushing your children to achieve, keeping your husband happy. I'd give myself an A- at present. There are a few things getting away from me these days. But I'll sort it out, in time.

David walks into the room and flips on the overhead lights, changing the setting for our talk. I had the lighting the way I wanted it. Dark. I blink.

"What are you doing? Turn the lights down this minute." I stand up, my hands in fists. The knife slipped between the couch cushions makes me smile. I'm a buffalo in disguise. It's like method acting, sort of.

Oh, come on, don't worry about the knife. I need backup, just in case I don't like how our talk ends. You'd do the same. It's really just for comfort, balance of power. Men are stronger than women in general. We need to make sure we have the advantage. He's never hurt me physically, of course, but he's never bought a house with another woman before, either.

Meanwhile, David glances at me, as if I'm coming on to him, as if I would like him to ravish me right here, on the spot.

I do look lovely this evening, but nothing could be further from the truth. I give him the look. He dims the lights. Sits down on the opposite couch. I sit, too.

Game on.

WEDNESDAY

ONE DAY UNTIL GRADUATION

16

12:27 a.m.

David speaks first. "So, why are you awake? Is something wrong?"

Yes. Several things, but first: "It's Betsy. I had a visit from Hoffman. He says she's mixed up with the wrong crowd."

David hands me an envelope. The Cove stationery again. "You may be right. This was in the mailbox." He pushes his hand through his hair. One of his nervous habits.

"So now you believe me? I'm not the one writing these."

"I do," he says as I take the envelope from his hand and pull out the letter. Same block handwriting: BETSY KNOWS THE TRUTH. SHE WAS THERE. SO WAS I.

I look at David as I toss the letter onto the coffee table, as if it were on fire. "What does that mean?"

"Hell if I know." David stands up, pacing. "Do you know who she's hanging out with? Who is her best friend? Have you seen Josh lately? I mean, this is kind of your area with the girls. Really, your only job."

Yes, it is. Was. Especially now, since you're never here. Keeping track of the girls, their friends and boyfriends, has been my life. "I've been distracted by grief, as Dr. Rosenthal would tell you, if you cared. But I do know Josh and Betsy broke up." I don't admit I only found this out the other day.

"What happened?" David asks. "I liked him."

I didn't. "You'll need to ask Betsy. There are a lot of things we need to ask Betsy about, it seems. Do you have any idea who could be leaving these notes?"

David stretches and yawns. "No. And what could Betsy possibly know about Mary's accident?"

"I'm not sure." But that's not entirely true. Betsy knows more about the evening Mary disappeared than she has told us. I know it. Sisters have special bonds. Sometimes, even I wasn't privy to their secrets. Of course, that's normal, I'm told. Dr. Rosenthal says adult children should have privacy, their own space. But I don't agree. There should be no secrets kept from your mother.

Stifling another yawn, David says, "Look, I know this is important. But I'm exhausted."

I bet. He's had a very busy day: an athletic morning followed by a relaxing romantic dinner and more, ah, romance, with just a smidge of work in between. Poor guy.

Too bad. I know where he went after dinner. I was there, too, watching from outside. The Port Streets are lovely at night. Even I like it in that neighborhood, sitting inside my luxury car. It's easy to blend in, to hide.

It's almost as if I belong on that street, in one of these homes, in that home. David and I had considered buying a house there but we chose The Cove to be closer to the beach and the ocean. I guess David just wants to have his cake and eat it, too. Such bad karma.

"Oh, David, I'm tired, too," I manage, stifling a yawn. Tired of your shit. I smile, use my nice new wife voice. "You need to help me. We need to confront her tonight together. A united front."

"It's one in the morning. Nothing positive will come from surprising her at this time of night. Let's go to sleep. We can talk to her in the morning. Coming?"

I stand up. "You're right. Nothing positive is going on when your husband waltzes in the door after midnight, most nights. Don't you dare walk away from me." My tone is a bit icier than I meant it to be. But it's late. I've been waiting so long and we're on the final countdown to graduation. It's time. I slip the knife into my back pocket. "We have more to talk about."

He turns around. His shoulders sink, he pushes his hand through his still-damp hair. "I'd rather not. Let's just get through this week, through Betsy's graduation, and then we can make some decisions. Not now." He stops near the bookshelves and I move between him and the path to our bedroom. That's as close as he's come to

revealing his plans. He looks nervous, his eyes dart between me and the hallway I'm blocking.

Behind his head, on the bookshelf, a heavy geode props
up my collection of ocean photography coffee table books.
It's a big rock. Drop it on someone's head and that would
be a deadly accident.

"I don't want to wait another week, another day, another hour. I've had it, David. You brought Kylie to the
memorial service, of all things. And then your parents
brought Elizabeth. Are you just trying to make me furious? Humiliate me in front of everyone we know? What's
the endgame, darling?"

David keeps the couch between us, walking backward
toward the kitchen holding his palms up as if I had a gun.
I wish. "You're not in a good state of mind tonight, Jane.
I think you ought to get some rest. We'll talk all of this
through soon, but not now, not tonight."

He's reached the kitchen island. I'm following slowly.

"Betsy tells me you went to Volunteer Day at school.
That was a step forward." David's hands are resting on
the island, as if he and I are chatting about our days,
casual-like. But he is tense. On alert. Almost as if he's
afraid of me. Weenie. The knife is just for my own protection, of course, in case I need to make something appear as self-defense. But I don't want to hurt him. I have
plans to execute.

"Did she also tell you I had a panic attack and had to go
outside because of her? Did she mention she yelled at me
in front of everyone? Did she mention she didn't apologize? Called me a monster? I was there to paint with her,

to help her. I love her so much and she's so mean to me. I only want what's best for her, for all of us." I'm shaking again.

They talk all the time, David and Betsy. I know they do. Why isn't she mad at David for being Mary's biological dad? He's the monster in our house. Instead, they're both moving forward without me. I put my hands on the island, imitating his stance. For fun, I bang my hands on the counter and he jumps. Funny how his face looks when he's scared. But why be scared of little ol' me?

"Jane. Stop it. You need to take a breath. Can I get you some pills? Xanax or something? You have a bunch in the medicine cabinet." David is dismissing me. He's not afraid of me, I suddenly realize. He's frustrated. I've stalked him all through our home, but he didn't even notice.

"No, I don't need drugs. I need answers. Honest answers. I'm so sick of this."

David yawns. "I'm going to sleep."

"I'm going to wait up for her." I'm not tired. But if I do get sleepy, I'll stay here on the couch. I don't want to sleep next to him anyway. Not ever again.

David is halfway down the hall, a safe distance away, when he yells, "Leave her alone. That's a bad idea."

You were a bad idea.

After the pouting girlfriend was out of the way, after David and I had three wonderful and romantic dates, I decided it was time to sleep with him. Well, not sleep, but you know. The question was where. I couldn't bring him to the low-life apartment complex where I lived, that was clear. I'd finally evicted my loser former boyfriend, Bobby, the guy who drove me from Arkansas to my dream of Hollywood. He thought we'd be together forever. He didn't even know about all the guys I'd been dating since we arrived in Tinseltown. Boys are idiots, especially high school boys, and high school sweethearts just never work out. That's what my mom told me. So of course we wouldn't, but he didn't know that at the time.

It had taken us five days to reach the sparkling dream of Hollywood because Bobby made us stop at any landmarks we'd read about in the history books in school. I'd never been outside of our town, so I had to admit standing on the edge of the Grand Canyon was just about the best feeling of freedom I'd ever had. My belongings were shoved in a trash bag in the back seat of his car. I'd never been so happy to see a place in the rearview mirror than when we left my hometown and my so-called adoptive family behind.

Bobby thought it was romantic I traveled so light. How I'd mesmerized him so much he'd seemed to forget I was an orphan with nothing but what was in the trash bag and a business card for a Hollywood talent manager was another sign of my feminine prowess.

"This is just unbelievable. Who knew this was just down the road from Eureka Springs?" Bobby asked, holding my hand at the edge of the canyon.

Well, everybody, everywhere knew but he was simple, sweet. I turned toward him. "It is. I've never seen anything like this."

"I'm talking about you, Delilah Jane. You, here, well… I'll remember this moment forever." He'd hugged me and then we'd screwed in the back seat of his car. I'm not sure how we did it, but it was steamy and sexy. I guess that's young love.

Bobby's parents freaked out when they discovered he was gone. He was all set to attend the University of Georgia in the fall, his momma and daddy's alma mater. He had a ticket to a comfortable future, a future that would not include a hedonistic trip to Hollywood with an orphaned beauty pageant contestant.

They shouldn't have worried so much. He was a means to an end, my ride to the coast. I sent him back to them, not a moment too soon. I couldn't stand living in the tiny rank apartment with a country hick one day longer. Once I'd hooked David, I set Bobby free. Broke, heartbroken and determined to never mention my name. I even kept his car when he flew back home. He'd loved the car, but I needed it more than he did. Besides, his parents promised him a new truck to drive to college to lure him back home.

I know he still thinks of me, at least in his dreams. They all do. He married a girl from Atlanta, Mary Beth or something. They have four boys. She's stuck, at least if you follow my mom's logic: Don't have more than two kids, Delilah Jane, or you can't leave him.

I'm down to one child: a mirror of my own story.

But she's not an orphan. She has her mom. That's all she needs.

Betsy and I are in a standoff, that's for sure. But this helpful note writer, anonymous as he or she may be, is on my side. I reach for the new note on the coffee table. It is clearly written by the same person as the first one. I am certain Betsy knows the author of these notes. I am certain she knows much more about a lot of things.

I will simply wait up for her. She must come home at some point. Graduation is tomorrow. I remember my own high school graduation day, a period and THE END on my life in Eureka Springs. The next day, Bobby and I were gone.

My heart thumps. My eyes open wide with the realization. Betsy has made the same type of plans. It's all clear to me now. She keeps telling me she is gone after graduation and now I know she's going with Bo. This is what Hoffman was warning me about.

Young people are so foolish sometimes. Add illicit love and, well, they become complete idiots. Like mother, like daughter. I'll save her from herself.

17

2:00 a.m.

I sit on the couch in the living room awake, waiting for Betsy. I've left my lookout only to use the bathroom and make a snack. I'm on a mission. I'm focused.

It's time to extract information from my daughter. But I'm going to need help. What exactly does the anonymous note writer think Betsy knows, versus what I know? David will be no help. But there are professionals who do this. People like Detective Branson.

I stretch. What if Betsy made it into the house without alerting me, somehow sneaking past me through the outside courtyard when I was having my snack, darting down to her bedroom undetected by going around the side? I need to check. I guess I'll let her sleep if she's down there. But if she's awake, I'll strike, cobra-like.

What if she isn't home? What if she doesn't come home at all?

My heart thumps and I pull out my phone. Text Betsy: Where are you?

Betsy texts: You'll never find peace until you let everything go.

What? I punch in her number. The phone rings twice before it's answered. By a man.

"Mrs. Harris. This is Bo—we met at school. Betsy is safe. She'll be home a little later."

"Give Betsy her phone this minute. She has a curfew. She's in high school."

"Mom, calm down. I told Bo you wouldn't like him answering. I'll be home late. Go to sleep. It's Seniors' Day, late start." Betsy's voice sounds like she is on drugs.

"I need you home this minute. I will pick you up." I remember she thinks I don't drive anymore.

"You don't drive. I'm fine. I'll be home soon."

"Listen, young lady. This behavior is unacceptable. You're out way past curfew and we need to talk. Come home immediately."

"You do know I'm about to graduate, Mom. Your reign is over. Mary and I both will be gone."

"Betsy!"

She's hung up the phone. When I call back it goes to voice mail.

Mary would never have pulled something like this. She

did have her secrets, true, but nothing like this. This could bring another embarrassment onto our entire family. Why can't Betsy be the straight A, popular, normal kid? No, she has to be an artsy loser dating a person she shouldn't.

Aren't the adopted kids supposed to be the ones with problems? Yes, they are, and they are good for the waistline. Betsy was the opposite.

I discovered I was pregnant three months after Mary's adoption. I'd made the mistake of removing my IUD and bam. My pants were tight, and soon my figure disappeared. I thought I'd dodged the pregnancy bullet and could only hope I didn't have my mom's penchant for thirty-pound weight gain with pregnancy.

But I did.

When Betsy was born, I wished for the best for both of us. Those wishes included, first, that I would lose the weight quickly and, second, that I'd be blessed with another little angel who I could mold into a successful, beautiful person who loved her mother. I dropped the weight quickly but lightning doesn't strike the same place twice, they say, although lightning does kill about forty people a year in the US, in case you wondered.

Carrying Betsy to term and delivering a healthy baby girl completed our family, I made sure of that with the doctor. Betsy was born with a smattering of my white blond hair, David's bright blue eyes and extreme colic that didn't resolve for months. She was sensitive to light, to sound, to touch. She was a fussy eater, a reluctant swimmer when the time came to learn and a clingy kindergartner when it was finally time for her to go to school. In short, she was a struggle.

Betsy was the opposite of vivacious, lovable, beautiful Mary. Mary was my golden child, I suppose, and Betsy had a hard act to follow. I guess you are born the way you are going to be. Life may make you into something worse, of course, especially if your older sister is almost perfect. Jealousy is a terrible emotion.

I need a distraction. I walk into the kitchen and open my laptop. There's a tab on the online newspaper I like labeled Accidents and Disasters. I go there when I can't sleep. A man died from a box jellyfish in Australia. The most venomous marine creature known to man, each tentacle has enough toxin to kill sixty people. One minute, you're snorkeling with your mates and the next, dead. Not a gidday. He's one of forty people who die this way each year.

Death by jellyfish makes me giggle.

I'm a bit slaphappy, I know. It's not funny. None of this is funny. I cover my mouth, shake with laughter until it stops, turning into something darker.

I stand up and kick the side of the couch. My hands clench into fists. I hate being out of control, hate it. I grab the knife from the table and slide it into the butcher-block holder on the kitchen counter.

This will be the last time I will be out of control. Ever.

18

9:00 a.m.

David hovers above me. "Jane. Wake up."

I open one eye. I've clearly dozed off but I'm not in my bed. I'm in the living room, on the couch. He's dressed in a business suit, as always. No tie. I'm not sure whether he's coming or going.

I sit up slowly. Disoriented.

"I brought you coffee." David points to the steaming cup on the coffee table, next to the letter accusing Betsy. I try not to let my stomach tighten with anger again. It's too early in the morning.

"Thanks."

"Did you talk to her?" He's hoping I handled the dirty work so he can skedaddle off to his new life.

"No. I called her but she was with Bo. It was weird."

"What do you mean weird? Who is Bo?"

"I don't know. I got a bad feeling. Like what Hoffman warned me about." I take a sip of coffee.

"I'm not sure what you're talking about. I'm going to go wake her up. It's her last day of school, Seniors' Day, where they all get special shit, right? What is she doing still asleep?"

I shrug. Take a sip of coffee. "She does whatever she wants these days." And you've created this, dear. David prided himself on being the disciplinarian, but clearly he has dropped the ball. He's juggling so much these days.

David stomps downstairs and I hear his fist banging on Betsy's door.

"It's graduation day! The day we've all been waiting for!!" David yells. "Upstairs. This minute." David is commanding when he wants to be. A glimpse of the old days, the happy days. The normal family days. Firm dad. Loving mom. Two beautiful girls.

I'm relieved to see Betsy rush upstairs, already dressed, sort of, in very short shorts and a crop top. She shoots me a death stare as she heads to the kitchen even though I haven't done anything. Her dad is the one yelling and she's blaming me. David is on her heels, so I follow them, bringing the note with me.

I watch her back as she makes coffee. David leans against the kitchen island. I pull out a bar stool and take a seat. This should be fun.

She turns slowly and stares at us, first David and then me. She notices the letter on the island and grabs it. "What the fuck?"

David yells, "That's what we want to know. What's going on, Betsy?"

"I have no idea who is writing these. It's some sort of crazy person. This is a sick joke. What am I supposed to tell you? Why the rocks slid out from under her? Why the current carried her away? What do you want from me?" Tears slide down Betsy's cheeks.

"Whoever is doing this, writing these letters, they know you." David's arms are crossed, he looks tired, maybe as tired as I am. "They think you know something you haven't told us."

"Unbelievable. I wish I was the one who died." Betsy rips the letter in half. "This is all insane. You two are both crazy. I hate it. I can't wait to get out of here."

I stand up, my legs shaky. "Think. Is there anything you haven't told us about that day, anything at all? We love you no matter what. Maybe you've blocked something out? Denial is a strong emotion." I've read that happens when you witness a tragedy, or think you might have caused it. Guilt can make you forget.

Betsy stares at me and then walks away.

"Get back here," David demands as we hear the front door open and Betsy is gone.

David stares at me. I see it in his eyes. He has finally had the realization: What if Betsy had something to do with Mary's death?

"What do we do?" David's voice is hushed. He locks

eyes with me. He is thinking perhaps that he doesn't know his daughter like he thought he did. "I guess we could call Detective Branson? Have him talk to her? Show him the notes."

My hand flies to my mouth. "What? No. We can't turn in our own daughter. Besides, he told me the case is closed. Period." I rub my eyes with my hands. I'm so tired. I'm also covering the satisfied look I can't quite get off my face. He believes me now.

David looks at the ceiling. "When did you speak with him last?"

Oops. I guess I'm busted. "Yesterday. I took him the first note."

"I told you to ignore the note. Betsy was afraid you'd do this."

She should be afraid, and I don't listen to you anymore. "Well, I took it to the detective. And now there's another one."

David sighs. "Mary fell and that's all there is to it. We need to leave it at that."

No, that isn't all. "What if Betsy does know something? God forbid, what if she saw something? Caused something? We have to consider it. It's what someone believes, it's what the note writer believes."

David looks at me, shakes his head. "I just can't imagine anything else but an accident. That has to be the truth. And besides, if this unnamed person really does have something on Betsy, he or she would call the police, right? Maybe it's just another girl in her class who is jealous of Betsy?"

"No one is jealous of Betsy." I mean, duh. I know, it's hard, darling, but try to focus. "There was nobody on the trail that day who remembered seeing them, at least no one who has come forward. Maybe the note writer was afraid to come forward until now, or still is?" I slide back onto the bar stool, suddenly exhausted. Why can't he see what I'm trying to show him?

"You think someone saw Betsy do something to Mary? You're wrong." He shakes his head.

More evidence. Men are clueless. "I just don't know." A tear works its way down my left cheek.

"I'm late for work." David moves slowly through the kitchen. "Don't push Betsy anymore. We need to just move on. If we talk to Branson we're just going to cast suspicion on our own daughter. Why would we ever do that? This is her graduation week. She needs to enjoy the final day of high school, not be confronted by her unhinged parents. Enough." He heads for the door. "I'm going to call Betsy and apologize. You should do the same."

"But what about the truth?" I am pushing him.

He stops, hand on the front door, and stares at me. "Leave it, Jane. I don't want to lose the only daughter we still have. I don't think I could survive that."

"I know." That's true.

That's what makes all of this so fun.

19

10:00 a.m.

My phone rings and caller ID informs me it's the school.
A shot of adrenaline floods my system. Something has
happened to Betsy or she has vanished.

"This is Jane Harris," I sputter.

"Hello, Jane, it's Angelica." The counselor sounds
happy.

"What's wrong?" I'm on alert, I should be.

"I'm calling with good news." Angelica's voice is lilt-
ing, a kindergarten teacher's voice. "Betsy is a finalist
in the school art scholarship prizes. Her work will be on
display tomorrow during graduation, and if she wins,

she'll get a thousand-dollar scholarship, too. It's so exciting I didn't even mark her tardy today during the Seniors' Day festivities. I covered for her and said she was with me finding out about being a finalist for the prize."

"Wow, great. I don't think I've seen her latest work. What's the subject?" In my mind I imagine a portrait of a teenage girl, gorgeous, except for the knife glinting in her hand stabbing her evil parents. I'm being macabre. But honestly, I watch a lot of crime TV these days, do a lot of online research about death. If you are going to be murdered, you're more likely to be killed by someone you know and, most likely, love. Almost half of all murdered women are killed by a romantic partner. Lovely, I know.

Even poor Brad was a suspect in Mary's disappearance, for a brief moment, those crazy three days when she was missing. But he was in Iceland on a family trip. I didn't know their little date, with Mary wearing my red dress, was special because he was going on vacation the next morning. No, I found that out after she died. He couldn't be a suspect. He was a dead end, so to speak, but still, he must have been traumatized by the suspicion. All of the strange men they questioned, the convicted child abusers and child molesters they rounded up and questioned were cleared. None of them knew anything about poor Mary. All the while she was drifting toward me in the California Current.

Focus on Angelica.

"It will be such a big, fun surprise for Betsy tomorrow evening. Well, really for all of you. All Betsy knows is that she's a finalist. I hope I didn't spoil it for you but I just love delivering good news." Angelica is so cheerful. "Well, I've got to run."

"Angelica, wait. Have you noticed Betsy hanging out with the wrong crowd?" She would know, wouldn't she?

Silence.

Finally, she answers. "I don't know exactly who she hangs out with, to be honest. A lot of kids drift between groups. Betsy seems fine. She's artistic, and smart. A lovely girl. You should be proud of her, how she's been able to pull herself together and complete high school even after losing Mary. She's one of the strongest young women I know."

Whatever. "I met a man named Bo yesterday in the gym during Volunteer Day. Says he's a substitute teacher?"

"Oh, yes, Bo is one of the kids' favorites. He's a substitute gym teacher and he donates his own time to tutor the kids."

Until 2:00 a.m.? I walk into the courtyard, smiling as I glance up. I don't have to worry about those murderous palm trees but I probably should be worrying about Bo. I could report this, get him in big trouble, if I wanted to. Maybe I will. Just need to get through graduation day first.

Angelica keeps talking, per usual. "You know, Mrs. Harris, a lot of kids struggle to navigate the pressures of high school and life in this pressure-cooker community. I mean, I don't know how they do it. Four hours of homework a night, sports, jobs, the pressure to get straight As. We all place so many expectations on them, parents and the district." Angelica sighs into the phone. I imagine her looking out at a sea of troubled teens. "I could talk about this all day but I'm sorry—I've got to run. Betsy is doing great, she's a wonderful young woman and she's about to graduate, so you have nothing to worry about. See you tomorrow night."

Oh, but I'm worried, and intrigued. Betsy has been a step ahead of me, hiding things from me. I'm accustomed to her Cs and community college–level achievements. I'm also quite familiar by now with her disdain for me. But a secret boyfriend, that's next-level stuff. I wonder if Mary knew about Bo? Has this been going on for more than a year? Is Bo what Mary was helping Betsy hide from me? I wonder if Mary was a fan of Bo, too? I answer my own question. No way my preppy daughter would like her sister to hang out with a man like that.

I know my Mary. Mary would have hated them together as much as I do. I decide I need to search Betsy's bedroom, so I hold the handrail (no tragic falling for me) and reach her door. It's locked. I presume the outside door will be, too. Foiled, I head back upstairs and grab my window to the world, while ignoring my actual windows and the views they could provide of the ocean. I open my laptop and search his name. Bo has a blog with about two hundred followers. He writes about sports, and teens talking to each other, and he has a whole series of do-it-yourself household fixes. How handy. He writes about parental pressure and the "false idea of perfection" forced on teens these days.

He hosts "talk-it-out sessions" at Point Park in the nature preserve section every Sunday evening, weather permitting.

My pulse quickens.

According to Bo's post, Point Park is the perfect place to "kick-it with nature." It's also a deadly place. Why would Betsy want to hang out there? The park is the scene of the crime, so to speak. Strange, and creepy.

Before I can stop them, memories from a year ago rush into my mind. The doorbell rang and the guard handed me the red leash still attached to a bedraggled and confused Cash. It was just before sunset, May 20, last year.

"We found him outside the back gate, Mrs. Harris. Poor fellow seems really frightened," the guard said, patting Cash's head.

Before I could do the same, Cash darted past me and into the house. No doubt thirsty and tired. "Thank you. I thought he was on a hike with my daughter. I don't know why he's alone."

"Well, it's just a good thing he was at the back gate, not one of the Pacific Coast Highway entrances. Lucky fellow seems unharmed, just scared." The guard tipped his green The Cove baseball cap and climbed back into the white pickup truck, The Cove Security printed on the side.

An hour later, Betsy had walked through the gate into the courtyard. Since Mary had returned from college almost two weeks earlier, the girls barely came through the upstairs part of the house anymore, opting for the side stairs and a quick escape. And they seemed closer, as if Mary's year away at college had been good for their relationship. Even though Betsy still had a few more weeks before school was out for the summer, they'd reconnected.

As for me, it was like I had tenants who I never saw.

"Thank God," I'd said, rushing to my daughter, pulling her into a hug. "Are you okay? Where's Mary?"

Betsy looked strange, distant. "I wasn't with Mary. Why?" Betsy was dressed in hiking attire. Gray shorts. Tennis shoes. White T-shirt. Actually, to be fair, it was an outfit you could wear anyplace in May at the beach. She could have been anywhere. Betsy's face had flushed, or did I simply imagine that. "I haven't seen her since breakfast."

"Cash turned up, alone, at the back gate. He left for a hike with your sister, hours ago. He's shook up."

"Poor guy. Where is he?" Betsy followed me in the house, the first such visit for her in a while. Cash cowered under the kitchen table.

"What's wrong, puppy?" Betsy cooed, crawling under the table, petting his head.

As I stepped closer to them I thought I heard a low growl. "Be careful. I think he just growled at you."

"I think that was directed at you," she snapped, helpfully.

I took a deep breath, smoothed the front of my tennis dress. "Look, I'm worried about your sister. It's dark. Please, if you've seen her, tell me. Tell me the truth."

Betsy ducked back under the table with Cash.

David walked in the door then, supposedly from work. It had been hours since Cash was returned to our home, hours that I'd been calling his phone, and he'd ignored me.

"Oh, David, you're home." He likely thought I was confronting him, the guilty jerk. But I wasn't. It was about Mary.

David stiffened, and looked into my eyes. "What's going on?"

"I'm worried something has happened. Cash is here. Mary isn't," I said.

"Betsy, what's going on?" David patted my back and wrapped an arm around me. I could feel his body tensing as if he wished he could push me away, as if he already had.

"I don't know, Dad. But Cash is acting weird, so is Mom. Did you call her phone?" Betsy crawled out from under the table and called her sister.

"Of course I called her. No answer." I'd tried it. It rang and went to voice mail. It still had battery life, then, and even though it had taken a big tumble, it still worked. For a short period of time.

"It went to voice mail. What do we do?" Betsy asked. She looked at both of us. Her parents. We are the perfect family, the perfect parents. We should know what to do. And yet we didn't have the answer. What do you do when your daughter is missing? It's everyone's nightmare, yet there aren't any standard steps.

David had jumped into action. "We call her friends. Betsy, start with her high school buds. Call Liz, and Brad. I'll call Morgan from USC. She's got to be around somewhere." David seemed pleased with himself.

"Someone must have seen her this afternoon." I look at Betsy, who turns her back to me and makes a phone call.

They didn't give me an assignment, so I made dinner, to keep myself busy. It's times like this when distractions help. I sliced carrots and onions, crying over the cutting board. It was such a long, sad night. We found out later, when Betsy gave her statement to the police, that she'd lured Mary to the park for a hike. Now I realize there is even more to the story. Maybe she wanted her sister to meet her secret lover. Mary must have been furious. Did their argument escalate to violence? One can only wonder—and only Betsy would know the truth.

We didn't find Mary that night. Or the next day, or for three days. A "Help Us Find Mary Harris" Facebook page was created and hundreds of people joined. We were celebrities. The police swarmed our home, interviewed each of us individually. As I mentioned, they ruled out Brad. But everyone else was a suspect at first. Once they cleared the family they pushed us to go on television, to put a face on the tragedy. Meanwhile, drones scoured the thousand-acre Point Park and preserve, aided by search and rescue teams. Mary's sorority sisters joined in the search, too, starting just outside the back gate where poor Cash was found.

I open my laptop and click on the video I keep on my desktop. It's an interview of David and me on the LA news station, pleading with the public for information. I don't turn up the sound because I know my words by heart. My face is a little swollen from crying, but my makeup is good. I looked and sounded the best, of course. I loved being in front of the camera. All of my acting experience shone through.

David looked horrible, almost like he was guilty of something besides not being home the evening Mary disappeared, not answering his phone when we needed him. The day of the interview, he let me do the talking. I'm wearing sunglasses because that is acceptable in these situations, I read, even though the press conference is being held inside at the station. They told us the appeals are most compelling from the mom, the kidnappers want to see my pain. I could deliver those lines easily.

David looked straight into the camera like a novice. Everyone knows you look at the interviewer. Duh. He has circles under his eyes, his dress shirt is wrinkled, as if he slept in it and he probably had. Betsy stayed off camera, safe with the policewoman who was omnipresent at our home during the search.

When it was time for my monologue, I faced the camera, because that's what you do. "Please. Please bring my daughter back. We'll do anything you ask. Her father and I, and her entire family, stand at the ready. We love you, Mary. If you can hear me, reach out and we'll come get you. We love our daughter. Please, bring her back home." David and his parents wrapped me in a hug, the first time we'd touched in years. I guess they wanted to be sure to have their fifteen minutes of fame. They're like that.

We didn't know then that the ocean currents would bring her home to us the next morning.

Those three days, waiting to find her, well, there is no description for those days. Or for the weeks after, as the sympathy poured in, as the meals were dropped off without stop, as the cards and flowers and donations surged, as we had a small, private funeral to bury Mary. It's all a blur now. It was a terrible trauma. I worried a little that I couldn't handle everything that happened. But then I found Dr. Rosenthal.

"You've lost so much, Jane. You're grieving. Your entire family is. I should see them all. Bring David and Betsy in with you. You all need to process what has happened," Dr. Rosenthal had advised.

I think Betsy met with her only once, but I can't really remember. Like I said, those were the crazy times, muddled by the numbing onslaught of pharmaceuticals. Let me be clear: I don't feel guilty about anything. I mean, I haven't been a great mother to Betsy this past year, but that's to be expected when a mother is grieving the loss of her daughter. As I mentioned, we'd been growing apart since before Mary died. Betsy seems to be dealing with Mary's death in her own special and sneaky way.

I knew Betsy and Mary shared some secrets with each other, and kept me in the dark. I didn't appreciate it when Mary hid her contact with her birth mother from me, and I don't appreciate Betsy hiding Bo. They should realize mothers need to know everything. That's what mothers do. We guide, we control, we listen, we encourage.

We always find out when our children hide things from us, big and small.

It's a mother's instinct to search for the truth. Knowledge is power, they say. And now you know almost the whole story. Almost.

20

11:00 a.m.

Cows kill twenty people a year in the US, which seems like a low number given what we do to those poor creatures.

Bees murder about one hundred folks and sharks kill less than one person per year, even though they get the worst rap. I wonder about chickens. Have they had any revenge? Uncooked, contaminated food kills more than five thousand people a year, and I bet a lot of that is chicken. Karma again. Makes you think.

And I am thinking. I need to figure out the relationship between Betsy and Bo. I need to find out what she is doing out with Bo until 2:00 a.m., although I suppose by now we can all make a guess. Besides that, what are they up to?

I suppose all younger siblings learn how to be sneakier than their older siblings. They watch what the older one does, what the older one gets caught doing, and then they do it better.

What has sibling rivalry caused you to do? Think about it.

A Google search doesn't provide an address for Bo. I'll need to track him down at school, or at the hardware store. I can talk to Angelica and find out his schedule. My head spins with possibilities as I walk through the courtyard to the front door. Could I set an even bigger trap? Perhaps so.

The dry cleaning is dropped off on Wednesdays, left outside on the bench below the sign indicating deliveries. This way, I don't have to talk to anyone. There's a note with my name on it stuck on top of the bright green dry-cleaning bag.

I hope they didn't find anything embarrassing in anyone's pockets, David. A condom here, a lipstick there.

I rip open the plain white envelope and pull out a note:

I know what really happened. Poor Cash.

My heart thumps in my chest as I scan the street. There is no one around. I leave the dry cleaning and rush inside. Why would the dry cleaner leave this? No, it wasn't him.

I take a deep breath. Is someone watching me? This is a note from a different person. An accusing person.

Calm down, Delilah Jane.

Or was this note left by Betsy? Yes, that's it. Of course, to throw us off her trail. She's bringing up the stupid dog again for some reason. First his bowl, now this. She's so ridiculous.

I rush into the kitchen, grab a brown paper bag. I practice my breathing. In and out. Slowly. Calm down from my anger. Anger triggers panic attacks, too, did you know that?

Did Betsy leave me this note? No, of course not. It is for Betsy. Betsy lured her sister to the park, took her to an out-of-bounds closed trail. Mary's old boyfriend Brad knows that she never went on out-of-bounds hikes. That wasn't her style. She was a rule follower, for the most part. Her college friends know that, they all wrote me notes, telling me how happy she was, so excited for sophomore year to begin. Just look at her Facebook memorial page. She's happy. Loving life.

Sure, Mary and I had a fight the morning she died, and this one was bigger than the one the night before with the red dress. This fight was nothing epic, just the typical mother-daughter kind of disagreement, but it was big enough that she raced out of the house, slamming the door.

"You can't stop me from seeing my biological mother. Don't try. And do not threaten her or me like that," Mary yelled. She stood in the courtyard, Cash on a leash by her side.

"Yes, I can. It's in the paperwork. You were never to meet, let alone go live with her. I will not allow it." I spoke calmly. I was dead serious. It would not happen.

"I like Elizabeth. She's brilliant and loving. Heck, anyone would be an improvement over you," Mary said as she turned and ran out the gate.

The memory of that moment clenches my stomach every time. But our last fight is not important, not anymore. The real question is, who saw her between the time she left the house and when she fell to her death?

Betsy did.

Betsy heard some of our fight that morning, I know. She appeared in the courtyard behind me.

"You're unbelievable!" she said before she followed after her sister.

She wouldn't talk to me ever again about what Mary told her, Mary's plans for the future. Nothing. Said it wasn't my business. Not then, not ever. But it was all my business. My girls are my life. Mary died before we cleared things up, we were still arguing up to the end. I bite my lip with the memory, still upset I let things with Mary get out of control. I cannot let that happen with Betsy. I won't.

So I'll destroy this note. We have the other two as evidence. Whoever wrote this one, well, I'll never know. I crumple the paper and toss it into the kitchen sink. I drown it in water and, once it's wet, mash it to shreds and feed it down the disposal. And then, like a lightning strike, I realize there is another person who likely doesn't appreciate the relationship between Betsy and Bo.

Josh.

Josh might know a lot about Betsy. He was always nice and friendly to me when they dated. And he came to the memorial service even though Betsy had dumped him already. Josh could have plenty of insights about my daughter. I wish I'd paid more attention to him, gotten to know his parents, the rest of the games people play when their kids are dating. Like Brad, Josh's family lives in The Cove, too, I discovered recently.

Perhaps Hoffman can help me connect with Josh? I know he'll have so much to tell me about my daughter, especially if she broke his heart. A lover scorned is a dangerous thing.

But first, I call Dr. Rosenthal's office. The bored receptionist explains the doctor is booked today, as always.

"Tell her it's a bit of an emergency." My hands can't stop shaking.

"Is it an emergency?" bored receptionist asks.

"Yes." My heart races as I try to stay calm on the phone. I realize now there could be two sides to the story, even though I've destroyed the latest note. I need to make sure my story is the one people believe, the truth. It's an integral part of the plan. Dr. Rosenthal will see things the way I do, but I need to reinforce it today. Now. I grip the phone, willing a positive response.

Big sigh. "She can squeeze you in at three."

"I'll take it." I exhale. Hang up.

Text Sam: Can you take me to the doctor at 3?

Sam texts back: Of course, Mrs. H. See you at 2:45!

21

12:10 p.m.

There are only two notes now, so let's just focus on those, shall we? Betsy knows more than she's told us, and Josh knows Betsy intimately. Trust me, I read his love notes to her. In a box, under her bed, the obvious place. But those love notes have stopped. The last love letter I could find from the poor boy was more of a goodbye of sorts, and it was written back in September. It was confusing and I didn't have much time to read it. All that I have seen on Betsy's phone this school year have been check-ins between the two of them, almost friend-level texts. Although Betsy does tell him she loves him. Has she been leading him on?

Josh, why didn't I think to talk to you sooner? I hope I'm not slipping. Of course I'm not. It's just hard with all these moving pieces, all those months of pills and grief. But I'm on it. On him. I hurry to my bathroom and apply concealer, blush and mascara. I pull my hair into a low ponytail. I wrestle on some athletic wear. Blue shorts, white T-shirt and finish the look with a trucker cap with the word *Thankful* stamped on the front.

I could be hiking, walking on the beach or doing just about anything on a warm May afternoon at my beach city. I have a flash of memory to what Mary was wearing the last time I saw her. Almost the same outfit, but black shorts instead of blue. A USC hat—the one thing we never recovered. I take a deep breath, finish tying my tennis shoes and head out. I will walk down to Hoffman's office. I will be a normal Southern California housewife, one who actually leaves her house every morning to walk in the sunshine and soak up vitamin D. It's all the rage these days, you know, getting vitamin D from the sun instead of a pill. Did you know it's possible to overdose on vitamin D? So many ways to harm yourself or somebody else.

At the clubhouse I pull open the door and all three staff members rise to greet me, an excessive display of deference they are forced to perform hundreds of times a day.

"Mrs. Harris. So good to see you out and about." That's Robert. He's nice. He didn't add anything about Mary, and that makes my heart relax.

"Good to be here. Is Hoffman around?" I smile. "I'm

thinking about signing up for the couples' tennis tournament."

"That's great!" Kathy has big glasses and big teeth. She reminds me of an enthusiastic horse. "Hoffman is in his office!"

"Thanks." I wave to them all and they sit down in unison, just waiting for another resident to come through the door to force them to stand again.

Hoffman's office is at the end of the hall, closest to the courts. Makes sense. I knock. When he opens the door, he doesn't mask his shock. "Wow, Jane. What do I owe this surprise? I hope I didn't upset you yesterday."

"Well, I needed to know. So thank you." I sigh and drop into the chair facing his desk. "And actually, I need your help. I want to talk to Josh, Betsy's old boyfriend. Can you help me get in touch with him?"

"Of course. Josh is back. Graduated with honors. I'll call his mom if you'd like," Hoffman says.

"Back? From where? Isn't he supposed to be finishing his senior year with Betsy?" I lean forward. This is an interesting development.

He leans against his desk, arms folded. "He went away to boarding school for senior year. Some fancy place back East and it was a great move. He's off to Princeton in the fall."

A light bulb pops on in my slow brain. I whisper, "He wasn't here all school year?"

Hoffman looks around, even though we are the only ones in the room. "It's not a secret. I mean, Betsy didn't tell you?"

Not exactly. "I do know they broke up recently." And now Betsy is with Bo. Something is nagging at the back of my mind, a worry that Betsy may be one step ahead of me. No, that's not possible. I focus on Hoffman. "I need to talk to Josh. Please, can you help me?"

"I'll call him now. And, Jane?" Hoffman pauses.

What now? "More bad news?" I lean back in the chair.

"No, not really. It's probably nothing—it's just the tennis ladies. You know how they talk. And since your falling-out with Melissa, well, I'm sure it's nothing." He flushes. We all know he loves the gossip as much as they do.

"What are they saying about me, Hoffman?" I feel my fists clench. I mean, you'd think we were all in middle school.

"I try to keep up with everything. Everyone. Help when I can. I mean, with a divorce rate of 73 percent in wealthy beach towns, I just want to help make a difference. Keep families together."

Oh crap. He's heard something about David. It's not surprising. "Tell me."

"I know you're under so much stress, and so much heartache. But I did want to tell you to pay some attention to your man. Somebody else seems to have her eyes on him. And she's making moves."

Kylie.

"What? Who? No, he wouldn't." I feign surprise. It was only a matter of time before people spotted them together. The memorial ceremony may have been the trigger.

"I don't know her name, but they have been seen to-

gether, at restaurants a couple of times. When they confronted him, David told the Stewarts, who live just five
doors from you, it was just a business dinner. But Jackie
Stewart talks, and now the rest of the ladies aren't so
sure. She's younger. I'm so sorry." Hoffman's hands are
palms up. He's just the messenger, I remind myself. None
of these women like me, and I know that. This just gives
them more crap to say about me. About us.

I cover my face with my hands. My lying, cheating
husband. At least everyone is on my side now. David is
so stupid. "He's my life. I can't lose him, too."

"Then you won't. I'll help you connect with Josh, we'll
get Betsy back on track, and then full-on romance for the
two of you. Have you been on vacation since—"

"No."

"Out to dinner?"

"Nothing like that."

"Well, no time like the present. If you were my wife,
I'd be wining and dining you, spoiling you rotten."

I swipe under both eyes, flash him a smile. I'm brave
and desirable. "First things first. Could you call Josh?
While I'm here?"

Hoffman seems pleased with an assignment and hurries
to the other side of the desk. The next minute he hands
me the phone. "It's Sandy. Josh's mom."

"Hello, this is Jane Harris."

"Hi, it's Sandy, Josh's mom. I'm so sorry for your loss."

"Could I come over, speak to Josh, if he's home?"
I meet Hoffman's eyes and then look out at the tennis
courts.

"He's here now if you want to pop over?" Sandy says, her voice sounding a tad British.

"Thank you. I'll be over in a few minutes."

Hoffman shakes his head. "Betsy and Josh were so cute together. Pretty perfect, if you ask me."

"Young love is destined to end. But yes, nice boy. Thanks so much for connecting us." I am up and headed to the door.

"You're a good mom, Jane. Betsy is going to be fine." Hoffman smiles. He's waiting for me to say something.

"Yes, as long as she listens to her mother," I say. "Maybe we gave them too much? I came from nothing, fought my way out of that stifling little town. I had my pick of men, never settled for one in high school like my girls."

Hoffman's staring at me. I must have spoken aloud. He says, "I can run you over to Josh's house if you'd like."

"Great, and sorry, for the outburst. I'm just beyond worried about Betsy," I add, following him out the door to the line of staff golf carts.

"Where did you grow up?" Hoffman asks once we're seated in the white golf cart with the green The Cove logo.

"Arkansas." I shake my head. "I worked hard to erase all of my past." Why am I telling him so much? *Stop talking.*

"I came from a small town, too. I know how it is."

Hoffman is kind. "I was a beauty queen, did you know that? Had my choice of suitors."

"I'm not surprised." Hoffman winks. Is he flirting?

My stories seem to have worked their magic. Uncharacteristically, I told him the truth. I'm out of practice. Despite everything that is happening, with anonymous notes and lying daughters, I feel my cheeks flush.

"Here we are." Hoffman points to a spectacular contemporary hugging the cliff.

A front-row property. I had no idea. I should have checked Josh's address sooner. Despite my admonition toward dating in high school, it seems this one could have been a good catch.

Maybe he still has feelings for Betsy. Or, maybe like me, he's just mad at her.

Anger can be a more powerful emotion than love, I've discovered. And revenge? Well, hell hath no fury as a lover scorned, they say.

Let's see how much scorn Josh feels, shall we?

22

1:30 p.m.

Nothing stands between the ocean and me except a coffee table, a thin balcony and a big drop. This house has been built with disappearing walls of glass. And they are gone.

Given my fear of the body of water in front of me, this is a nightmare. But I need answers. My palms are sweating but I'm practicing deep breathing and ignoring the view. Instead, my eyes focus on the Picasso above Sandy's head. When Josh speaks, I stare at the Miro. This place is a challenge for my late-in-life mastery of artistic masters. But so far, I'm two for two.

Cultural education wasn't part of my upbringing, as you may have discerned by now. I filled that gap with online courses, visits to the art museums in LA and, of course, travel to all the most important cities of the world courtesy of David. Just ten years ago we celebrated our anniversary on safari in Africa. It was all first class, the meals gourmet, the wine divine. And each day on the game rides we'd watch animals hunt and kill each other. When a baby elephant charged our open safari jeep, David jumped across the seat to shield me. My hero. There really is nothing like the circle of life to bring you closer. But I digress.

Not only am I awkwardly terrified by their spectacular house and its perch, I'm also underdressed, based on Josh's khakis and white pressed T-shirt, and Sandy's black designer dress. I look down at my shorts, my casual go-for-a-walk-in-the-neighborhood attire. Who knew I'd be popping in for high tea? There isn't anything I can do about it right now. But I am a quick study. If I ever visit the Hamiltons' home again, I will dress accordingly.

"So, Josh, I didn't realize you have been away at school." I can't take the small talk anymore. I reach for a finger sandwich perched on the edge of a three-tiered silver tray. Yes, we're drinking tea, and eating cucumber finger sandwiches. This must be a regular afternoon thing for these people because they didn't even know I was coming over until a few minutes ago. I'm losing patience. I need to ask some questions.

"Josh has been home about two weeks now," Sandy answers for her son. She seems both proud of him and wary of me, both at the same time. Her eyes dart to her son as if to be sure he is still there. "We're just so very happy to have him home for the summer. He's off to great things in the fall."

"Thanks, Mom. It was an adjustment, changing schools for senior year, but it was worth it." Josh nods and shoves a crustless cucumber sandwich into his mouth. Apparently they didn't work on manners at boarding school. "It's nice to be back. You know, doing whatever you want, for the most part."

Sandy clears her throat. "Boarding school has a very regimented routine, day and night. Josh learned so much, met such fabulous people. Of course, he missed his friends back here, like Betsy. But he's going to Princeton in the fall because of his dedication to making a positive change."

Josh nods. "Great time. What can I do for you, Mrs. Harris?"

"Well, first, welcome home and congratulations on all of your achievements. Betsy never mentioned you were away." I take a sip of my tea. It's cold.

As cold as the stare Josh is giving me.

"I'm not surprised." Josh shoves another sandwich in his mouth.

Sandy's head tilts in my direction. "If I may be frank, Josh needed a break from your daughter. She broke his heart."

Josh coughs, choking on a sandwich. "Oh my God, really, Mom? Betsy is fine, she's just mixed-up."

Finally getting to the heart of it. I ask, "You mean because of Bo?"

Josh's eyes grow wide and he leans forward, elbows on knees. "Yes, him. He's the reason Betsy and I broke up. Well, and when I went away to school that didn't help. We still talked almost every day, but things changed, because of him. I was there for her after Mary died, but I guess she needed more."

Sandy stares at her son. "What's going on, Josh? What are you talking about?"

I brush imaginary crumbs from my lap and stare down at my tennis shoes. "I understand this is hard for you, that you and Betsy were a thing for a while. And I'm sorry you kids broke up. I didn't know Betsy was spending so much time with that teacher." Of course, I already know she's in a relationship with that man. I wonder if Josh is still a sucker, if he still believes her after all of this. I take another sandwich, chew my bite of the cool cucumber slowly.

Josh flushes. "Oh, gosh, I don't know that. I mean, I think he was hitting on her, but Betsy and I still had a thing. We went out at Christmas break, and talked almost every day." He puts his plate on the coffee table and leans back.

He's telling the truth. They did text all the time. I saw their messages. But nothing from Bo, nothing. Did Betsy keep Josh around to trick me, as a beard, for one reason only: to hide Bo from me?

"It got really confusing at the end. She said she just wanted to take a break." Josh shrugs and looks at his mom.

Sandy stands up. "It's time for Josh's piano lesson. Nothing like music to soothe a broken heart."

"Mom," Josh says sharply. Poor guy. Momma's boy.

At least I'm not a walking Hallmark card of motherly advice. It's time for me to go and deal with Betsy, my little heartbreaker. "Thank you for the tea, Sandy, and, Josh, I'm sorry it ended up that way. I'm sure she'll come around and realize everything she gave up here." My hands encompass their stately home, the art, the view and Josh, of course.

Josh doesn't look so sure but he escorts me through the all-white mansion. When we reach the front door, he whispers, "It's nice seeing you, Mrs. Harris."

"You, too." I pat his arm.

He whispers, "You should ask Betsy more questions. About everything."

"I don't understand?" I look into his eyes.

"Mary's death was not an accident."

My heart thumps, leaping out of my chest. "Did you leave me that note?"

"Josh?" Sandy is at the door.

"Goodbye, Mrs. Harris," he says and the door closes between us.

I'm left standing on the front step of the mansion, heart racing. What does Josh think? What does he know? Did someone see something, someone the police haven't talked to? That seems impossible given the monthlong investigation.

Every lead was followed. Every coincidence ruled out. The investigators pursued every angle, documented everyone near the scene of Mary's death. They even went as far as pushing a dummy of Mary's height from the edge of the cliff, marking where it fell versus a dummy that slipped from the edge. The results were strikingly similar. In the end, the detectives decided Mary didn't have any enemies, wasn't suicidal and that it was a tragic accident. They were almost correct.

I start walking down the street, away from the ocean. If I walk through the park, through the tunnel, up the steep set of stairs, I'll be home in ten minutes. I check the time. I could have Sam pick me up down here. He's at my beck and call.

I text Sam from the park bench. As I wait for my ride I realize I need to talk to Josh again, without his mom. Whatever he knows, I will make him tell me. He's a bit soft—I mean, he plays the piano, for heaven's sake—but despite the politeness and the finger sandwiches, I can tell he's also very angry. They say you can recognize yourself in others.

Sam pulls up to the curb and hops out to open my door. "Good afternoon, Mrs. H. I hope everything is okay. You usually don't see the doctor twice in a week."

He closes the door behind me and slips behind the wheel.

"I'm afraid everything isn't fine." I almost tell Sam about the latest note, but I don't. It's destroyed, like it didn't exist.

Sam says, "Anything I can do to help? Want to talk about anything? Has something happened?"

Poor guy. It's almost as if he thinks we are friends, confidants. Let's see, well, there's this. "My husband bought a house for his girlfriend."

"Really? Wow." Sam's eyes are big, but fortunately glued to the road.

"And Betsy's old boyfriend thinks Betsy pushed Mary off the cliff." I shrug.

Sam pulls into the parking lot without saying a word. "Betsy didn't hurt Mary. I'm sorry about your husband."

"You don't know anything. You're a Lyft driver, for heaven's sake," I blurt before I can stop myself. My anger acting out again. Besides, he needs to remember his place, but I need him on my side for one more day. "Sorry."

Sam opens my door, but he doesn't make eye contact. And he doesn't say a word as I walk toward the doctor's office.

He'll be fine. I have other things to worry about than hurting my driver's feelings. Besides, how dare he doubt my facts, my truths. This is my story, my family, not his. He's a Lyft driver. I shake my head and clear my thoughts as I step into Dr. Rosenthal's office. Later, I will question Josh again. He has more information that can help me.

But first, Dr. Rosenthal needs to be enlightened.

23

Dr. Rosenthal stares across her desk, taking in my new facts. I've tried to weave a story from what Sandy and Josh have told me, and what they didn't. I lean forward in the La-Z-Boy. I didn't even extend the footrest today.

"I'm afraid Betsy may have killed her sister." I say it with a shaking voice.

"No."

"What do you mean, no?" I'm tired of people saying no to me.

I try to imagine the scene. The Point is majestic, but it's illegal to hike there because the ground at the edge of the cliff is so unstable. In the spring, giant coreopsis invade the typically barren land, bursting with bright yellow. The legal part of the hike circles the point, a fair distance away from the coast. But toward the end, as you near the ocean, you can hear the roar of waves, and you stop at the Hiking Trail Closed. Danger. sign nailed to a post blocking the path. The coroner's estimate is that Mary fell just before sunset.

"Jane. Talk to me."

I blink and look at Dr. Rosenthal. I say, "Betsy could have been there with her sister, perhaps they went to the park, maybe so Betsy could introduce Mary to Bo. I'm almost certain that was Betsy's agenda. I can see them, walking together along the path, quickly jumping the fence warning them of danger while encouraging Cash to do the same. I imagine their conversation was intense, a hushed disagreement, making them unaware of their surroundings."

"Sisters hike together all the time. It's normal. Your girls are normal." Dr. Rosenthal leans forward. Is she trying to stop me?

"I wonder, what were they talking about? Was Mary threatening to tell us about Betsy's new boyfriend? Did Betsy push her over the edge in a fit of rage?"

"Jane. Stop. I need you to listen to me," Dr. Rosenthal commands.

I blink. I'm listening.

"You cannot accuse Betsy of this. Mary died of a tragic accident. End of story."

I shake my head no. "I got another note. Yesterday. The note said Betsy knows more than she's telling us."

"Who could be doing this to you, to her?" Dr. Rosenthal looks concerned. Her brows knit together, lips purse. "I mean, it has been a year since Mary died. Why now?"

And then I know. Josh and Betsy broke up. The spell she had on him broke. So he wrote the first two notes. He repeated the same words just now at his home. He is trying to tell me to look at Betsy, to ask her more questions. He thinks she's guilty. He has access to The Cove stationery. His dad is on the board. Did Betsy somehow keep him under her spell, leading him on until he came home from boarding school and learned the truth?

Despite myself, I feel a spark of pride. She's my daughter. And then I realize something else. The third note really pissed me off. And I have no idea who it was from. It was on different paper, so maybe it was from Betsy, to throw me off.

All in all, it's clear she is messing with me, even if she didn't write the third note. I really hate that. Perhaps I've underestimated my younger daughter. But not anymore.

Dr. Rosenthal must have asked me a question, but I wasn't listening. "Jane?"

And then I have another dawning. Who else besides Betsy would want to help throw me off track? Her boyfriend, Bo, that's who. I smile at my brilliant detective work.

But my happiness doesn't last long. Betsy is such a disappointment. I feel the emotions mix in the pit of my stomach, sadness and anger mixed. She's trying to outsmart me. Silly girl.

Dr. Rosenthal is talking again. "Did you show both notes to David? These are real, right?"

I hate it when she doubts my lucidity. "Yes, of course they're real. Betsy ripped one in half, in fact. Seems like the action of a guilty person."

"Jane," Dr. Rosenthal scolds me.

She thinks I'm imagining the notes. I understand why. She is accustomed to grieving, confused, despondent Jane. A woman suffering from "complicated grief" and all its many symptoms, well documented online and easy to research.

It is complicated. "I showed the first note to Betsy and David. They laughed at it, at me." I shake my head.

"Why would they laugh at you?" Dr. Rosenthal drops her head so she can look at me without her readers.

"They always do. They gang up on me." True. "But I think Betsy might have hurt her sister. She always was jealous of Mary's success, Mary's life. Mary was the favorite daughter, so it had to be hard. Betsy's uncomfortable around me, like she's hiding things. Betsy does know more and that's why she had to make fun of the note."

Dr. Rosenthal seems concerned, her fingers tap the desk. "You are accusing your daughter of murder?"

When you say it like that it's so dramatic, so diabolical. "No, well, I don't know anymore, I just know they were fighting just before Mary died."

Dr. Rosenthal takes a deep breath. "That's a serious charge, Jane. You'll need to go to the police."

"No, I would never do that." I already have.

She presses, "What does David think?"

My face falls and I rummage for a tissue. Time to turn on the faucet. "David isn't home much these days."

Smelling another delicate and potentially juicy topic, Dr. Rosenthal takes the bait, as always. Isn't this what she went to school for? To hear me spill the juicy details of my husband's illicit affair? Of course it is.

"Tell me more, Jane. It's okay."

I break down, sobbing. "I…just…"

"What is it?"

"I don't think he loves me anymore," I manage to tell her. This is true. I know it.

Dr. Rosenthal writes something down. "He seemed very committed to the marriage when he was here." She looks through her notes. "Oh, my, that was almost ten months ago now. I thought I'd seen him since. Time flies. We need to bring him in for a session, a couple's session."

Tears stream down my cheeks. She hands me another tissue.

"What evidence do you have for your feelings? Remember, we don't always perceive people and events as we should when we're mired in grief. That goes for both Betsy and David. I'm sure Betsy has an alibi for when Mary died."

Well, I'm right about both of them, Doctor. "David is having an affair. I have photos of the two of them together. And Betsy, well, this is just awful."

Dr. Rosenthal looks shocked. This is all bad form, I know. Screwing around on your grieving wife, murdering your sister. I start crying again.

"Really? Are you sure about David?" She looks at her notes, and back at me.

Yes. I've been spying on him for months now. And there's Hoffman. "The tennis coach. Told. Me. He works at The Cove, he knows everything." I sob.

"This man told you Betsy killed Mary? And that your husband is cheating on you?" She has stopped taking notes.

I nod.

She looks at me.

"Well, sort of."

"Jane. Have you been drinking again?" She's twisting her glasses around her finger. It's mesmerizing.

"No. I mean, I've had a little, but I'm really much better." That's true. It's time. You could say the memorial service really opened my eyes. Or, you could say, my eyes were fully opened when David crossed that threshold with Kylie in his arms. In truth, as you know, I never was as grief-addled as I seemed. "The fog is lifting. I need to take control of my life. And I need answers, about Mary's death. And David, too."

Dr. Rosenthal lets out a big sigh. She wants me to let it go. "We know what happened to Mary. She died tragically. Let's address David. What is your plan for confronting him?"

I won't be confronting him but I do have a plan. I realize looking at her that she doesn't get me at all. I mean, that's partially my fault because I haven't told her the truth all along. I get that. She underestimates me. Everybody does. "What do you suggest?"

"Perhaps you could bring him with you, to the next session? Tell him it's time, since he hasn't been in for ten months. We'll see if he can express what he's going through. Sound good?" Dr. Rosenthal's glasses are back on her face, framing her wise owl-like eyes. She has a PhD and I'm just a high school graduate. But there are several different types of intelligences in the world. There's book smart. And then there is a different smart. Street smart. People smart.

"You think my husband will waltz in here and admit to you he is having an affair?" I shake my head, the tears long gone, just like any hope of salvaging our marriage. The only thing left is revenge.

"I think if he shows up with you there is hope for your marriage. As for Betsy, you need to take your time, really think about what you're accusing her of doing. That's a very serious charge. I just can't imagine it."

I've never seen Dr. Rosenthal's eyes so big. She's a bit freaked out, I think. She's heard more from me than she bargained for. I sniff. "I know. I've said too much. Just forget everything."

"I'm sorry, time's up." She walks me to the door and, for the first time ever, touches my shoulder. "Make another appointment, please. Come in next week, or sooner, if you need to. And bring David. And Betsy, too. We can clear everything up. This is important. I think you may have things mixed up, Jane."

No, it's you who have things mixed up, Doctor, but you'll figure it all out someday when you review your notes. As for the future, neither David nor I will visit this office again. And of course, Betsy wouldn't be caught dead here. I wonder if Dr. Rosenthal will miss me and our chats? I know she'll never forget our last session together today.

Did you know therapists are compelled to report child or elder abuse, but otherwise secrets are safe with them? Unless she is subpoenaed or compelled by a judge to testify, that is. It's a fine line, society's "need to know" versus a patient's rights to confidentiality. Sometimes people need to know there is a monster in their midst.

I'm glad I'm not a shrink. And I'm equally glad I don't have to pretend to need one anymore. There's nothing wrong with this noggin that a little revenge can't fix.

I feel better already.

24

4:00 p.m.

Sam can tell I'm in a mood, and doesn't try to chat with me. It's nice, this understanding we have. This is a comfortable, respectful silence. The deferential employee, employer relationship I love.

I look out the window and up at the steep faces of the rugged mountains surrounding our beautiful beach community, walling us in from the real world, sheltering us from the big cities beyond. Trapping us when fires rage, luring us to the edge when we think there is no other choice. It's a romantic and dramatic life we live on the California coast. This is the perfect setting for the little drama playing out in my household these days. All we need is a big bank of fog to roll in, drop the temperatures and give everyone the chills. Setting is everything, don't you think?

I think of my husband and what he believes will be his new Port Street setting. Such a shame. He used to be completely under control. In our relationship, until recently, I was the maestro. From the beginning I'd told him I don't sleep with men on the first date. A lie. By the time our third date rolled around, he was desperate.

"Hey, gorgeous, what are you doing today?" he'd asked when I answered the phone after three rings.

"Oh my goodness, is this really you?" Of course, I knew it was. I covered the mouthpiece and threatened Bobby with a death stare and a finger held to my lips. Quiet. He was so lame. A means to an end.

David picked me up an hour later in his black BMW convertible (of course), at the address I'd given him. I stood outside of "my" condo building. David drove us to Geoffrey's, a restaurant nestled on the edge of the sea off PCH in Malibu. I knew at the time he was still holding on to pouty lips sorority girlfriend, making sure his about-to-be ex-girlfriend was spending the weekend at home in the Palisades. (You always need to hedge your bets, David tells our girls. And he certainly does, as you now know.)

The date was perfect. We exchanged stories, told each other about our families (sort of) and our lives (not completely). We shared a bottle of expensive champagne. And then another. He didn't seem tipsy, he'd just been a frat boy, so his liver was in shape, but I pretended I was. And that's when I told him, with a tear rolling down my cheek, that he was the best thing that ever happened to me.

I meant it. When he asked me to come home with him, that it was time, I shook my head no. "I can't."

"We can take it slow, Jane. Promise. I'm a gentleman. Just come home with me."

I'd pretended to deliberate as I watched the sun plunge into the ocean, as his knee pressed against my leg, the heat spreading through my body. I remember coaching myself, as my mother had once done during pageants. *Pace yourself, Jane. If you want the prize, you cannot be too eager. The trophy is so shiny, Jane. But you must not grab, you must make them want to give it to you.*

I touched his hand lightly and then pulled away. "I better not. I have work in the morning. But can I see you this weekend?" I blinked and stared into his deep blue eyes. I have a work ethic, too, David.

"Of course." His eyes twinkled with desire.

I was familiar with that look, both then and now. It's my superpower. I'll bump into guys I dated in the past, or a friend of a guy I dated in the past. They all still give me the look even if they've been married for years. They still feel my power.

Sam pulls to the curb in front of my home in the "most highly sought after" community in Orange County. I'm just repeating what's in the brochures. I try not to believe any hype but my own. "Thanks, Sam. See you tomorrow. I'll let you know if David decides to drive me to graduation."

"Big day tomorrow." Sam waves without smiling and

slips back into his car. I think he might still be mad about my outburst. I wave as he drives away. I probably won't see him again. Sam has been a great crutch this past year. But like most things in life, there is an end date to his usefulness. And it's now. I imagine an expiration date stamped on his forehead and chuckle.

It's also funny Sam is talking about tomorrow. He doesn't realize there is still so much more left of today.

25

I walk through the front door and check the time on my phone.

It's late afternoon on a Wednesday. The question is where are David and Betsy. I don't expect them to be home, of course. Not anymore. But I do like to know where they are.

I have to admit I've been focusing most of my time on David's whereabouts, not paying enough attention to Betsy. I'd assumed, wrongly it turns out, that she had been where she said she was. Hanging out with the other losers in her high school class, painting canvases of random things, wearing dark clothes and occasionally getting a tattoo when I've forbidden her to do so. I guess I also thought she'd been spending time with Josh, but now I know I was wrong about that, too.

But it's not my fault, not really. The last time I'd seen Betsy and Josh together it had been at Point Park the day Mary died. I had just ducked off the path when they rounded the corner. I'm not sure how I could have explained my presence there if they'd spotted me, because as I've noted, I'm not much of a hiker and I never go to Point Park. I've certainly never hiked up the trail to the top of the Point. That's off-limits, everyone knows that.

So it was happenstance, I suppose, that I saw them. Betsy was ugly crying, tears running down her face. I do remember that. Josh had his arm around her, comforting her. I was crouched low, behind a rock, with no place to go until they moved along. I hoped there weren't any spiders lurking around me, and I especially hoped there weren't any snakes. I remember I could hear my heart thumping in my chest.

"I need to make her understand some things. Why are you here?" Betsy said to Josh, through her tears.

"I love you. Betsy. I followed you here so we could talk."

"I need to fix things with my sister, okay? Then you and I can talk." Betsy had lifted her head from Josh's shoulder, scanned the hiking path, looking for Mary. "I hope she comes."

"She will. Don't worry. I deserve to know the truth."

Josh patted Betsy's back. He wasn't acting very romantic or comforting for a boyfriend. But Betsy did look awful.

"I promise." They hugged in the middle of the trail, trapping me behind the rock. Betsy's back was to me, Josh faced my direction, his head on her shoulder, hands wrapped around her waist. He didn't look able to comfort anyone, in my opinion. But clearly, I was wrong about him. I thought he was from the wrong side of the highway, so to speak. A kid from town. It's a shame, really, that I didn't know he was a rich kid. I would have encouraged their young love.

Then again, I didn't know it was ever threatened. Those pills just made me slip a little. But no longer.

That day I crouched behind the rock for what seemed like hours but was likely only a few minutes. Finally, they broke apart, Betsy heading one way down the path, Josh the other. You understand why I didn't tell them I was there, right? I didn't want to disturb their special moment.

I didn't know where exactly Betsy was going but I did know she was meeting Mary, to help her understand something, where she was coming from. I knew that much. I'd heard Mary and Betsy fighting the night before, of course, standing in the hallway outside Mary's bedroom. I wish I'd heard more, I really do. I wish I'd known about Bo, his intentions where my daughter was concerned. I would have stopped it sooner had I figured it out. I should have hidden another bug, in both of their rooms.

Don't act all superior and pretend like you haven't spied on your kids. All parents do it. We eavesdrop during car pool, we put tracking spyware on their phones and in their cars. We tell them who to be friends with, and who seems to be acceptable to date. And sometimes, when they are hiding secrets from their own mother, we listen outside their bedrooms. My mom told me she was always watching me, and I believed her.

Problem was, then and now, my family is hardly ever around anymore. The snippets of information I picked up during the two weeks Mary was home last summer, the short two weeks before her accident, were spotty at best. The girls whisper-argued. There was never one text between Betsy and Bo, or between Betsy and Mary, for that matter. I didn't know he existed then. I didn't know the actual cause of the friction between them. All along, I thought Betsy was sticking up for me, telling Mary not to move in with Elizabeth. I thought they were fighting over Mary's birth mother, not some ridiculous ponytail-wearing hardware store employee.

When I'd finally knocked on Mary's door they'd pretended to be tired and kissed me good-night. Little traitors. I couldn't push them because I wasn't supposed to be listening at all. The only thing left to do was to follow them the next day. You would have done the same.

Back then, I'd focused my attention on Mary, because that was the pressing issue, her move to LA, her move to Elizabeth. I'd already been watching David, of course.

That left little time for Betsy and her secrets.

There was never one text between Betsy and Bo.

I didn't know he existed then.

But now I do. I'm on to you, Betsy. Now it's your turn.

26

I call Hoffman. He answers on the first ring. "Twice in one day. What fun. How can I help?"

"My visit with Sandy and Josh was helpful, thank you."

"My pleasure. Let me know what else I can do. Anything." He's flirting. I'm sure of it now. That is wonderful. He's crazy about me. I guess I always knew it, sensed it, but I had David. And truth be told, Hoff is not my type, not for the long run.

But right now, sure. "Well, I do have one more little favor. I need to talk to Josh, alone, without his mother hovering. I think he wants to tell me something. Any ideas?" I need to find out what Josh saw the day Mary died.

"I have a tennis lesson with him tonight. A private. Why don't you come down as it's ending. We could pretend you're having a private lesson, too. And you can talk to him. Maybe have a lesson after? It would be great for you and me to get some exercise."

I smile. Bingo. "You're so smart. I love this idea. And yes. I'll bring my racket. We can volley a little after I speak with Josh."

"His lesson is six to seven. See you then."

"I'm looking forward to it, Hoff," I murmur before hanging up. I have managed to wrap him around my finger like I used to have David. I'd focused on befriending Hoff the moment we moved to The Cove. And it's paid off nicely. Some women are girls girls. Some are guys girls. I suppose you've figured out where I fall. I've always enjoyed the company of men over women. I'm sorry to say. They're just, well, easier.

I imagine Hoff's smile and enjoy my hold over him. Power is such a trip. But I have more to do before my "tennis lesson." First things first. And that means my husband.

Besides the evening when Mary disappeared—as you'll recall, he'd come waltzing home late, supposedly "after work" but smelling of her perfume—there had been other clues that David was having an affair. For months, ever since Mary left for college, these clues, these little nuggets of information, had come to light. They seemed so innocuous at first. It was easy to overlook them.

Sure, I had that sinking feeling that I was missing

something and that wasn't like me. I don't miss things. I'm always watching.

Maybe it was simply denial. I still don't understand why I wasn't good enough for him anymore. I figured perhaps it was just a temporary reaction to Mary heading off to college. They had been close, and I know he missed her. Maybe he envied her escape. But he's mine, and an adult. He should have gotten over it.

He didn't. The business dinners that lasted until after midnight or the late hours in the office working on a special deal started soon after Mary left for freshman year. But the more telling signs were his new commitment to working out, the spring in his step. He must have opened a new credit card, had the bills sent to the office, because there was nothing tangible, not at first.

The yoga classes were a slip, but otherwise, he didn't make many mistakes.

It was the little things that hurt the most. The reluctance to hug me. To touch me. To kiss me. Those things were there. Despite the fact that I was a catch. As Hoffman will attest, I still am today.

I guess it all came together when we spent our last Christmas together as a family, in Telluride. During the day, David skied with Mary and Betsy, and that wasn't abnormal. I, of course, am not a big fan of the sport, having grown up in the Deep South. I would be back at the condo, waiting for them to come home and regale me with mountain adventure stories, their cheeks rosy from the cold. And they did. But at night, David would close himself off in the office, spending hours on the computer.

The newly password-protected computer. While the girls and I went to dinner without him, trying to ignore his absence. I was on to him after that trip.

I spent the spring worrying and scheming. It's easy, really, there are all types of spyware apps on the market. I began to read his texts, track his movements, in real time. And I discovered disgusting proclamations of love, of course. But I also found more.

I discovered that my husband and my daughter were also keeping a secret from me. And that secret was worse than any affair. That stabbed into the core of my existence. They were figuring out how Mary could work for and live with Elizabeth James. Mary loved her more than me. She even told me so, one of the last times we talked. Mary spoke her words quietly, but they are burned into my heart:

I love and respect Elizabeth. She's brilliant. I'm going to be just like her, Mary said to me.

I forbid it, I said. You're not thinking straight, Mary. You're irrational. Psychotic. You need to rest.

I don't have to listen to you anymore. You are a terrible mother and I'm so lucky to have another role model. Even Kylie would be an improvement. At least she's normal.

My daughters are my life, the very reflection of my success as a mother. Even thinking of this sends me into a rage again.

It's never been that satisfying to kick things, or punch walls. I used to do that when I was younger and broke too many toes and my hand a couple of times. I still enjoy throwing things—like plates or small bookends—at people when I'm angry, but neither of them were home then, nor are they now. My heart pounds.

Living well is the best revenge, I tell myself, unclenching my fists. My shoulders have shot up to my ears and I coax them down. I'm proud of the self-control I can muster when I need to, and I do. I still have a lot to do before my tennis lesson.

In fact, I have a lot to do before graduation tomorrow night, when we all enjoy the culmination of Betsy's activities, both at school and outside of school.

She'll be so surprised.

27

5:00 p.m.

The yoga class begins at about five minutes after five, every Wednesday.

The teacher is late every week, the class attendees perpetually on time. An interesting and upside-down dynamic, but I decide she must be a good teacher or they wouldn't put up with it.

I wouldn't put up with it. I do know it's important to have a proper instructor because yoga taught incorrectly has the potential to kill you. It's tragic, but true. There are endless stories of injuries to backs and limbs, but consider the danger of overstretching the head and neck. Consider the shoulder stand where you raise your legs into the air, and the plow where your feet go over your head and touch the floor behind you. Both, seemingly innocuous poses. But reductions of blood flow in your basilar artery can cause a fatal stroke. It's happened many times.

Through the window I see the teacher unfurl her lime-green mat in front of the group. I count ten students lined up on their mats in a row, facing toward the back wall and the tardy teacher. Their backs are to me, feet stretched out in front of them. As they begin their sun salutation series A, I watch for the upward-facing dog of the man on the far right side of the room.

According to a Columbia University study, yoga's extreme bending and contortions resulted in back, shoulder and knee injuries, neck injuries and strokes more often than death.

But one can always hope. David is wearing ridiculously short shorts for a man his age, no doubt picked out by Kylie. She's on a pink mat to his left, in an all-white, skintight getup. She's not "normal," she's a show-off. As for David, this whole yoga thing is new. Just like his haircut, his waistline and where his loyalties lie. They don't touch each other here, not in front of all of these yogis. They act as if they're just friends taking yoga class together: just a couple of buddies doing downward dog.

Mary's death seems to have accelerated their romance, added some sort of tragic fuel to his need to escape from me and our life together. As if Mary's death ended our family. But that is not the case. His actions destroyed our family, our marriage. And I will make him stop.

David and Kylie have been taking this class for six months, at least that's when I found out about their standing date. Because even though this studio is two beach towns away, and I've been grieving, and I don't have any friends, I'm not stupid. My husband would never take a yoga class, and yet a package showed up in his credit card transactions. A package for two.

Satisfied that they're busy, I walk behind the studio to the lot where we've all parked. Cozy. There's David's black Tesla. And a few spots down, Kylie's brand-new white Audi with its temporary plates. She's only twenty-eight. She shouldn't be driving an Audi, but she is. And I know her sugar daddy. I touch its smooth, new finish. I look around quickly, and slip the tracking device under the front right wheel well. The magnetic case grabs on to the metal with a satisfying click. Without access to her cell phone, this is the next best thing.

I open my car door, conveniently parked next to the white Audi. In case there is a camera back here, which I doubt, I was simply bending to pick up my keys. I resist the urge to do something more with my keys to Kylie's pretty car and back my car out of the parking space. I have more work to do.

Assuming they both survive yoga class stroke-free, they will grab a pressed juice at the shop next to the studio. Then, depending on their mood, they'll either grab a to-go meal from the sandwich shop or step into their favorite little Italian bistro. You know, the one I ordered in. It's so romantic it makes me want to throw something. But I won't. I clench the steering wheel and turn onto Kylie's street.

This is another almost too perfect community, if you ask me, filled with multimillion-dollar homes boasting grassy yards, trees and even sidewalks for kids. At the beach, we don't have space for sidewalks. My stomach turns as I park in front of her next-door neighbor's lovely home.

This home has a lot of space for a single woman in her twenties. But I know she has big plans. They both do. They text each other about their dreams all the time. I just simply cannot believe he was serious. He bought this house for her, for them. Not for us. Not for a fresh start.

I open the car door and my hands clench into fists as I remember David's text promise to help her fill a house with babies someday, while of course leaving one room free for Betsy. They wouldn't want her to feel left out. I'm not even an afterthought. Not a consideration. Instead of consoling his poor, grief-stricken wife, David thinks he's moving on with a new model home, and wife.

Because poor Kylie will never be David's next wife. Her dreams are about to become her worst nightmare.

We should start by calling Kylie by her real name, Nancy Finch. Nancy was born in some tiny town in North Dakota, made her way to Vegas after high school and landed a fabulous sugar daddy. Herbert Holiday struck it big with his casino and hotel complex. He was known to be cheap, until little Nancy came along. She married him when she was twenty and he was sixty-five. Gross, right?

There's more. Turns out Nancy Holiday has a pending

warrant out for her arrest in Las Vegas. Can you imagine? And these weren't just a case of passing around a few bad checks at the grocery store or nail salon. No, Nancy forged her sugar daddy's name on at least ten checks, paid herself hundreds of thousands of dollars. When he died suddenly—tragic accidental overdose of Viagra mixed with his heart medicine—Herbert's grown and estranged kids got control of the estate. That's when they discovered he'd been conned. Of course, by then, Nancy had taken her newly minted breasts and disappeared.

Until now.

I smile as I walk up to her new, move-in-ready home. And how did I piece all of this together? Bottom line: it just takes one to know one. I'm on my computer all the time these days, and it's not just researching tragic accidental deaths. Now you know what else I'm fixated on.

Poor David will be shocked. Fortunately for him, this love nest is in both of their names. So once she's gone it will belong to him—and me because actually I own half of everything that's his. Even this stupid house.

I walk up to the front door. I feel like I'm on a movie set, as if nothing is real. I peer through the front door window and note the bleached wood floors and the overly white interior. It's shabby chic, so ten years ago really, but they bought it furnished and you get what you pay for, I suppose. On the front porch, to my left, a cozy wicker couch and matching chair, so I could just sit down and watch the activity on this quiet street. But I'm not going to wait for them to come home. Don't worry, I'm not going to be violent or anything. There won't be a rabbit on the stove. That's just not my style. You know me well enough by now, don't you?

I open the bronze flap and shove the envelope through the mail slot, waiting until it hits the floor. It lands perfectly, faceup, addressed to Nancy Finch Holiday in big block letters. I check my phone, and Kylie's car and David's car are both on the move. Yoga is over, and so, I'm afraid, is all of their fun.

I hurry down the walkway to the street, my heart thumping. This has been the most excitement I've had in a long time. I pull away from the curb and head back home to the more exclusive community where I belong. Kylie thinks she can just take, take, take without working for anything. And she's been lucky so far. But not anymore.

As I let her know in my anonymous letter—yes, I also pen anonymous notes—

I've outlined all the facts. Her real name. The crimes she's been charged with. The warrant for her arrest. And I also let her know, helpfully, that the exact same information will be delivered to the Orange County sheriff's office. I wish I could have stayed around, I wish I could hear how she'll explain the letter to David.

If I know her, and I feel like I do, she'll hurry inside after unlocking the front door and scoop up the letter before David sees it. She never parks in the garage even at her apartment, a low-class move that David seems not to notice. He has other things on his mind when he follows her inside.

I predict she'll be gone by the morning. She'll wait

until David comes home to me tonight, what was to be his last night at our house.

I can't wait until after graduation when you're all mine, Kylie texted yesterday.

Just two more nights of this hell. And I'm all yours, David texted in reply.

I'm assuming I'm the hell he refers to, but who knows. Makes me sick. And angry. Wouldn't you be, too? I mean, I could understand a little fling. We all grieve in our own way. But buying a house with her? That was the straw that broke this camel's back. I had to strike tonight, their first night as official owners of their dream home. I mean, it's so poetic.

Tonight, David will leave their love nest reluctantly. Climbing out of bed, he'll stop and smile at Kylie, promising tomorrow night, after Betsy's graduation, he'll finally be able to spend the entire night with her, wake up with her in the morning and every morning after. They'll finally be together and not in her cheap Balboa apartment. He'll take a moment to wash up in the master bath—offering "dual sinks, a vanity area, large soaking tub, oversize shower and generous closet."

Kylie will jump out of bed, pull on her bathrobe and hurry him out the door. She's had the note on her mind, of course. With shaking hands she'll pull the letter out from under the stack of catalogs and junk mail. She'll open it and read the truth: she's been found.

She'll skim the note another time, noticing for the first time the cc: Howie Holiday. Herbert's son is her worst enemy and her biggest threat. She'll understand a copy of this letter has been sent to her ex's son, the one out to get her. *Hello, Herbert Holiday Jr. I'll call you Howie. Meet Nancy Finch Holiday, aka Kylie Dorn want-to-be Harris, now residing in a fabulous Port Street home yada yada yada.* I was sure to enclose a recent photo of Kylie/ Nancy. Just to bring it home for him.

Of course I attached the address of the love nest in my letter to him, in case he'd like to snoop around online. And he will.

She will know she has to go, and fast, the little home wrecker. She'll drive the white Audi into the garage, closing the door behind her. She'll work for a couple of hours, filling the car with everything of value she's received from David, and from Herbert before him. And then she'll climb into the front seat, with tears in her eyes, and drive away.

I pass through the gate and take a deep breath. There's such comfort in this extra line of protection. I realize the guards pay little attention to who comes and goes. I mean, there are more than five hundred homes in The Cove, and so many different shifts. I'm just another blonde house- wife. And I have a transponder on my car to automati- cally open any of the nine community gates. Even at the main gate, where I am now, the guards barely glance at those of us using the "residents'" lane.

But still, it's nice that no one could just walk up to my door and slip me a note. Not unless they live in The Cove, or have business here. That's why I know my anonymous notes are from people on the inside—one way or another, they have access to The Cove.

Josh used The Cove letterhead and he lives here. That's easy. Who wrote the third note? It doesn't matter, not really. It will all be over tomorrow.

The home is a sacred, safe place, or should be. Mine is guarded, protected by me, or by the literal guards roving our community 24/7. Poor Kylie. Her multimillion-dollar home is vulnerable, like she is. David can't protect her, nobody can. Her anonymous note could be from just about anyone.

I close my garage door and sit for a minute in the car. David's car isn't here, of course, it's now parked in front of the lovely home on Port Chelsea Place!!

He'll be home a little earlier than usual, tonight. I know, it's supposed to be a night to celebrate their new home, but Kylie will be distracted, anxious to read the letter. And David, focused on tomorrow's graduation and imminent liberation, won't mind enduring one more night of hell at home with me.

Poor guy. He thinks he has it so tough.

He has no idea what tough really is. Tough is when you lose everyone you love, one at a time.

That's tough. Some people can't survive it. David already admitted he couldn't. Remember that?

28

You can accomplish so much in a day, if you have a plan and know how to execute it.

I'm sure you're wondering how I kept myself from confronting David, how I was able to keep all of Kylie's secrets to myself, especially when I had to see her at the memorial service. Especially once I saw my husband carry his mistress inside their new multimillion-dollar home. Yes, that was tough.

And I wanted to surprise you.

You have to agree: I am a great actress. In fact, if things had worked out, if the lousy LA manager had been a real talent scout and not a creep, I would have been a star. But you have to roll with the hand you're dealt. And I was dealt a future with David. Things weren't bad, not really. Not until David and Mary, and Mary and Betsy, and David and Betsy started keeping secrets from me.

No one keeps secrets from me. No one. And I will figure out Betsy's secrets. She's the key to the last mystery in my mind. I mean, I discovered Mary's secrets. And David's. The person in peril is Betsy. And she doesn't even know it. It's my duty to help everyone see the truth.

I walk into the courtyard, look around for Cash, before realizing he's gone. The dog was really sort of a traitor at the end. He was. No one can deal with a dog that growls at you, no matter the "trauma" he suffered. I mean, come on, get over it. We've all suffered. No one goes through life without some sort of struggle.

Except for maybe the kids who grew up behind the gates of The Cove. Mary's and Betsy's childhoods were blessed. Josh's, too. How could Betsy be so stupid to throw it away with a con man like Bo?

Well, in Betsy's case, like I told you, she got her father's crazy gene pool. They're stingy, selfish liars. All of them. David. His parents. His daughter. She might look like me, but she is all of them. It's too bad.

I check the time. I need to get changed for my tennis lesson. I hope I still have an outfit that works. I mean, I quit the team long before Mary died, so it's been a while since I've worn tennis whites.

In my closet I rummage through my old tennis drawer and pull out a dress. I know this will look great on me.

I slip it on, the fit is nicer than a year ago, it pulls over my head without a tug. I admire my legs, long and lean. Maybe I will volley a bit with Hoffman. Or maybe we'll go have a drink? I do have a lot to celebrate tonight. But first, tennis, anyone? It's your turn to play with me, Josh.

29

6:40 p.m.

I drive down to the tennis courts, even though I could easily walk. My car is like a traveling home, of sorts. I have many things I may need. I like the notion of being prepared. It's why I installed a false floor in the trunk of my car. Lift up and I have everything I need on my nighttime expeditions. Flashlights, high-powered camera, black sweatshirt and sweatpants: the usual stuff. I learned so much from Mr. Wyatt, during my first job helping out at the gas station after school. I knew how to modify my luxury ride now, just like I knew what to do to my mom's brakes all those years ago. It's so easy to cut a brake line if you know what you're doing.

I pull into a parking space and check the app. David is still parked. Betsy is on the move, driving north on Coast Highway. She's past the gates for The Cove, so she's heading elsewhere. I'm not clear if she knows her father is leaving me tomorrow. I don't know if Kylie and David have given Betsy a tour of their new family home. Has he shown Betsy her new bedroom? I haven't tracked her car to that neighborhood, but they have both been good at keeping secrets from me, so I wouldn't be surprised.

My body stiffens with rage. That would be so terrible, I try not to imagine it. Even though it won't happen now, just the thought of them starting over without me, it's enough to push me over the edge. I shake my head, try to push my temper back into its box. There is no time for it, not right now.

It's time to focus on Josh, and Betsy by proxy.

I can hear the tennis ball thwacking on the court before I spot Hoffman and Josh playing. There are four courts, but only one is in use. Most of the time, all the courts stand empty, just begging for some action. The green metal gate squeaks as I open it and Hoffman spots me, waving. "Hey, Jane. We're just finishing up. Watch Josh's serve. It's impressive."

I walk to the bench at midcourt and sit down. "Let's see it, Josh." I say it in my most motherly, encouraging tone.

Josh looks terrified. As if his mom is going to catch him here, with me, watching him serve. I hope she doesn't actually pick him up after his lesson. Hoffman would have warned me if that was the case, right?

Josh serves into the net.

"Focus, son. I know she's distracting." Hoffman smiles at me.

Am I? I guess so. I shoot Hoffman a big smile.

Josh serves again, clearing the net, but the ball lands a foot out. He shakes his head and his shoulders droop. "I'm done for tonight, Hoff."

"No problem, kid. Your serve is coming back. Can't force it."

Hoffman and Josh walk over to my bench. Hoffman says, "Great job today. We'll work on it again tomorrow. I'll pick up the balls. You two know each other, right?"

I scoot over and pat the bench. Josh sits beside me, wiping his forehead with a white towel. "You have more questions, right?"

He's so stupid he's likable. I pretend to sigh, sniffle a little. I hate sniffles. "I do. If you don't mind?"

Josh slumps beside me. He knows he can't hide from me anymore.

"Thank you for the notes. I was so lost in grief, I just didn't see the truth." I pretend to dab the corner of my eye with a tissue.

Josh takes a deep breath. "I didn't want to see it, either, Mrs. Harris. Because it's horrible."

30

6:50 p.m.

My heart thumps wildly in my chest. Horrible, he said. I love horrible. Calm down, Jane. I shake my head, cover my face with both hands. I pretend to recover. "Why don't you start from the beginning?" I speak softly, in a comforting, motherly tone.

Beside me Josh's right leg is bouncing up and down as if it's on a miniature trampoline. He's so jumpy, if I said "boo" he'd make a run for it.

I turn to Josh. I'm not sure why he isn't speaking. Patience is such an overrated attribute. I'm glad I don't have any. No wonder Betsy dumped him. I try again.

"Josh, it's important that I understand how to help Betsy." I smile and pat his bouncing knee. "I know you want the same."

Josh shakes his head. "No, I'm sorry, I don't want to help Betsy. I want to help Mary. Well, I wanted to. But it's too late."

I feign shock. "What do you know about Mary's death? Tell me. Please."

Josh takes a deep breath. "This is what I think. Betsy told Mary about her secret relationship with Bo. Mary didn't approve. Betsy wanted Mary to meet Bo at the park, so she could convince Mary he was a good guy. Betsy didn't tell me any of this, though." He wipes his face with the towel. A dramatic pause.

I feel like shaking him. Come on already. "And?"

"I followed her to the park, she'd been acting distant and I wanted to talk. She sent me away. She was crying, really hard. I thought it was just a girls' fight, you know, between sisters. I didn't know about Bo, not the real relationship. I thought Betsy still liked me, all this year, even though I was away at boarding school, I still believed her, believed her lies. I believed we were together. I didn't even take a date to my senior prom at boarding school. I'm such an idiot. I believed her when she said she couldn't fly out for it. She said you wouldn't let her."

Interesting. I wouldn't have allowed her to go across country to hook up with Josh, but she never asked. She was just using Josh. "She didn't mention prom to me."

Josh sighs, or exhales loudly. One of the two. "I thought

we were a couple until a couple of weeks before Mary's memorial. That's when she finally decided to come clean."

I look over at him as he wipes his face with the towel again. He's heartbroken. "I'm sorry. I didn't know about any of this. I thought you two were still together, too."

"Yeah, I know. Betsy knew you spied on her through her phone. Mary told her all about it. My mom did it, too. Does it, too. That's why we only do fake messages on text. We all use encrypted apps."

"What? Really?" That makes sense. I never saw a text from Bo.

"We all use it, well, when our parents are like you. We make sure to text once a week or so, just to keep you satisfied."

I shrug. I am what I am. "I love my daughters. That's all."

"Mary was great. I know she was on my side. I know they were fighting about Bo. That had to be it because otherwise they were really close. They fought the night before Mary died, and again that day."

I swallow. "I heard them, that night, but it was muffled. I couldn't tell what they were arguing about."

"That morning, the day Mary died, I followed Betsy. She was acting suspicious. She canceled our bike ride. Said she was busy. Told me she was going on a hike with her sister and she'd call me later. But I had to follow her. That's when I caught up to her, crying on the trail. And then I left. If I had stayed maybe Mary would still be alive."

Josh pushes his hand through his hair, shakes his head. There were so many people in the park that afternoon.

"What happened next?"

"I caught up to Betsy on the trail. She was alone. Freaking out, crying. She told me she was meeting Mary, that they'd had a fight. She told me I needed to leave her alone. Give her space." Josh takes a big drink of water. "I was such an idiot. I still believed her. Believed she loved me even on the day she was introducing her sister to her new boyfriend. She promised she'd tell me the truth."

I pat his hand. "No, Bo is not her boyfriend."

"Yeah, that's what I thought. I still believed her. This whole year. Even after what happened to Mary." Josh turns and looks at me. "Betsy lied to me, and she's lying about what happened to Mary. I know it."

I look straight into his eyes. He believes everything he's saying. "So you wrote me the notes."

"First, I confronted Betsy. The day before Mary's memorial. I know, it was bad timing, but she won't return my texts, my calls. She sort of ghosted me." Josh looks up into the bright tennis lights. "I asked her if she was with Bo at the park the day Mary died. She said no."

"But you don't believe her? Why? Do you have proof?" I try to keep the smile from my voice.

"Mary sent me a text. But I didn't get it until after I'd left Betsy in the park. There is lousy cell service there. I left and drove home, and the text came in. Mary told me that Betsy was confused. Told me not to worry. Here, I saved it."

He hands me his phone with Mary Harris's, my daughter's, text message saved. Their whole exchange is there.

Mary: I'm with Betsy. Don't worry. I'm on it.

Josh: Thanks Mary. You know I love your sister. Tell me what to do and I'll do it.

Josh: Any updates?

Josh: Mary? I'm worried. I called you. Please text back.

I hand the phone back to Josh. My stomach flips. "Mary must have died before she got your text message. She was in the park. No cell service."

"I know. When Mary didn't answer me, I drove back to the park and waited in the parking lot. I figured I'd thank Mary, maybe talk to Betsy. Who knows? I probably thought we'd get together that night, Betsy and me." Josh leans forward, elbows on knees.

"You didn't find Mary, right?"

"No. All I saw were Betsy and Bo. Walking into the parking lot, together."

"From Point Park? On *that* day?" I ask, trying to ground him. He seems very far away, like he's in a trance. I look across the tennis court. Hoffman is sitting on the bench opposite ours. He's on his phone checking email or texts. He senses me watching and smiles. I smile back and turn to Josh. "The afternoon Mary died? Why didn't you tell someone? Say something?"

"Betsy told me not to say anything about that day, that she'd get in trouble." Josh kicks the ground with the tip of his tennis shoe. "She's afraid of you."

Not afraid enough. "Me? I think we should be afraid of her."

Josh swallows, shakes his head. "I loved her. I would do anything for her. I went to boarding school a few weeks later. Betsy convinced me I didn't see anything. She told me she loved me and that we'd be together when I came back, after I graduated. But we aren't. And I know what I saw. Despite the fact Betsy led me on all this time, texting me that she loved me, she didn't. They were together, in the park, the afternoon Mary died. And I have some of the last texts Mary ever sent on my phone."

"I guess those texts didn't really help—not without the context around them." He can provide plenty of context now, if I don't spook him.

"I didn't show the police. I didn't want to get Betsy in trouble. And besides, I'm sure they downloaded Mary's data, all her texts." Josh looks around the tennis courts, out toward the street. I know he's checking for his mother.

"Yes, we did see all of her texts. The ones to you didn't mean anything at the time, I suppose. Well, I'm glad you're finally telling the truth. It's always good to do the right thing, no matter the consequences." I pat his shoulder.

"I loved Betsy. I probably still do. That's what I told the police when they interviewed me back then. And I loved Mary, too. I kept Bo a secret. I didn't want to stir up any trouble."

"I know." But come on.

"Mary had it all figured out. She freaked out about Bo. I mean, he's a teacher. It's sort of gross."

Mary was such a good daughter, so protective of her younger sister. "But Betsy wouldn't listen to Mary?"

"I guess not. I'm an idiot."

Yes, you are. I pat his back. Keep talking, idiot. So here we are. "Do you think Betsy and Bo killed Mary?"

"What? I mean, I can't be certain of anything. I just know Bo wanted Betsy to bring Mary to him. And she did. I was there. At least for a part of it."

I smile and lick my lips. The air has turned chilly around us. Hoffman still waits patiently across the court. A chill runs down my spine. I'm finally getting proof. The text messages. The eyewitness.

"Bo killed Mary?" I whisper and then cover my mouth.

"No. Well, I don't know." Josh turns to face me.

My mouth drops open. I shake my head no. "No," I whisper. My eyes are wide, staring at him. Challenging him to be certain of what he is saying.

"I didn't see Betsy kill Mary." He pauses. A tear rolls down his cheek. "But Betsy was meeting her there, Bo was somewhere waiting, and then Mary died. I wanted to believe it was an accident. But now I don't think it was." Josh begins to cry, a quiet, hopeless sound. "They were so mad at each other anything could have happened."

Ah, yes, the Harris temper. From their father. "Did you follow them? Did you witness Betsy push Mary off the point?" I tilt my head. Is he confused or will he stick to his story?

"No, I left and didn't come back to the park until after dark. But I know your daughters. They were yelling, so mad. Betsy was furious." He sobs. "When I left the parking lot, Betsy and Bo were the only ones I saw."

I pat his shoulder. "Thank you for telling me. This isn't your fault. But the truth has to come out. It's been a year."

Josh wipes at his face with the bottom of his tennis shirt. He's a mess, but he knows what he saw. "I know. I was such a fool. I saw Betsy with Bo, and I still kept her secrets, still comforted her that day. I believed her when she told me there was nothing between them. That Bo was just a friend. I didn't tell the police anything. I lied to them. I thought she loved me."

Wow, he's so malleable. David's a man of steel compared to this one.

"I should have told you sooner, but I didn't really see anything. And Betsy was being so nice. We were back together, at least that's what she said. She loved me."

Despite the situation, I feel a swell of pride in my heart. Betsy is her mother's daughter after all. "You could have called? I wondered where you were." A lie. But I should have tracked him down sooner, I realize.

"Betsy and I talked all the time. She was so sad about Mary. I didn't want to think there was anything more to the story than that." Josh kicks the ground. "What are you going to do, Mrs. Harris? Betsy hasn't been herself since Mary died. It must be so hard on her. I mean, the guilt must be eating at her," Josh adds. He pushes off the bench.

"I'm sure it's hard to live with a murder, even if it was an accident, a fit of rage." I stand up, too. I mean, I wouldn't know, but I can imagine how stressful killing someone could be, especially someone you love. Haunting.

"I don't think it was an accident, Mrs. Harris. I think Betsy pushed Mary off that cliff, maybe with Bo's help. Maybe alone. And you don't think it was an accident, either." Josh looks down at his feet.

Correct. "I never did. Mary never went up there to that point. Never," I agree.

"Do you think I should go to the police?" He swallows. He certainly is facing a big moral dilemma at such a young age. And the kid still has to live here when he comes home from college break. If he tells he'll be labeled a snitch. And who knows what Bo will do to him? Bo could be dangerous, don't you agree?

"I can't tell you what to do, or stand in your way. It's my worst fear come true." I look down at the bench, pretend to gather my thoughts. "Tell your mom what you know, she will tell you what to do." A sob racks my body and I bend over. "My God. My only living daughter is a—" I falter, unable to say the word *murderer*. "What if Betsy and Bo lured Mary to the Point to murder her? My God." I break down, inconsolable sobs. Full waterworks.

"The stupid thing is, I still love her." Josh lets out a big sob as he walks away. I lift my head from my hands so I can watch his back as he crosses the tennis court and waves to Hoffman. He opens the metal gate and disappears into the night.

I sit up and take a deep breath, collecting myself. I knew he might have the piece I was missing. He puts everything together in a way even Detective Branson will understand.

Most likely, Josh will drive home and confess everything to his mom. He'll sob, and cry, but his mom will insist that he do the right thing. They will call Detective Branson first thing in the morning and Josh will implicate Betsy in the murder of her sister. It was a crime of passion, of course. She'll probably be able to get off with a little time served, with a good attorney. Everyone knows she was angry, her new love was threatened. Teenagers in love do very bad things.

What I can't believe is how much Josh still loves Betsy, even after everything she's done to him. I mean, I guess I can understand. I thought David would dump the bimbo, start over with me. That was my original plan. I thought we could reconnect, be a family again. Now I know the truth. Josh and I were both delusional, in denial. But not anymore.

This is all working out perfectly. My devious daughter has hung herself. And Josh will be her executioner. I should probably feel sorry for Betsy.

But I don't.

31

7:30 p.m.

Hoffman crosses the tennis court and sits on the bench next to me. He hands me a green The Cove sweatshirt.

"Thanks." I grab it from him and pull it over my head. I do have the chills.

"How'd everything go? Did he tell you what you needed to know?" His eyes are green speckled with brown, I just noticed. "Are you okay?"

I force a smile. He is so kind. "It's terrible. Everything is a mess. Especially me. I'm sorry, I must look like a wreck."

"You look beautiful to me." He leans lightly against me and I can feel the warmth of his body through the sweatshirt.

Our bare legs almost touch. It's been so long since a man has been kind to me. I deserve this. "Thank you. I should probably get home, skip the lesson." Even though I want to do more than play tennis with this young man. I know he can feel the zing of energy bouncing between us. It's nice. But he's not my type.

"What did Josh say? Can you tell me?" Hoffman is both kind, a little sexy and the designated gossip of The Cove. Everyone knows that.

Be good, Jane.

I speak quietly, slowly. "He said Betsy killed Mary. He was there."

"No." Hoffman shakes his head. His eyes are huge.

"I know, that's what I said." My body shakes with a deep chill. I can see Mary's face, angry, self-righteous. And then she's falling.

"What are you going to do? Did you tell him to keep it a secret? If the cops hear about this it could be bad. You could lose Betsy, too."

I nod. Look into his kind eyes and tell a little fib. "I told him to keep what he knows a secret. I told him to do it for Betsy. He still loves her, it seems, even though she has a thing with Bo. You were right about that, I'm afraid."

"That guy. He's like almost my age. So wrong." Hoffman cracks his knuckles. An annoying little habit, but nobody is perfect.

"So wrong." Hoffman is like half my age, but I'm an adult. "You know what else is wrong?" I place my hand on the bench in the small space between the two of us. My pinkie finger touches his thigh.

"There's more?" Hoffman wraps his arm around my shoulders. It feels nice. I let him keep it there.

"My husband closed escrow on a lovely house on one of the Port Streets for his mistress this week." I sigh, slump against him. I am quite a tragic figure.

"No. That same woman he was spotted with, the one I warned you about?" Hoffman seems stunned. A house on the Port Streets? That's far more serious. That's commitment. "You need to confront him. How could anyone cheat on you?"

David is an idiot, that's how. "Thank you."

Suddenly the court lights shut off and we're plunged into darkness. I jump and Hoffman pulls me to him.

"The lights are on timers," he murmurs before his lips cover mine.

I enjoy the sensation, the zinging stars in my head. His hand cradles the back of my head. I'm dizzy. I need to pull away and I do.

"Wow," I manage. I'm not lying. It's been so long since anyone has kissed me with raw desire.

"Sorry, I couldn't stop myself. I hope you'll forgive me." He stands and helps me up.

"Of course. I just need to sort out my life. I know I need a fresh start." I'm flirting with him and I'm irresistible. It's not his fault he feels this way, even though he is way below me. I mean, me and a tennis pro? Come on. That's a housewife/country club cliché I'm not going to partake in.

We walk in silence through the dark parking lot to my

car. He says, "I hope everything works out. You know where to find me if you need me."

I click the car door open and hurry inside. I can't let him kiss me again. Once, an accident. Twice, well, people will find out. I can't have an affair with a staff member of The Cove. I'd be ruined here, and all over Southern California. But it doesn't matter because I'm out of here, soon. I wave through the window as I pull away.

After graduation, after everything unfolds tomorrow, perhaps I'll explore the neighborhood where Elizabeth James lives. After, of course, I facilitate her quick departure. It's amazing the havoc a lawsuit from one disgruntled patient can cause. I've already found her. And she's so angry. But that's later. After I get through all of this mess. Then, after Elizabeth is dealt with, I will start over, find love again. And I'll aim high, much higher than a tennis pro.

There are so many more men like David out there. If she's smart, and I know she is, Kylie will be leaving her Port Street home soon to find a fresh catch. Maybe she'll head east and stop in Scottsdale. There are plenty of rich men golfing their retirement days away in Arizona. Sounds dreadfully boring to me, but they have money. She'll try to keep one state ahead of the Holiday children. They'll catch her, eventually, I know, because I will track her.

Poor Kylie. She'll remain hopeful until the day the cops show up at her new lover's door. Even then, she'll flirt with the male officers, and try to talk herself out of trouble. Her new lover may try to save her, convinced there has been some kind of mistake. But I'll help him learn the truth with a well-timed letter.

The ending for her is all just so predictable.

I'm not finished with David yet, though. He hasn't suffered yet, not really. Sure, Mary's death devastated him, but he had Kylie on the side to distract him, to make him feel young again. And they were going to have more children. He'd have a chance to be the father of another little girl. Perhaps they'll name her Mary?

And he still has his loyal, annoying parents. Has he already introduced them to Kylie, told them about their future? Did they tour the new home? They'll all be so heartbroken by Kylie's disappearance. Gone without a trace, without so much as a note goodbye. Sigh.

I wonder about tomorrow. When he discovers Kylie is gone, will he still attend the graduation ceremony? He must, right? He has to be there to support Betsy. I mean, he doesn't even know yet that his precious daughter, the one he talks to more than he does his wife, is a murderer.

But he will discover the truth soon.

I see Hoffman in my rearview mirror, standing in the dark parking lot, watching me drive away. It's so nice to feel wanted again. Too bad it's by the wrong guy. Poor man. Somebody should warn him that I am not what I seem.

Nah, why spoil our fun.

32

8:10 p.m.

I'm hungry. All this activity stirs up my appetite. Of course, the house is dark when I pull into the garage. Only the exterior landscape lights seem to welcome me home. No one else is here. No one else cares.

I walk through the front door and flip on lights to illuminate the courtyard and continue into the kitchen. Of course, since they're on my mind all of a sudden, I focus on the "art" David's parents gave us for our wedding, a ceramic pitcher I'd like to break. They'd been in Italy, unable to attend our ceremony, of course, a trip they organized after we'd picked our wedding date.

They did, to their credit, have me figured out almost from the start. It's too bad. I had been hoping for years of fake cheer, of holidays spent at their huge oceanfront home, the girls unwrapping piles of presents in front of their three-story live Christmas tree. We'd go to the club, where my mother-in-law, who would insist I call her Mom, would introduce me to all of her bridge club friends. My father-in-law would beam at his son and tell him he married above his rank, that he wished his wife had been so beautiful in her day.

Okay, he wouldn't say that, not in front of her. But a girl can dream. They never did welcome us over for holidays, and didn't include us as a couple socially in anything at the club. David and his dad play golf every week, and I know he goes to lunch with his mom at least once a month. They don't include me. Never have.

I hop onto the kitchen counter, carefully climb onto my knees. The stone is cold and hard on my bare legs, but I ignore the sensation as I reach up and grab the pitcher from the display shelf. I don't feel much these days, except anger. I feel that deep in my bones.

I place the pitcher on the counter. It's a rooster or something birdlike. "From Tuscany," David had said at the time as he unwrapped the gift. "Aren't they great? They didn't have to bring us a gift. I think they'll come around."

He'd pulled me to him, so young, so hopeful. We'd just returned from our two-week honeymoon in French Polynesia. We were tan, relaxed.

"Maybe we should invite them to dinner this week?" I suggested. I'd already won, David and I were married, without a prenup. I didn't stand to gain anything by alienating them. I wanted them on my side. Their generous resources could have been nothing but an additional blessing.

But alas, David's parents are an interesting pair. I hadn't fully appreciated their strong wills, their joint and unified hatred of me. By now, twenty years later, they simply stare at me with contempt. At the memorial service they eyed me stone-faced. But they know they need to behave in order to see their only grandchildren. Grandchild.

I think they blame me for Mary's death. I'm a convenient scapegoat, I suppose. I don't know why I feel that way. Intuition, I suppose. It's the way they look at me now, their loathing has an added element, like when they averted their eyes when I saw them at the memorial service, for example. Their behavior is something akin to fear. If so, they're going to be utterly shocked when it turns out that it's Betsy's fault. That Mary was murdered.

The social scandal alone isn't good for people of their age. Will they visit Betsy in prison? I'm getting ahead of myself, of course. Betsy won't go to prison. How ridiculous. We'll get her a good lawyer. Rich people don't get locked up, at least not most of the time.

I stare at the ugly rooster pitcher again. I hate the thing. I pick it up and hurl it toward the sink. It crashes into the sink—half in, half out—and shatters into a satisfying array of ceramic shards. David will get the message. This is what happens when you break your marriage vows. Things start to shatter.

The scene reminds me of the broken wineglass the

other day. I dropped it on purpose, of course. Hoping to elicit a caring response from David. I wanted to see if he felt anything for me at all anymore.

And he proved he still does. He swept up the glass and took care of me, even if he did leave for her house shortly after. But still, there is something between us. A small flickering flame where there once was a roaring fire.

He'll turn to me, I know he will, when things unravel. We've been together for so long. Sure, he's strayed, but he'll come back to me soon. He won't have any other choice. Goodbye, Kylie/Nancy. And then, when he's lost everything, when he finally needs me again, I'll go in for the final knockout blow. I'll move to LA and leave him all alone. Heartsick. Miserable. Destroyed.

I walk across the littered kitchen floor. The hard stone helped create sharp, tiny pieces. As I walk across them with my tennis shoes, I hear the satisfying crunch. Hopefully, David will be in a happy mood again when he arrives home and he'll clean up after my latest accident. One night to go before he thinks he's free, so I bet he'll be happy to make sure the kitchen is in good shape for his last day here with us, his family. I can just imagine David and Betsy celebrating her graduation by eating breakfast together tomorrow morning, despite the fact it's a meal she says she doesn't eat anymore but does when David asks her. Frustrating.

I hope I've set things into motion. I'm counting on my hunch that Kylie won't open the letter in front of him, counting on her to be like me. Putting my faith in my husband's mistress, such an odd thing, isn't it?

I need to change into sweatpants, wash the makeup from my face. I wasn't playing tennis tonight, of course not, family. I have been home all night, as far as they're concerned, just waiting for them to join me.

They're so clueless.

In my bathroom I stop in front of my mini-shrine to Mary. I stare into her dark brown eyes. I try to understand again why she would go against my wishes. The one thing she promised never to do. My red dress wasn't the problem. Taking it and wearing it without my permission was wrong, but not the betrayal I couldn't forgive. Mary was ungrateful and unyielding in her betrayal; David smug and condescending in his. Together, they were moving Mary to LA to be with Elizabeth. Unacceptable.

I feel my pulse race and take a deep breath. That's the past. Mary is gone. I need to focus on now. If David had continued to keep his silly romance quiet, that would be one thing. I could allow him a dalliance, a way to blow off some steam. I mean, it's not easy losing a child and I was busy with my own pharmaceutical escape. But purchasing a home, promising to start a new life. That's unforgivable.

I'm certain Betsy, my dear little girl, has been in on all of the secrets, first Mary's and now David's. And now I discover she has a big secret of her own. Did she really think she could hide Bo from me, leave me for him?

They are all traitors. I pick up the picture frame of smiling college Mary and drop it on its face on the bathroom counter and punch the back until I hear the satisfying sound of breaking glass. Then I walk to the closet and change clothes.

Maybe I'll wait in the courtyard tonight, wrapped in a blanket. I don't expect either of them to be home too late. It's a big day tomorrow. A day of celebration and a day filled with so many surprises.

33

As I sit outside under the stars, enjoying the warmth of the firepit and the absence of killer palm trees, I wonder about other dangers around me, what other tragic accidents could happen out here in the courtyard. The palm trees could kill, sure, but they're gone now. What else? I check my phone. Before I do a Google search, I open the tracking app.

Betsy's car is heading this direction on Coast Highway from the high school. Despite the fact she has outsmarted my spyware, she hasn't found the physical tracking device on her car yet. So take that, Betsy. I guess her art class is finished for the evening? Or was it a tutoring session. Or should we just call it what it is: a date with Bo, a guy old enough to know better. Wherever she's been, she's coming home. David's car is still parked at Kylie's new house. Charming.

I do know that for once Kylie and I are on the same page!! She's as anxious to have him come home as I am. Perhaps he's napping right now in their new cozy bedroom and she is hiding in the kitchen, reading my little letter. I'm almost positive that, by now, two out of three of us know their little affair is over. Only my poor husband is in the dark.

Speaking of dark, I search: What can kill me in my courtyard?

Well, I learn that there are six common garden plants that can kill you, including the oleander I have lining the edge of the fence. Who knew these fragrant flowers as well as each part of the plant is poisonous? Even a small amount of the leaves can be lethal. Sprinkle a little oleander leaf and flowers in your spring mix salad, perhaps? Edible flowers are all the rage these days, adding color and texture to formerly boring salads. If someone put an oleander in my salad, I'd probably swallow it down without question. I love lantana, and it's on the list, too. Adorable orange-and-yellow flowers. I have some in the backyard. Ingesting the tiny green berries can kill you, too. I'm surprised more dogs don't die from accidentally eating these toxic pretties but I know some do. One has.

It seems like I could concoct quite a toxic appetizer from my yard. Of course, killing someone by feeding them poisonous flowers and leaves and berries wouldn't be an accidental death. But it would be surprisingly easy. The rest of the search results deal with snakes, rats, frogs, toads and even the pocket gopher, whatever that is. All are a bother, but not deadly. I'm safe for now as long as someone doesn't offer me a courtyard salad made of local leaves and berries.

I hear Betsy's car arrive outside and pull the blanket up to my chin. I could pretend to be asleep, but why not try to have a conversation with the daughter I've discovered I don't really know at all.

My daughter the murderer. It just doesn't sound right. My daughter the accidental murderer. Better.

"Mom?" Betsy spots me the moment she steps through the gate. She looks wary, like a small dog cornered by a pit bull. She looks like she thinks I'm going to tear into her. But I'm not the one she should fear. Josh is the one with all the information, keeper of her secrets. The one scorned.

"Good evening. How was your night?" I smile and stretch. She doesn't know how to take my pleasant tone.

She closes the gate. Feeling safe. Welcomed. "It was great. All the AP art kids stayed and helped finish decorating for the grad party. I mean, it's still going to be lame but it looks good."

I wonder if she'll have a chance to enjoy it. "Good. Well, are you hungry?"

"I grabbed a bite with a friend on the way home." She smiles. From the look in her eyes, I realize who the friend is.

"Bo?" I ask. My voice isn't judgmental anymore. I'm no longer bothered by her association with the loser gym teacher or any of the myriad of secrets she and her sister kept from me. After tomorrow, it won't matter.

She smiles. I've put her at ease. She thinks I'm getting used to the notion. She's wrong, so wrong. "He's coming to the graduation ceremony tomorrow, isn't that sweet?"

She's eighteen years old. It's not illegal what he's up to, but it's certainly not socially acceptable. Not here. Not most places. That alone could make him complicit. "Great. I'll save him a seat."

Betsy laughs. She thinks I'm kidding. I'm not. "Okay, well, I've got to get some sleep. I'm a finalist up for some special award at the ceremony tomorrow. I don't know if I'll win, but we'll find out tomorrow. It comes with scholarship money."

"Wow, that's great." Of course, Angelica told me about the award. I'd forgotten with all the excitement. "Mary won several graduation awards."

Betsy deflates. "I know." And then, "I wish she was going to be there tomorrow. I miss her so much. Every day."

"Me, too." It's true, I do. Even with the betrayal. I miss how we were, how our family was until everyone started pulling away and leaving me, disobeying me, growing up and moving on. Taking secret meetings in Santa Monica with birth mother bitches. Hanging out with sneaky older men. Buying a love nest with their younger girlfriend. My husband used to be so handsome. They were such cute little girls. We were the perfect family.

"Is Dad home?" She's walking through the courtyard, unaware she's smelling the sweet scent of deadly olean-der. There is danger lurking right in front of her eyes.

"No, he's visiting someone on the Port Streets. Not sure who? Said he'd be home in a little while." I stand up and turn off the firepit, following Betsy to the door. "You don't have any idea who Dad would be visiting over there, do you?"

Betsy looks surprised I mentioned the Port Streets, surprised I'm zeroing in on him. But teens are selfish, so she's worried only about herself. She recovers from the shock and says, "Um, no, I don't know what Dad's doing. See you in the morning. Oh, and, Mom?"

"Yes."

"After the grad party a few friends and I are going camping. Just a couple days. Thought I'd let you know. Good night."

"You don't want to ask permission? You'll need money, a car, supplies. You need my help." I stare at her, chal-lenging her. But she just smiles.

"I don't need anything from you. I'm all set. Good night."

"Good night," I say and wave to the little liar as she makes her way downstairs.

Now I know a couple of things. Betsy has been to David and Kylie's new house. I wonder if she picked out a bedroom? Probably. She doesn't realize that if I hadn't gotten rid of Kylie tonight, Kylie would have cut Betsy out of David's life as fast as you can say: I'm pregnant!!!

They'd start over, with a new baby girl, and Betsy would be as discarded as I am.

I'm doing her a favor, again. And what does she do to repay me? Sneak around with Bo. Preparing for a little camping trip, are we? Ha. She'll see that won't be possible. Betsy thinks she is one step ahead of me, the little liar.

Tomorrow is going to be such fun.

34

10:00 p.m.

I've opened a bottle of wine, poured a big glass.

I had to be careful with all of the broken pieces of crappy rooster littering the floor. But I managed. The area in front of the refrigerator was barely touched by debris. I have a good aim, strong arms thanks to my clandestine garage workouts.

I sit on the couch in the living room and wait for my husband to come home. It's a familiar pose, a familiar scene, but tonight is different. My anger has dissolved like sugar boiled in hot water, the rage that has fueled me for the past year is being replaced by another emotion. I believe the feeling is satisfaction, the offshoot of success-ful revenge. Of course, I can't be sure, I don't have any tangible evidence of my vengeance, yet. Kylie's car is still parked at the Port Street house. And so is my husband's.

Retribution is coming my way, though, so let me hear a hallelujah. Don't think of me as spiteful, please. Re-member all they've done to me. You'd do the same if you were in my shoes.

I open my app. Oh, look, David just left Kylie's house. He's still ten minutes away in light traffic. I open my banking app—there is an app for everything these days, am I right? Oh, what's this? Betsy's savings account has surged. Is she trafficking drugs? I need to freeze her ac-count. This amount of money gives a person freedom, an escape. Should I go downstairs and confront her? I imagine Betsy washing her face, admiring her expensive graduation outfit, opening her closet and pulling out the maroon cap and gown she'll wear over her dress. She's so excited about tomorrow, and the future. The future.

And then I realize: That's a graduation check from Da-vid's parents, I just know it. She's made a mistake and deposited it where I can see it.

She's become too confident. She is so relieved tomor-row is here, I could sense it as we spoke in the courtyard. She's leaving me, just like David. David is moving in with Kylie while Betsy and Bo will go "camping" in the early morning after her graduation party.

So romantic, don't you think? But it also seems like she's running from something, doesn't it? Heading for the border before Detective Alan catches up with her, perhaps? It's not like I didn't suspect her, but now I know for sure.

She's just lucky I'm saving her from this awful life on the run that she thinks she wants.

I take a big gulp of my wine. There are some things and people I cannot control, of course. And exact timing is out of my hands tomorrow except for the graduation ceremony, which begins promptly at 4:30 p.m. I cannot neutralize my in-laws, not completely. While they have been marginalized, I cannot prevent them from coming to the graduation ceremony, and obviously, I can't stop them from giving Betsy this great big check. All I can do is freeze her funds. It's for her safety, really.

I hear the garage door opening. My man is home. How wonderful.

I've kept the lights on tonight, so he can see me, hear me, right away. He walks into the courtyard and heads toward me, toward the front door. He looks inside and spots me on the couch. I see his shoulders tense, but he has to finish. He must come home one last evening. He steels himself and pushes through the door.

His hair is wet from the shower. His tie and suit jacket are not with him. He must have left them at his new home. He's so careless because he thinks he's almost free of me. If he was a whistler, he'd be whistling. The word I'd use to describe him this moment is *smug*. Smug, satisfied and superior. Three words. Sue me.

"Good evening, Jane. Excited for graduation tomorrow?" He sets his briefcase on the floor by the front door as if preparing for a quick escape.

Not so fast, dear. "I'm wonderful. And yes, it will be a great day tomorrow. Betsy has been so busy. I'm sure all of her hard work will be rewarded. I hope you've eaten."

"Yes, I did earlier. So I think I'll just turn in. Big day tomorrow."

Poor David. He's so tired. I don't even think he feels guilty anymore. Somehow he's rationalized his affair with Kylie and he'll tell friends he stayed with his pathetic wife as long as he could, long enough to get his youngest daughter through high school. But he just had to leave.

Poor Jane, he'll tell the guys at the club. She's gone mad. I did all I could for her, but I had to save myself. You know what I'm saying, dude?

Oh, David. You are so wrong. You are mine, all mine, until I'm finished with you. You should realize that. Oh, and just to prove my power, watch this.

"Oh, David. I accidentally broke something again. I'm so clumsy these days. I didn't trust myself to clean the kitchen. I was afraid I might break something else but I'd hate for Betsy or you to cut yourself in the morning. Do you mind sweeping up?" I'm so pathetic. Helpless. But he thinks this is the last of it. His final night of penance before freedom.

Big exhalation. "What did you *drop* this time?"

"You'll see." I smile and take a drink of wine as he saunters into the kitchen.

A moment later he's back, broom in hand, eyes flashing at me. "You did this on purpose, I know you did. My parents gave us that rooster for our wedding. It was an expensive antique. Priceless."

I stare at him. Had I known it was worth something, I would have thrown something cheaper. Oh well. "I never liked it anyway."

He holds the broom like a golf club, and tries to resist a retort. And fails. "They feel the same about you."

I put my hand on my chest, feigning surprise. I don't want to fight with him tonight. I just want him to sweep up the mess, perhaps cut himself superficially on a jagged piece of broken porcelain. And then I want him to sleep on the couch, where he belongs. "I'm going to bed. You can sleep on the couch."

"Fine with me," he yells.

I grab my wine, the wine bottle, and head toward the bedroom. I can feel how much he wants to tell me to stop, to make me obey him, to make me fall in line. But he's never been the strong one, not from the very beginning. And besides, he has a mess to clean up in the kitchen.

I smile, imagining him with his broom and dustpan. He'll check to see if the rooster can be glued together, salvaged in some way. But it can't. Some things are too far broken to fix. Roosters. Marriages. Lives.

I know he'll be gone when I wake up in the morning. The next time I see him will be at the graduation ceremony.

My bet is he won't have Kylie on his arm. We'll see.

THURSDAY

GRADUATION DAY

35

10:00 a.m.

I'm alone upstairs in the kitchen. The couch was empty when I came through to make coffee. I'm not even sure if David will sit with me at graduation after our grand finale fight over his parents. We'll see.

Sam's text was the first of the day. "Do you need a ride to graduation, Mrs. H.?"

I decide to be polite in case someone needs to interview him later. He'll remember me as a grief-stricken mom, terrified of sitting on the ocean side of cars, terrified of driving, of leaving the house.

I text: I'm going with my husband. And good news. I'm going to start driving again. It's time. Best wishes on your education. Nice. Dismissive. Hopefully he'll go away and I won't have to block him.

He texts: Okay. Thank you. I've learned a lot driving you this year, watching over you. Getting to know you so well. Congrats!

Does he think he knows me? I suppose he thinks he does, silly boy. And congratulations? Oh, I suppose he means congratulations on Betsy's graduation. Whatever. It's her achievement, not mine. A fleeting moment of success in the midst of a lifetime of Betsy failures. Does Sam want a tip? I need him on my side, proof of my complicated grief, you know, just in case someone would ever suspect me of anything. Which nobody would, of course.

I text Sam: I'll mail you a tip.

Sam texts: Thanks. And Jane?

I don't have time for this. I text: What?

I'm standing in the kitchen—the very cleanly swept kitchen—wearing shoes just to be cautious. I'm also wearing a brand-new dress. It's blue, like my eyes, bright and clear this morning. My makeup is perfect and my hair is curled in waves. I'm ready for what could turn out to be one of the best days of my life. I need to look good. And I do.

Sam texts: I know what happened. You do, too. Poor Cash.

I swallow, jab at the letters with shaking fingers as a chill races down my spine.

I text: Are you threatening me? I don't understand. I didn't do anything to Cash.

The doorbell rings. I have no idea who would be here, but I take three deep breaths. Sam is an idiot dog lover, that's all. I shouldn't have kept him around so long, let him become like part of the family. Well, now he's gone. Good riddance. I search for his contact and block him. Ha.

I saunter out to the gate and open the door. It's a huge bouquet of red roses. How lovely. I imagine them being for me, from Hoffman.

The deliveryman says, "Here you go!"

"Why, thank you, they're gorgeous." I take the vase from the deliveryman. It's heavy and awkward. I hope I don't drop it.

I make it to the kitchen and yank the card from its plastic pitchfork and tear it open.

Betsy. Congratulations on your graduation.
The future will be beautiful, like you.
Xo B

They're for Betsy, from Bo. How sweet.

"Mom, are those flowers for me?" Betsy stands behind me, reading over my shoulder. Just a moment later and the card would have been gone. And the flowers would have been mine.

"Why, yes, they are." I slip the card back into its holder. I turn to Betsy. "Are you hungry, honey? Today's the big day. I'm so proud of you and everything you've become."

Betsy's brow furrows. "Okay, well, not what I was expecting to hear from you, but I'll take it."

"Can I make you something, anything? I want to help you celebrate your special day." A salad from the courtyard, perhaps? I'm kidding. "It would mean a lot to me to spend a little time together this morning. I mean, you'll likely be just as busy after today as you've been the past year. What are your plans? We'd talked about starting college early? Jumping right in this summer."

Betsy pulls open the refrigerator door. Grabs the orange juice. "I'm not going to college this summer, that's for sure. I need a break from everything. I'm going camping, and then we'll see."

I'm hurt. Or at least I pretend to be. I drop my eyes, slide into a bar stool, grip my coffee in both hands. I almost make a tear. It makes her feel bad and I'm glad. "You do need a job, of course. You'll be off the gravy train. No more allowance."

I open the refrigerator and pull out the carton of eggs. I'm hungry. She is, too. We will have eggs and toast together. It will be special. Our last meal, with her in high school, that's what I mean.

"I know I'm going to get a job after I travel a bit. Grandma and Grandpa gave me a big graduation check. They told me at Mary's memorial service that they gave me more than they gave Mary even because I've been through so much. They know I need to get away. They're so great."

"So great." I pull out a pan. I imagine David Sr.'s and Rosemary's round little heads as I squeeze the eggs. Crack. Crack. "One or two eggs?"

"I'm not really hungry." Betsy sighs. "One. And toast. Thanks." She's on her phone, no doubt texting Bo with their secret messaging app. She smells the roses. She takes a photo of them and then a selfie with the roses behind her. She smiles as she sends the shots to him. "I'll go get ready for school while you make breakfast. We're supposed to wear our graduation outfits for photos at noon. We'll all be a mess by the ceremony."

Likely you will be at least, but I don't tell her that. She is the opposite of dainty. She'd never last in the South. Well, I guess I didn't, either. "You'll be wearing a gown. It will cover everything up."

"Good point." Betsy hoists the huge vase of roses into her arms and seems to float out of the kitchen.

While Betsy is downstairs getting ready, I make us breakfast. And set two places next to each other at the table. We'll both face out to the ocean. And I'll try to be fine with it. It's sort of like our last supper as mother and daughter. After today, my nest will be empty.

I stare out the window to the huge, dark, cold ocean on the horizon. It looks so perfect. I take a deep breath and fight off the panic attack. It's time for me to move on from that, too. Everything will come to light, and it will be a new season of mourning. This time, though, I won't hide out and lose weight. No, this time I'll give interviews, up my social media game. I've already reached out to a few industry people, starting to circulate my name. And those new head shots next week will be fabulous.

"Thanks for cooking." Betsy walks into the room. She is beautiful, just not as pretty as Mary or me. She wears a purple dress that hugs her petite and perfect figure and, believe it or not, dressy heels instead of army boots. She's even removed the nose piercing and has regular earrings in. She looks like the girl I imagine her to be.

She pulls out the chair and sits down. Her arms palms up on the table reveal her Mary tattoo on one wrist, and on the other wrist, the infinity symbol matching Bo's. I know she's feeling powerful, revealing her tattoos to me, taunting me. That's fine, she can have the morning, I'll take tonight.

"You look beautiful, honey, you really do."

"You seem surprised." She chomps a bite of egg on toast.

"What does that symbol mean again?" I resist the urge to grab her wrist, flip her palm over.

"We are all one." Betsy chews another bite.

We are all definitely not one. Some of us are in charge, some of us dependent. Some of us are smart, some clueless. Some beautiful, some, like Betsy, not. That's what separates us all: looks and intellect. I pretend to eat, pushing my meal around on my plate. The silence between us is heavy, debilitating.

"What time should I get to campus? To get a good seat?" Yes, this is small talk. If I don't keep it light, I'll throw something.

"I don't know." She's shutting down. Our time together is over. "I've got to run. See you there. And if you arrive before Dad and the grandparents, try to be nice and save them a seat. Okay? For me?"

"Sure, honey. Anything for you."

And then she's out the door. I check my app and Kylie is almost to San Diego. I wonder if David knows she called in sick. Probably not yet.

I grab our dirty dishes and carry them to the sink. I hope to hear some more good news yet this morning.

My phone rings. It's an unfamiliar number. My heart thumps with anticipation. This is going to be the best day ever.

36

11:00 a.m.

It's not who I expected.

"Hi, Jane, it's Hoff. Just calling to check in on you. That kiss last night was, well, great."

He's still turned on. He's calling me on his way into work. He thought about me, us together, all night. I have that effect on men. Meanwhile, I'd forgotten all about him.

"I'm doing better, thank you. And listen, nobody can know about our little rendezvous. I was never there at the tennis courts, okay? Or about the wonderful kiss." Deep, throaty laugh.

"Of course. Your secrets are safe with me," he says with a whisper of desire. "Say, I'm also calling to give

308

you a heads-up. Sandy, Josh's mom, called me to cancel her tennis match today. She's driving Josh to the police station. She assured me he didn't do anything wrong. I just thought you should know."

Good boy. "Oh, goodness. Well, I know Josh had some things to tell the police. The poor guy was so torn up last night. I guess he has to do what he has to do." I look at the ceiling. My heart feels heavy, but just for a moment. It's all her fault. We all get what we deserve in the end. "Say, Hoff, I need to get going. Today's a big day. Graduation."

"Of course, so sorry to bother you."

"You aren't a bother. Let's talk tomorrow? Maybe get together for a little tennis or something?" I suggest. That should keep his heart thumping.

"Can't wait," he says, hanging up.

He's going to have to wait forever, poor guy.

37

11:30 a.m.

All this waiting time has me thinking, making sure I've
planned everything correctly because it's both Betsy's and
David's special day today. And then I think about Mary,
how I smashed her photo last night. And why.

At first, I thought David's parents had broken the law,
that they were the ones who connected Mary with Elizabeth James. But it was much closer to home than that. I
suspected something terrible was being hidden from me
when I overheard a snippet of conversation. I'd walked
into the kitchen and David didn't see me. Mary was away
at USC, she'd been there a couple of months. David, Betsy,

Kylie and I were back in Orange County, settling into what would be the new normal. I didn't know Kylie's name yet, but I knew she was there, like an itch you scratch but it still itches and you don't know why. Much like I didn't know about Bo yet, just that Betsy was drifting away from me.

Much like I didn't know what secret Mary and David were keeping from me, but I knew it was a big one.

"I'll be happy to pay for a DNA test, honey. But I don't think you'll need to go that route. I have an idea where to find her. But I don't want you to get your hopes up. I'm not sure if she's open to meeting you," David said into the phone.

He didn't know I was standing behind him, fists clenched. He didn't know what I heard but he sensed me in the room. He turned and we locked eyes, his face flushed a bit. Only someone who has known him for more than twenty years would notice his unease, so of course I did.

"Your mom just walked in and I've got to head for my workout. Why don't you call me at the office in the morning and we'll get those classes straightened out? Yes, I know it's important." What a liar. "Love you, too, honey."

After he hung up he looked at me. "Heading to the gym."

"Yes, I heard. What did Mary need?" I resist the urge to put my hands on my hips. He could have handed the phone to me, let me speak to her. But they both hung up, guilty.

"Just some help scheduling classes. See you later." David's urgency to leave for "the gym" surprised me then. But of course, I didn't yet know about his lover, she hadn't taken form. She was still a guess, a hunch, an itch.

There were all sorts of secrets brewing in my house and I couldn't stop them.

Of course, Mary didn't need to order the DNA test kit, not when David could just call his parents and find out Elizabeth James's current address. And then, to finish stabbing me in the back, David gave our daughter her birth mother's email address and contact information. I would never want anyone to find me, especially if I had given my own child away. Unfortunately, Elizabeth didn't share that sentiment.

And so it began. My daughter Mary emailed Elizabeth. At first, it was very stilted, their correspondence, each testing the other's purpose, the other's willingness to connect and have a relationship. Even though she was busy with freshman year in college, and all the social positioning required to pledge a good sorority, she still obsessed about this forbidden woman. And their bond grew stronger online until, finally, they arranged to meet.

Mary was home for Christmas break. The next day we were flying to Telluride. It was December 22. I didn't know it but that day, that email, would be the beginning of the end of our family. Elizabeth agreed to meet Mary after the Christmas holiday.

I think you probably know by now that I tried everything in my power to stop it. As soon as we returned from Telluride, before Mary could arrange to see Elizabeth James, I was stalking her. I drove to LA, sat in front of

Elizabeth's home. I went to the Saint Joseph's Health Center in Santa Monica, where she had privileges. A lesser hospital, I'd note. I mean, I wished Mary's genes had been at Cedars-Sinai, but oh well.

And then I started threatening her. I called her cell phone, told her not to make any contact with Mary Harris. That she had signed a confidentiality agreement. That my client—I pretended to be a private investigator—would throw the book at her, lock her up, send her up the river. She hung up on me eventually, but I thought I'd gotten my point across.

Elizabeth James became my fixation, much as she became my daughter's. I did my best to try to stay one step ahead of her, and Mary. But it wasn't enough. They met for the first time a week after Mary returned to college. And my heart broke each time they had lunch, or coffee, and, eventually, dinner. It was my worst nightmare transpiring, and yet I never imagined she would decide to stay with Elizabeth for the summer, that she'd pick Elizabeth over me so completely. So finally.

Mary and Elizabeth met for coffee early in the morning on the day Mary died, the morning after she and Brad went on their special date, the date she wore my red dress on. My daughter didn't even try to hide the fact of her relationship with her birth mother. A relationship I forbade her to have.

"You can't stop me, Mom!" Mary had screamed at me, defiant, angry. Resolved. "I'm an adult. This is my life and Elizabeth will be a part of it. She's my role model. A doctor and everything! I'm taking the internship and her offer of housing. I can't wait for my summer away from you. I've learned so much this year away at school. Most moms aren't like you, not at all."

I'd grabbed her wrist, yanked her toward me, ignoring the low growl from Cash. "I am your mother. Your only mother."

"Let go of me. Now." Mary jerked her arm free as the stupid dog showed his teeth. And then they were out the door, leaving me shaking with anger.

I was out of control of my own daughter. This was a conspiracy that started long ago. I'd been a fool.

Betsy had appeared upstairs next. I didn't know if she heard Mary and me fighting, but she probably did. The air was thick with tension. Between me and the girls and between the two of them.

"Where do you think you're going?" I demanded. "Are you hanging out with that woman, too?"

"School. Duh. And then a hike with Mary. At Point Park," Betsy said, charming as always. "You're not invited."

I had smiled. I'm in control, they weren't. "I'm busy anyway. But, if I break free, maybe I'll come along. Surprise you girls."

"Oh my God. Don't you dare. Leave us alone," she screamed and ran out the door.

And that's the last time I ever saw Mary.

I never go to Point Park.

At least that's the story I tell.

I check my phone. Sam hasn't messaged me back. And then I remember, I blocked him. I'm in charge. Goodbye, stupid dog-loving Lyft driver.

Good riddance.

38

4:15 p.m.

The parking lot is almost full when I pull up to the high school. The ceremony doesn't begin for another forty-five minutes, but like our children, we parents are overachievers. We all want to be in the front row, or as close to it as possible, to witness our little creations' latest achievements.

It's just so exciting, isn't it? I know I can barely contain myself, but it's not because of the long and boring ceremony. No, not that. I'm excited Kylie has made it into Mexico!! She crossed the border, can you believe that? That means somebody is really freaked out. She probably will end up staying down there. Meeting a rich snowbird, maybe from Canada, who falls madly in love with her and her physical assets, just as she's falling in love with his yacht and the staff of gorgeous young men. One can only hope. But that is the life I wish for her. Out of my way.

I'm smiling as I walk toward the auditorium. That's when I spot him. Detective Branson. I suppose the police always attend graduation of the local high school kids, right? But detectives don't, do they?

"Hello, Mrs. Harris. Beautiful evening for a ceremony. You must be so proud of Betsy." He tips his hat.

"I am. She *pushed* through somehow this year. With everything that's happened. She's *stronger* than she looks, that's for sure." I couldn't be more witty if I tried. I'll admit, I worked on that little statement for a bit.

"I'll see you inside." He stays rooted to his lookout spot as I keep walking toward the doors.

They are letting parents into the room already, even though I'd anticipated having to wait outside. My new blue dress, a tight-fitting number, is drawing attention, along with, I'm sure, the four-inch heels I've added to my ensemble. I look as though I could be jetting off to a film festival instead of joining the masses in an uncomfortable wooden auditorium chair. Oh well. That's my next life, act two. Starting tomorrow.

I walk about halfway down toward the stage and find a row with some empty seats. I wonder, who deserves my kindness? Well, David will need a shoulder to cry on. He's already having a terrible day and it's about to get worse. My in-laws? Sure, why not. Those wretched people should sit next to their son, watch him as he falls apart. I know that will hurt them, too.

I sit on the aisle. They will all cross me to sit down. They all already have.

I search the growing crowd for a familiar face and spot Sandy and Josh. I'm shocked they're here. Josh feels my stare and turns. He won't make eye contact, and I'm certain he knows I've learned of his chat with the police. I smile at the back of his head.

A hand on my shoulder. I look up into the face of Sarah Murphy. Why is she here? Is she always lurking around school? She needs a life.

"Jane, don't you look gorgeous. Congratulations on Betsy's graduation. I heard she won a special award. Aren't you just the proudest?"

Oooh, Sarah, I am not. "Yes, it's wonderful. Can't wait to see what it is."

"Me, too. Okay, enjoy. I saw David in the parking lot. He should be right in," she adds.

"Oh goodie." My smile drops as she walks away.

"Jane, are these seats for me and my parents?" It's David. He looks like hell. Like he's frantic with worry. Like the love of his life just fled across the border. Of course, he doesn't know where she went. And I'll never tell.

I stand. "Welcome to the happy Harris row."

He crosses in front of me and debates about where he should sit. Three seats down is where he'd like to be. But that would force one of his parents to have to sit next to me. He takes one for the team and sits next to me. Our legs touch for a moment before he yanks his body to the side. He is wringing his hands. I'm not kidding.

"Is something wrong? I mean, you should be happy, it's your daughter's graduation day." I smile and pat his knee. His face is all sweaty, like he's been running around town. Which he has been. I've been following along on the app as he drove between romantic interlude spots. Of course, he kept circling back to the house, their new multimillion-dollar home. Like something would be different, this next time he drove by. Like she'd magically appear in an apron in the kitchen. Sorry, David. Your dream is dust.

"Everything's fine," he says with the enthusiasm of a man who's lost everything. But he hasn't, not yet.

"David, are we to sit with you?" Mr. Harris doesn't even greet me. He and the wife stand stiffly at the end of the row in front of us, ignoring me. Me, the one who saved them seats. Me, the one who gave them grandchildren. Well, one grandchild.

I guess they gave me the other one. And then, because of them and their son, she's now gone. I stand up and they cross in front of me, giving David polite pecks on their way in.

I glance to my right, appraise the crowd. Yes, we are drawing attention. Ah, the tragic Harris family. So much loss. So much to come.

And then I spot a surprise. What is Sam doing here? He's standing along the wall of the auditorium, close to Detective Branson. Now I'm a little concerned about him. Clearly, he wrote the third note and he thinks I hurt Cash. What else is he up to? Shouldn't he be driving people around and making money so he can better himself? I doubt he's even taking college classes. That was likely a lie. I watch him scan the crowd. Maybe he had a crush on Betsy all along. That must be it. I hope I told him enough about Bo and Josh to let him know she's not available.

Of course I did. I told him a lot. He's wasting his time being here. But who cares. The plan is in motion. The cast of characters is assembled. Sam is irrelevant. Let the fun begin.

39

Betsy is in the middle of the class: in grades, in looks, in the alphabet, in the seating inside the auditorium.

So when she walks across the stage and receives her diploma, she has a medium level of applause. She's smiling, which is unusual. She's decorated the top of her graduation cap with a big red heart, like the painting I accidentally knocked off the wall in her room. I clap and wave and take a photo. I'm the vision of the proud mom.

But she isn't looking at us, her family. I follow her smile and spot Bo leaning against the wall of the auditorium underneath the exit sign, right up front on the right side of the stage. Perhaps he's volunteering with the ceremony, but he really should have to sit down like the rest of us. Their eyes are locked on each other as Betsy steps down from the stage.

Betsy goes back to her seat in the auditorium to watch the remainder of the class procession. If she wins the award, she'll be back up on stage again, like Mary was, several times, if I recall correctly. Betsy really shouldn't get her hopes up, though. She's not a winner. That's why I snapped some photos for her to remember the good times. I look toward Bo, his casual coolness almost too much for me. He must have felt my stare and looks my way and smiles. I turn away.

Standing against the same wall as Bo, but ten rows up, Detective Branson is busy scanning the crowd. Beside him, Sam is doing the same thing. My heart thumps. I wonder what they are looking for? I mean, we are all in our assigned spots, except Bo. Perhaps the detective is positioned close enough to grab Bo if he makes a run for it. A girl can dream.

Beside me, David is frantic, restless. He's having trouble sitting still. He pulls out his phone, then puts it down. He managed to clap for poor Betsy as she walked across the stage, but then his attention was back to his phone.

"Excuse me, I have to go to the bathroom. I'll be right back." David crosses me, again, and hurries up the aisle. I need to remember to tell the Vegas police their suspect has hightailed it to Mexico. I pull out my phone and send myself a note to do that tonight. I'll send Herbert Jr. Kylie's latest location at least. I'm not sure how long the tracker will keep pinging me, and from the looks of it, she's so scared she's going to just keep driving, stopping only for gas and likely paying cash. She's not an idiot— she simply met her match when she went after my husband. Bad choice!!

On stage the principal is introducing Angelica and the other counselors who will present the special awards to select members of the senior class. This part also takes forever, if I recall. Perhaps we'll start with Arts, an A, it could happen? But it doesn't.

David reappears, slides into his seat next to me. His parents look relieved to have the buffer back, despite how lame he is. I smile at them and they both lean back in their seats as if they've seen a ghost, eyes darting away.

It occurs to me that they really are afraid of me. I actually like that. Perhaps I'll use that to my advantage someday soon. They're old. I think I told you what happens when you scare someone who has a heart condition like David Sr.'s. Huge flow of adrenaline, and you're dead. So let's say I know that David Sr. is afraid of me. What if I sneaked into their home one night, woke him up as I stand next to his bed, maybe with my favorite little knife, and he has a heart attack, would that be murder? Of course not.

I'd just come over to check on them, a worried daughter-in-law, because they hadn't answered my phone calls. Old people fall and get hurt all the time. We've all seen the television ads: *I've fallen and I can't get up.* I was worried, that's all. In the confusion of the 911 calls and the ambulance ride to the hospital, the fact I had a knife wouldn't be remembered by Mrs. Rosemary Harris, would it? No, but after he died, she'd be gone shortly after. They're actually that disgustingly committed to each other. And then David would get everything, and I'd get half of it. I lean forward and look down the aisle. Rosemary stares back at me.

If only looks could kill, Rosemary would get rid of me for sure. I smile at her and she looks away. I win.

"And now, for the Arts awards." Angelica is at the podium. This is it. Poor Betsy's probably convinced she'll win. "And the Senior Arts Scholarship winner is…" Onstage, Angelica is having trouble opening the envelope. It's like we're at the Academy Awards or something. She's the one who wrote the name inside there—she doesn't need to open the thing to know the winner, yet we all sit and wait. "Betsy Harris. Betsy, please come on up to receive your award!"

I can't believe it. My girl. An artist. She's like me. Oh my gosh, I cannot believe she won. She is a reflection of me, after all. A winner. I stand up at my seat and clap. I know that's not really allowed, but I'm so proud and surprised that I can't help myself. I love my daughter. Betsy's onstage now, so I should sit down. I look left and right, taking my bows in front of my adoring fans before sitting back down.

Angelica's arm is around Betsy's shoulders, sharing in her spotlight, the place where I should be. Betsy grins.

"Betsy, you don't even know which of your paintings won this grand prize for you, do you? Ladies and gentlemen, Betsy Harris is a prolific and talented painter. She is the first student ever to earn a perfect five on the AP art subject test. We wanted you all to experience the caliber of her work." Angelica nods and the curtain behind them opens.

Projected on a huge screen is Betsy's winning painting. My hands are shaking and I'm having trouble catching my breath.

Angelica says, "Betsy's painting titled *The Hike* is oil on canvas and depicts our spectacular Point Park nature preserve on a beautiful Southern California day. A young woman and her dog enjoying nature. It's simply breathtaking."

As the audience applauds, I gulp for air. How could she do this? Paint a picture of Mary's last few moments? Beside me, David is biting his lip. He leans over. "Is that a painting of Mary? Of Mary and Cash on that day?"

"There's something very wrong with Betsy. I've been trying to tell you this all along. She's sick." It's as if she is confessing via canvas, surely I'm not the only one who thinks so.

The applause dies and the auditorium is silent as Betsy makes her way back to her seat. There is no one in this room who doesn't know how Mary died.

Everyone is wondering if that is a painting depicting that day.

Angelica starts talking again. She's always talking, justifying, equivocating. Annoying me. She says, "As Betsy makes her way to her seat, I want to thank her for her bravery this year. She's been through a lot. Using art to express your emotions is the best way to heal. Some of us write our truths to understand ourselves better. Betsy paints them." Angelica beams. "And with that, our ceremony is concluded. Parents and family members, please meet your graduate outside on the quad. Seniors, are you ready? You're officially graduated! Enjoy the after-party! You've earned it!"

Graduation caps soar into the air as the graduating class celebrates. A cap falls into the aisle next to me with a thud.

David says, "She uses art to heal. That's all it is. And she likes that park. She says she feels free there. She misses Mary."

I stare at the evidence still projected on the screen in front of the auditorium. She's screwed.

I'm so glad our daughter had that little taste of freedom with her visits to the park. I stand up and smile at David. "Of course. That's all it is."

40

Rosemary and David Sr. push past us out of the aisle, patting David on the arm.

I know they're heading Betsy's way, toward the front of the auditorium, despite the instructions to "meet our graduate in the quad." The rules don't apply to them, they're rich and old. Entitlement in action.

Beside me, David is lost. Now I know what the word *crestfallen* looks like. He's checking his phone again. He's looking for voice mails, texts, an email, anything from Kylie: his dearly departed. He lets out a big sigh as crowds of people push past us to exit the auditorium. The graduates are exiting through Bo's door. How convenient for him. He's there, ready to scoop Betsy into his arms. Poor Bo. He doesn't understand what is in store for Betsy. Her award-winning painting is just the final gift to all of us.

"Should we go find Betsy?" David sounds like he needs a drink, his voice is scratchy with stress. I have a water bottle in my purse. But it's all mine.

I can't keep the secret to myself any longer. I turn to him, lean close to his ear and whisper, "Kylie's gone!"

His eyes pop open. It's funny, actually, the look on his face. A mixture of anguish and anger: *Anguisher?*

"What have you done?"

I created a new word. I smile. "What do you mean? What have I done?"

David grabs my wrist. It's a subtle power move, the move of a weenie. "I demand an answer. If you hurt her I swear I'll... Just tell me."

"The question is, what have *you* done? You're the last one who saw her, right?" I take a step toward the exit and he grabs the fleshy part of my arm above the elbow: The place where all bad guy actors in the movies grab the weak actress before they do something awful to her. He's no villain, though. And I'm no damsel in distress. I jerk my arm away. He grabs it again.

"I'm serious, Jane. Where is she?"

"How would I know where your lover is, darling?" I smile and tilt my head, and give him my best Kylie impersonation. "All I know is she's no longer going to be bothering me!"

I notice a few people are watching us, our escalating

fight. I'm sure it's uncomfortable for them to witness such a display of rage at what should be a happy celebration. In polite society, domestic disturbances are kept behind closed doors for everyone's benefit. But David can't hold it in any longer. I can see it in his eyes, dark and shiny. He has come undone.

Don't you dare feel sorry for him.

My arm is throbbing under his grip. I'll have a bruise. I say far too loudly, "Let go. You're hurting me!" I knew that would turn some heads. I'm a damsel in distress, in a vibrant blue dress. Ha.

A man I don't know, but one of the gentlemen who overtly appreciated my outfit earlier, stops walking and asks, "Is everything all right here?"

David drops my arm and I smile at the man, flash my best flirtatious smile.

"Yes, I'm fine now. Thank you."

"Good. Such a happy day, isn't it?" the stranger asks. He's looking at David.

David shakes his head. "Oh, yes, it's a terrific day."

It's time to get to Betsy. "Let's go find our daughter, shall we?"

"After you," the man says, walking between David and me.

I add an extra swing in my step, just for fun. I know the stranger is appreciative. I wish I could explain the happiness I feel in my heart right now. I'm coming back to life. And it's fantastic.

41

7:00 p.m.

I feel the stranger's eyes on me as he follows me out of
the auditorium. I recount all his assets as I sway my hips.
He has silver hair, I love that, an in-shape body almost
as nice as David's, and he's wearing a well-cut, expensive designer suit. A glimpse at his left hand and the bare
ring finger is encouraging for the future. Perhaps he is a
widower, or a never-married, wealthy tycoon just looking for his perfect match: me. Of course, he must be here
because a kid of his just graduated, so there is some sort
of family around, I realize. But a girl can dream.

"Have a good evening," he whispers once we're outside

in the quad. "I'll be keeping my eye on you." He slips his card between my fingers and my knees almost buckle. I need this. You have to understand, it's been a long year of grieving in my house.

"Please do," I say, tilting my head to my best camera-ready side as he disappears into the crowd.

David tries to grab my arm again, he wants to interrogate me about Kylie/Nancy, but I see Betsy. It's almost as if the crowds have parted for us and I run to her, giving her a big, final graduation hug. No one comes between me and my daughters.

"Darling, I'm so proud of you. And that painting, well, that's something, too." I'm beaming with pride, and something more, excitement.

Bo is standing next to Betsy, of course. They've probably been whispering about drinking margaritas on a deserted beach in Mexico. He shakes my hand. "Mrs. Harris, your daughter is incredible. You must be so proud."

Ick. I fake smile at him while David moves in to give Betsy a big hug. "Way to go, kiddo. Did your grandparents find you?"

"They did! And I already thanked them for their generous graduation gift! They're the best." Betsy thinks she's going to use that money to go on a big, long vacation with Bo. I can see her dreams as clearly as if they were my own.

"Oh, that's what the deposit was for. There is so much fraud these days. I wasn't sure, so I froze your account." I smile.

"You what? Dad, oh my God. I'm leaving tonight. Fix it." Betsy points her finger at me.

I chuckle because David isn't paying attention, didn't hear his own daughter. He's texting his lover. "What, honey?"

I sense another presence enter our little social cluster. And here he is, the costar of our show, Detective Branson. Cue the *Law & Order* music. "Hey, Betsy. Alan Branson. Good to see you again. Congratulations on your high school graduation."

Branson is in plain clothes. It's clear at first that Betsy doesn't have any idea who he is. Then she realizes and her eyes fly wide open. Beside me David looks like he's going to be sick. He's gawking at Branson.

"Thank you. Yeah, it's super exciting." Betsy's unnerved as she shakes the detective's hand and then turns to Bo. "We probably should get going. To the grad party."

Sam appears over Branson's shoulder. He really hasn't learned his place in life. "Hey, Betsy, congratulations." He gives Betsy a high five, and she returns it. Everyone is just so happy.

"Thanks, Sam! Nice of you to be here." Betsy is anxious to get away, I can tell. "So, um, see you all later."

"Actually, Ms. Harris, we're going to need you to come to the station with us." Branson flips out his badge, TV style, and Betsy's face crumbles.

"What? No. It's grad night. A party. Whatever it is can wait," Bo stutters. He's as shocked as Betsy that the cops are here for her. For them?

"We'd like to speak with you, too, Bo." The way Branson says his name is priceless. Like there is something distasteful on his tongue.

Oh my goodness. I'm *loving* it. I cover my mouth with my hand so no one can see me smile.

Next to me, David snaps out of his haze. "That's not happening. I'll call my lawyer. I don't know what's going on here but my daughter will enjoy her graduation party."

"Tell your lawyer to meet us at the station. Let's go, young lady." Detective Branson isn't taking no for an answer.

"Wait. I don't understand. What are you talking about? What's going on?" Betsy cries. Several heads in the crowd turn to watch us.

"It's better not to make a scene," Branson deadpans, even though he's the one who is doing this, here, now. I guess he doesn't think murderers deserve graduation parties, only diplomas.

"Dad, come with me?" Betsy is shaking now, hyperventilating. Bo's arm is around her but she just wants her daddy. How sweet.

"We have the painting, sir." A young cop trots up, carrying the original of Betsy's prizewinning art.

"Escort Bo here to the station," Branson tells the young guy, pointing to Bo. "Mrs. Harris, we'd like you to come down, too, if you don't mind?"

"Of course. That would be my pleasure." I'm thrilled to be invited to watch the rest of the story.

Standing behind Betsy, close enough to witness the drama unfold but a safe distance away, are Josh and

Sandy. His eyes are wide, his head slowly shaking back and forth. His mom holds his hand.

"What are you charging my daughter with?" David says.

"She's not being charged, sir. We want to talk to her about what happened the day Mary died. Some new evidence has come to light." Branson is cool as a cucumber.

"What? The silly notes. Ignore them. I never should have told you about them." I deliver my line perfectly and then cover my mouth again.

"No, there's more. A witness. I'll explain at the station. Let's get going."

Betsy's terrified, I can tell. I'm her mother, I know these things. "Betsy, what is going on here?" I ask, shaking my head.

"Mom, I don't know. I don't understand." Betsy is crying, tears ruin her perfect makeup. "Dad, do something!"

David is stunned as if he has been shocked in the heart, stingray style. "I'm calling the lawyer."

Betsy turns her head. Is she looking for an escape? She sees Josh. I watch him flinch and then turn away. "No. This is crazy. I didn't kill Mary. I loved Mary. Bo was there, he knows."

Bo nods. "I was."

Did Branson roll his eyes, or was I imagining it? "Of course you were, son. And so was our witness. So many boyfriends, so little time. But the thing is, she wasn't with either of you the whole time, was she? No, there was plenty of time for a big shove."

With that, Branson has his hand on Betsy's back and he's pushing and walking her through the crowd.

By now, everyone has stopped talking. All eyes are on us, my little family imploding again. I suck in my stomach, keep my eyes on the ground. I'm so glad I wore this dress. I follow behind Betsy, Bo and David. We're in a single file line on our way to the finish line.

Focus, Jane.

Betsy is crying, big sobs shake her body. Bo is trying to comfort her while looking bug-eyed and terrified. David's on the phone, no doubt talking to the expensive attorney we used before, when the cloud of suspicion briefly hung over us, before the death was ruled a tragic accident. Or maybe he's calling Kylie. Who knows?

David grabs hold of Betsy, pulling her into his arms. "Mr. Jones will meet us there. Don't worry. This is all a big mistake." They're hugging in front of the police car, like idiots. What a photo op. Want to look guilty? Hug as you get in the back of a police car. That shot will explode social media. They won't be able to escape it. Ever. As I watch students take the shot on their phones, I keep my back to the crowd.

"One of you can ride with Betsy and Officer Trippit. The other two can ride with me." Branson opens the squad car door.

"Dad. Please. Come with me." Betsy's losing control, she's breathing funny. Maybe a panic attack? She could get that from me, I suppose. She sits down on the back seat while her dad walks around to the other side of the squad car. Another great guilty-looking photo op.

I have to tell her something. I look around, make sure most of the kids already recorded their video. I lean down, close to Betsy's triple-pierced ear. "Pull yourself together. People are watching. You overcame your fear of heights to go up there with Mary, and do what you did. You must be good at self-control sometimes, although from your choice in men, I'd say most of the time you aren't."

I stand up, and I'm about to close the door to the squad car, when Betsy screams. She points at me. "You did this. You gave them the letter. How could you?"

No, dear, it's how could you? I close the door to muffle the ridiculous accusations. I mean, come on. Who are you going to believe? A teenage almost runaway with tattoos and nose piercings or me? A girl who has always been jealous of her prettier, smarter and more accomplished older sister? It's so hard when you aren't the favorite daughter, I'm sure. Of course, you wouldn't believe her, but you would believe a poor grieving mother suffering from complicated grief who gave everything she had to her daughters to assure their happy home.

I peek into the back of the squad car. Poor Betsy can't open the door from the inside, and David's side is closed, too. Both of them are trapped, pointing at me, hugging each other.

Detective Branson hits the side of the squad car and it pulls out from the curb. Roll the credits. A drone shot starts on the back of the squad car and turns to a quick close-up of my sad face, flies into a wide shot, taking in the high school, the seniors turning back to the celebration at hand, and then higher over the coastline and the ocean, finally passing over Point Park and fading to black.

Great flick.

"Let's head over to the station, Mrs. Harris. I know this must be so hard for you." Alan turns to me and sees a mom who's now lost two daughters, a gorgeous woman in a tight dress, standing all alone at the curb.

I sigh, wipe the pretend tear from under my eye. "I'm just in shock."

"You told me there was more to the story, that note proved it. Turns out you were right. How'd you know?" Branson studies me, a little too closely. "I mean, had you seen her painting? That was really disturbing."

"No, that was the first time I'd seen it." The truth. I step back from him. "A mother's instinct, I suppose. I just didn't want to believe the truth, even when it was right in front of me."

"It happens. Well, let's go. Um, Bo, you're coming with us?" Detective Branson hurries across the street to his unmarked nondescript car. I slide into the front seat. Bo can ride in the back like the criminal he is.

I blink my eyes and feel the same attraction shoot between us from a year ago. I have him right where I want him. How wonderful. I give him the gift of my warmest smile. "Thank you, for driving me, Alan." Behind me I hear Bo on his phone. I don't know who he's speaking with, but he should be careful. Branson is listening, and so am I.

We drive in comfortable silence, except for Bo's "uh-huh, uh-huh," until we pull up to the police station.

Branson gets out of the car and comes around, opening my door and then Bo's. Bo is out of the car, hurrying
toward the front door, before I even step out of the squad
car. Branson extends his hand, helping me. So chivalrous.

"Say, Mrs. Harris, did you walk your dog the day Mary
died or was he with Mary all day?"

"Gosh, I can't remember. That day is such a blur, such
a terrible memory." I am not lying.

"Okay, well, think about it and let me know if you remember anything. You told us during your interview the
dog was with Mary all day until security brought the poor
fellow home." Branson tips his hat and I follow him up
the walkway to the station door.

Why is he so concerned about my late dog all of a
sudden?

It's probably nothing.

The cruiser carrying distraught David and about-to-
be-behind-bars Betsy is empty at the curb. She's probably being booked, or whatever it is they do with suspects
these days. I feel nothing but proud of myself, for brilliant
alliteration and much more. My plan worked flawlessly.

My future in LA is bright, and even brighter if Mr.
Gray Hair wants to come along. I'll try to write some
more of my story for you, but I'm going to be so busy,
it's best we just end our chats here. Stay out of trouble.
And always remember, the opposite of love is hate despite
what they say, respect your mother's wishes and never,
ever cheat on your spouse.

The End.

42

11:00 p.m.

I said The End.

Oh, what now?
I'm finished.
Moving on.

"Let's go inside." Branson holds the door open and I step inside the police station. I don't see any of my family.

"Let's go to the conference room down the hall. Bo,

have a seat. Someone will be here for you in a minute," Branson says.

That's right. I deserve a conference room. Bo is an accessory or something. He should sit out there in an uncomfortable guilty chair. Waiting.

As we walk down the dingy hall, I smile. Betsy is about to be put behind bars for a very long time. David will be destroyed by the loss of both Kylie and his only daughter.

Branson pushes on a metal door and in we go. It's cold and a dirty yellow color in here. I would have preferred the waiting area where Bo sits.

"Why am I in here?" I ask.

"I need to tell you your husband has been rushed to the hospital. Potential heart attack. His mother rode with him in the squad. I'm sorry. They tell me he's going to be fine."

"Well, I need to go to him." I stand up, grateful for an excuse to get out of this place. Rosemary went with her son to the hospital, I'm sure demanding the best heart specialists and the best room for her baby. She really makes me sick. I wonder what her weakness is besides her son. Will his death be enough to ruin her, too? We'll see.

I didn't know until recently that David suffered from the same heart problems as David Sr., although who couldn't have guessed that? David's young at forty-four, but still, almost thirty thousand people in the US will die suddenly this year of circulatory system diseases. He's been through so much stress and done so many bad things, am I right? I mean, he destroyed our home, our perfect family.

"Sit down, please, Mrs. Harris. Your husband is stable. They have him under observation. Probably just anxiety. Again, sit down, Mrs. Harris," Branson commands.

I don't like his tone. But I sit.

The door opens and a bedraggled-looking David Sr. shuffles in. Branson pulls out a chair across from me. We stare at each other in silence.

"I'll be back shortly. Betsy's attorney is with her now." Branson is gone.

How long will we be forced to sit in this ugly conference room, my father-in-law and me, waiting for an update from our attorney? I imagine Bo has come and gone, advised to find a lawyer and not to leave town. So much for their romantic escape.

I wish I had the chance to change into something a bit more comfortable before I came down to the station but I didn't give it any thought. I was too excited about today's events unfolding to shove a change of clothes in my bag. I won't be here long. I mean, a sexy dress can only be attractive for a few hours. After it has served its purpose, the dress should be slowly slipped off your shoulders and dropped to the floor by a handsome stranger with silver hair as you sip champagne in an oceanfront mansion at sunset. And if that doesn't happen, it becomes completely uncomfortable.

I drum my fingernails on the cheap metal table, hoping to get my father-in-law's attention, or at least bother him a little. He's motionless, eyes down. A lump of despair.

Branson's back. "Mrs. Harris, can we speak with you?"

He looks exhausted, too. He's not even squeezed into a tight dress.

"Of course." I stand and David Sr. looks at the ground.

"Sir, can I have a squad car drive you to the hospital to go see your son? There's nothing you can do for Betsy right now. Her attorney is here. She will be fine." Branson is so nice.

David Sr. has tears in his eyes. "Yes. Okay. But if Betsy needs anything, you'll call me?"

"Yes, sir," Branson says as David Sr. shuffles to the door of the conference room.

They're acting like Betsy's mother isn't standing right here. "I'll be here for Betsy." My father-in-law shakes his head and keeps walking. Branson shuts the door behind him and we're alone. No doubt he's been planning this all evening. It's just me and Alan.

I bat my eyelashes and swing my leg so he can see my high heel, my thigh. Sharon Stone comes to mind. No, I'm not that naughty. "So tell me, what are you charging Betsy with? Is it involuntary manslaughter? Like a crime of passion thing? They were fighting a lot that week, my girls. It's been tough their whole lives because Mary was good at everything she did and, well, poor Betsy. You can't imagine how difficult it was raising the two of them, trying not to always point out Mary's superiority. Betsy can be very hard to love. But I can't believe Betsy took sibling rivalry this far." I smile, but then tuck it away. This is serious stuff.

Branson says, "Josh told me you and Betsy fought a

lot, too. And you and Mary argued. Josh said you weren't very nice to the girls, from what he saw."

He is such a weenie. "What? He didn't even come to our house. I didn't even know they'd broken up, that's how much I saw him. He doesn't know anything." Oh, except, I can't undermine Josh. "But he knows what he saw that day in the park."

"Sort of," Branson says. "Josh saw Betsy, consoled her on the trail, before she met Mary."

I know that's true, I saw them hugging on the trail.

"Mary showed up a little later. She had the dog with her," he says.

Sounds right. "Yes. I know now she was trying to make Betsy break things off with Bo. Totally inappropriate relationship."

"Yes, Betsy agrees her sister wanted her to stop seeing Bo."

Mary was such a good girl. Except.

"Mary disobeyed you. She started a relationship with her birth mother, a relationship you forbade, is that true?"

Betsy is such a tattletale. "I was upset, yes. I'm Mary's mother. Not that woman."

"Were you in Point Park the day Mary died?" Branson looks at me.

I look up at the mirrored wall behind his head and wonder who else is watching. "Do I need an attorney? Are you accusing me of something? Can you get Mr. Jones over here? Who's watching me from behind that mirror?"

Branson strums his fingers on the table. "Mr. Jones is

Betsy's attorney. You'll need your own. Or you can just answer the question."

"No. I told you I wasn't at the park. I was home all day." I swallow. I feel like he's accusing me of something.

"Is that a fact?" Alan leans forward and cracks his knuckles. So irritating.

"It is. I'd like to go now."

"Not so fast, Mrs. Harris. What if I tell you there is video footage of you dropping your dog, Cash, off at the back gate of the next community over from The Cove on the day you swore you were home all day? Would you be surprised? Actually, as you know, it was more violent than just dropping the poor dog off. I have a video of you shoving the poor dog out of your car without stopping, on the day Mary died. What would you say about that?"

"Wrong. I didn't do that. I would never hurt Cash." I glare at Alan. How dare he accuse me of such cruelty? Besides, he knows I was home all day. They've already investigated all of this. Case closed.

"Well, I just got to thinking. That was a far way for the pup to travel with a leash on without getting tangled up. And he came home pretty fast, as I recall, before Betsy, before anyone else. It was almost like someone had him in her car, and then realized it would make her look guilty. Are you following me?"

"No. It didn't happen."

"So I went over to Diamond Bay security office. Asked one of my buddies there if I could watch their video from that day. Lucky, 'cause if I'd been just another month later, they would have taped over the footage."

I meet his eyes. "You're seeing things. I was at home. Waiting for Cash and Mary to come home from their hike."

Branson shakes his head. "It's a good thing Sam was paying attention during your little drives. He tipped me off about the dog. My nephew is smart. Going to make a good detective someday."

My face tries to register surprise, so I cover it with my hands. Sam? Alan's nephew? "Are you talking about Lyft Sam?"

"Yes, Sam Branson, my brother's boy. He's studying criminal psychology in school. Can't wait to have him join the force. He's done great work on this case. Observant. He was worried you might hurt Betsy before we could bring you all in today."

"Sam doesn't know anything about me." I wrap my arms around myself and lean back. "I'm done here."

Branson leans forward. "Mary and Betsy didn't talk for long. Mary wanted Betsy to come home with her, but Betsy wanted to stay and hang out with Bo. Mary decided to blow off steam, go for a hike on her own, as you know. Betsy and Bo were together in a different part of the park when Mary died."

"Oh, really? How convenient. Betsy has such a vivid imagination. Always has. She's hard to trust. I'm sure Bo is the same type." I shake my head. "You can't tell me you're going to believe that guy about anything."

"He has photos. Selfies of the two of them. I'll get forensics involved, but it was one of their first dates, and the first time they'd, well, you know, messed around."

Branson taps the table again. "They didn't come forward last year, for obvious reasons. The photos are geo-tagged and time-stamped. It fits. We didn't know about Bo and Betsy's relationship during our initial investigation. But now we know all about him. And we believe him. He has a lot to lose by confessing to a relationship with a student, but he came forward because he loves your daughter."

"Oh, my. Poor Betsy. He's a predator. I want to press charges. She needs to be protected from him. Arrest him immediately, Alan." I bat my eyes and lower my head, a grieving mother of a victimized daughter.

"We'll deal with Bo. Right now, I'm focused on you." He flashes me a big smile. He does want a date.

"Okay, I'm listening." A chill runs down my spine.

He leans forward again, palms on the table. "I'm thinking you were there. I think you followed one or both of your daughters to the park that day. You weren't just furious with Mary. You were fighting with Betsy, too, right?"

"I didn't know about Bo then." My face flushes, but I tamp down the anger percolating in my veins.

"No, but I'm sure you were mad about something else. You have an anger issue, Jane. You spy on your girls. Try to control them. You play mind games to keep your daughters off balance, confused. Dependent on you. It fits a pattern I've seen before, your type of personality. Personality disorder, that is."

"No, that's not true." I stand up, tired of this talk, of this blue dress, of this ugly conference room. "I'm going home."

"Not yet, Jane. What did you do to Kylie Dorn?" Branson asks. "Did you hurt her?"

Okay, that's it. I lean forward, meet his stare. "You mean Nancy Finch? That's her real name. She's alive and well somewhere in Mexico. You people are so stupid sometimes. She's a wanted criminal, a check forger, and she's been waltzing around in our community. I did us all a favor. I'll tell you where she is and you can arrest her. Look, I'm a hero. I'm tracking her." I hold out my phone and open the app. I'm just about to show him where Nancy/Kylie is but Branson stands up.

I watch as he nods his head and the conference room door bursts open. I'm suddenly part of a low-budget cable-TV cop show. Three uniformed officers swarm in, one on each side of me and the other blocks the door.

I watch Branson's lips moving but I can't hear anything, not really. Time is slipping or something is. Everything is hazy. I sit down.

He taps the table. "Your Kylie story better hold, Jane, because I'm starting to realize most everything you say is a lie."

"Wrong. I'm the one who has been wronged here." I can't believe this.

"Jane Harris, you are a suspect in the murder of your daughter Mary Harris. You have the right to remain blah, blah, blah."

He finally stops talking and it's my turn.

"Look, you were right the first time. It was a tragic, awful accident. Mary slipped, that's all. I mean, she was too close to the edge. About seventy-eight Americans die every year falling from cliffs." I turn on the tears. My knees give out and the officers on either side of me catch my fall, helping me into a chair.

"We know you were there, Jane. You followed your daughters, I bet you tracked them like a predator hunting her prey. In this case, your own flesh and blood. We've been working the case again, thanks to Sam's instincts. We've been digging around, and we found a new witness, Jane, someone who spotted you on the closed trail. She didn't come forward before, because like most of society, she could never imagine a mother hurting her own child. None of us could. She thought she was mistaken, that it couldn't have been you running down the trail with the dog. But it was."

"How *Law & Order* of you. A mysterious new witness? How convenient," I blurt, but my heart is racing as my memory flashes to a woman jogger.

Focus, Jane. Get yourself under control. He knows nothing. You know I'm innocent.

I fold my arms across my chest, and stop the tears. I will pivot, I'm a master of it. I match his steely gaze. "So what if I was there? Maybe I was the one trying to get Mary away from the edge. I barely saved the dog. I couldn't save Mary. It was her fault. I tried. Maybe it was just a horrible accident."

My mind reminds me of all the tragic deaths from falling over a cliff. The Grand Canyon claims twelve people a year. There is danger everywhere. I look up, and for some reason, Betsy, David and Bo are now in the room. I thought she was locked up, David was dying of a heart attack and Bo was packing his car, preparing to run away to avoid prosecution. This is disconcerting.

Bo's arm is around Betsy's waist, a gutsy show of affection to display in front of me. How dare he. David's face is ashen. I really thought he died. He should have. His blood pressure must be so high. Those little pills he's been taking for the past two days weren't what the cardiologist prescribed. Once he carried Kylie over the threshold, I swapped the pills. Who knew how much he needed them? Shame I didn't have a couple more days.

"How could you? You killed our daughter?" David mumbles. He doesn't look good. There's still hope.

Does he really think I'll answer him? Incriminate myself. I'm not stupid. He should know that by now. He should shut up. "I didn't do anything. Mary's death was a tragic accident. You really shouldn't air our dirty laundry in public, David. Do you want me to tell them all about you and Kylie? Or how about all the abuse I've suffered? He hits me!" I point at David to give my accusation extra weight.

"No, I don't." David glares at me like he wishes he could take a swing at me, proving my point.

I smile at Detective Branson. "You should arrest him for spousal abuse, Detective. I need a restraining order, at the very least."

Betsy takes a step closer to me. "I felt sorry for you after Mary died. I still didn't like you, but I tolerated you. But now I know you're sick. And you're dangerous." Betsy is shaking again. It's not even cold in here. "You spied on us. Thank goodness Mary found out right before she died. She put it together. The only way you found out about Elizabeth was by spying on Mary's texts, emails. You're awful."

"It's not spying when it's your own kids. All parents do it," I say to my ungrateful daughter.

"And all kids who have spying parents figure out how to get around you. Did you know there are all types of encrypted texting apps, Mom, not just the one your spyware traces?" Betsy says.

Bo pulls Betsy closer to his side. "Thank goodness you insisted on that."

I glare at them. "I would have stopped him, that's for sure. Arrest him for statutory rape! My daughter's in high school."

"I'm eighteen years old, Mom. And I'm finally free from you."

"Oh, what a bunch of hooey." She's so full of crap. I point at my daughter. I know they all realize she's guilty. "She was with Mary before she died. That's why she painted Mary and Cash on the hike. That was just before Betsy killed her sister. It's creepy. That must be why it's so bad. It's like a confession."

Betsy leans against the predator, Bo. "Deep down I knew you are pure evil."

I look up at my daughter, the daughter who shares my same eye color, my hair color, my only biological creation. I brought you into this world and I can take you out of it. My mom loved that line, too, or am I only imagining it.

"Your subconscious wanted you to confess. It's okay,

Betsy. We're here to support you. I'll visit you all the time in prison."

Betsy glares. "I don't ever want to see you again."

"How silly. I'm your mom. Our bond is forever. It would help if you had talent, something I could be proud of when it comes to you. I still can't believe you won an award for that ugly painting. The teachers must have felt sorry for you."

Betsy smiles, like she's in control. That's disconcerting.

She leans forward, stares me in the eyes. She never does that. "But you see, Mom, I was with Bo. We have photos together. Poor Mary. The last person she had to see on earth was you. And you pushed her off the cliff. Terrifying."

I stand up and lunge at my thankless daughter's throat but the two officers grab my wrists.

Betsy, Bo and David jump like startled babies as I scream, "She's a liar! They both are lying! They all are."

Betsy doesn't seem to be afraid of me right now. She should be, stupid girl.

"No, Mom, we aren't lying. You know it. Everyone here knows it. A new witness has come forward placing you at the park that day and they have the video of you abusing poor Cash. I mean, you're the one who wanted the investigation opened up for some reason, I guess so the cops would come after me for Mary's death, and now you've been caught in your own trap." Betsy shakes her head, still trembling, weak.

"You should be quiet now, Betsy." I know she's afraid of the evil-eye look I just gave her, I've trained her well.

For some reason, though, she keeps talking. "Of course you showed up that day at the park. Of course you followed us. You must have loved the fact Mary and I were fighting. She didn't understand the peace I'd found with Bo. I didn't understand why she'd start a relationship with her birth mother when you were enough to deal with. We would have worked through it all, if you hadn't killed her."

I shake my head. I'm pivoting again. "Both of you were out of control. I was trying to help, that's all, but I wasn't at the park. I never go there." I look around the room, trying to find the camera.

"You're lying. You always lie. Mary and I were pawns in your sick world. Home was never happy. Your only goal was to tear us down, make us dependent on you. We were always afraid, always wrong and never sure why. I knew you never loved us, especially me. But I never imagined you'd be capable of this." Betsy shakes as David wraps his arm around her shoulders.

David blurts, "My God, I'm so sorry. I should have moved out sooner, taken you with me." He looks like his heart may be seizing up again, he's gray, shaking.

"You are pathetic. Both of you. I'm the only one who really loved Mary. I knew what was best for her." Even if what was best meant pushing her over the edge of that cliff. I look into Betsy's eyes. I whisper, "You're my only daughter now, my only focus. But you're such a disappointment. Maybe you should join Mary? I'll help."

Betsy screams. A sound much more appropriate for a horror film, not in this claustrophobic conference room. She needs to learn a bit about acting. I glare at her.

"Take her away," Branson says as I shake my head yes in agreement.

"Goodbye, Betsy. I hope you make friends in there. I'll visit." I look at the detective. "It will be good for her. She always was such a difficult child, hard to love. Not almost perfect like Mary."

Something isn't right. I look around and everyone is staring at me. Perhaps I got my lines wrong? I never do that. "What?"

Detective Branson's eyes are steely, dark. "I really can't believe you'd kill your own daughter. Only a monster would do such a thing."

I meet his eyes. I flutter my eyelashes, then rethink that and start to cry. Someone yanks me to standing and now I'm weeping loudly as they force handcuffs on my wrists.

"Of course I wouldn't do something like that, Detective, you know me. No one loved Mary more than I did. My husband cheats on me and my daughter is about to run away with a teacher and she tells lies about me. I've suffered so much. Don't you see what they've done to me? I'm innocent. I demand to talk to my lawyer."

They're leading me down a dingy hall, but I'm not worried. I know I'll get out of this mess in no time. Mark my words. I'm smarter than all of them. Besides, I still have so much more to do. I need to visit Elizabeth, put her in her place. Find Mr. Gray Hair and flirt. Take all of David's money through divorce, among other things. My new head shots are going to be great.

This isn't the end.

EPILOGUE

I'd do anything for Mary but share her.

I said that from the beginning, but apparently, no one took it seriously.

A mother's love is singular, all encompassing.

There is no sharing.

I loved her the most. Period.

She was the favorite daughter.

Wherever she is, I hope she understands.

I doubt I'll ever get to explain things to her.

I'll be in a different place. Not here.

They'll never be able to keep me here.

I'm street smart and beautiful. I'll hire the best lawyer.

I'll be back in Hollywood soon.

I'm destined to be a star.

* * * * *

DEAR READER LETTER

Years ago, just after my family and I moved to the West Coast, I was lucky to become friends with an amazing woman, Malibu City Council member and clinical psychologist Laura Rosenthal. As you may have guessed, Laura is the inspiration for the doctor character in THE FAVORITE DAUGHTER. One evening Laura joined us for dinner on a night my husband and I were discussing the baffling character traits of someone we knew. We just couldn't figure this person out.

"Well, that sounds like a classic narcissist," Laura said.

At that, the light bulb turned on and it has been shining brightly in both my imagination, and in real life, ever since.

Maybe you're more aware of this than I was, but narcissists are everywhere in our society. Some estimate narcissists comprise 10 percent of the population and experts believe access to social media is creating more: Selfies are a narcissist's best friend.

Although it may seem terrifying to some that I enjoy getting inside the heads of these types of people in my most recent novels, to me, it's cathartic. Since first learning about narcissists from Laura all those years ago, I've somehow become blessed with a superpower: I can spot a narcissist. I'm not sure it's a gift or a curse, but it's true.

I also enjoy writing stories with unreliable narrators, and Jane Harris, like Paul Strom in BEST DAY EVER, is at her core a very unreliable person, among other things. These characters are obsessed with perception. Everything they show to the world is carefully calculated to portray perfection, even in their marriages, even when their lives may be falling apart. Narcissists suffer from a self-esteem problem coupled with low empathy. Failure is unacceptable, especially with their family, where they expect unflinching loyalty and subservience. Grandiose self-worth, vanity and entitlement are the foundation of the disorder. When any of this is challenged, rage is the result.

A special, terrifying subset of narcissist are those called "malignant narcissists." Erich Fromm first coined the term in 1964 to describe the "quintessence of evil." Some of the most difficult narcissists to spot are malignant narcissists who are mothers. She often gets away with her abuse because she is unseen to all but those she controls, her children, and no one wants to imagine a mother could be the monster in her own home.

No one wants to imagine that, except as a starting point for a novel, perhaps.

I asked my friend Laura if therapy works with narcissists. Her answer: It's a pretty tough one to fix because they cannot see themselves for who they are and cannot take responsibility. When things go wrong they blame other people, so therapy is tough. They aren't motivated to change. They like themselves just the way they are.

I hope you enjoyed Jane's story. She wants you to believe she is the perfect mother, a loving wife, a connected and compassionate member of her community. Did she convince you? And who is her favorite daughter?

Thanks for reading,
Kaira

ACKNOWLEDGMENTS

Thanks to you, the reader, who makes this job of my dreams a reality. I hope you enjoyed the story.

To the book clubs, book bloggers, reviewers, bookstagrammers and Facebook groups—across the globe—who support authors like me, thank you. Your words and stunning photos provide the energy books need to make it into readers' hands.

Thank you to my team at Graydon House, Harlequin and HarperCollins. It has been an unbelievable honor to bring this new imprint to life with you. A special shout-out to my editors, Margo Lipschultz, Melanie Fried, Charlotte Mursell and, especially, Michele Bidelspach: sometimes it takes a village. This book did! My heartfelt thanks, too, to Lisa Wray for her thoughtful guidance and support. And to Katie Shea Boutillier for making this possible.

Special thanks to Andrea Katz, Nancy Stopper, Ann Marie Nieves, and to my beta readers Elizabeth Paulsen, Tijana Hamilton and Melissa Cavanaugh. To my husband, Harley: I couldn't do this without you and I'm so proud of you for being the change.

And, finally, a note to anyone wondering if it's too late to pursue the life of your dreams: it's not. Go for it. Only you have the power to make your dreams come true. This book is one of mine. And for that, I'm so grateful.

READER'S GROUP DISCUSSION QUESTIONS

1. We're all unreliable narrators of our personal stories, whether we're comfortable admitting it or not. For example, most of us are on social media, where we share our filtered and carefully curated version of our lives. The perfect couple. The perfect day. A perfect illusion. Is Jane Harris that much different?

2. Does Jane have a favorite daughter? Why or why not?

3. At the beginning of the story, Jane tells us she's working on being a better mother, a better spouse. Is she trying to fool you, the reader, or herself?

4. Was Elizabeth James attempting to "steal" Mary from Jane?

5. In our society, we elevate and treasure mothers, almost to a point where the ideal of what a mother should be obscures the actual reality of who she is. Do you think that's part of how Jane was able to keep her true self hidden for so long? Was it hard for you to imagine a mother who isn't what she seems?

6. Betsy is a step ahead of Jane in this story. Is she just like her mom, as Jane claims? Or has Betsy become Jane's complete opposite?

7. Do you feel at all sorry for Jane? Why?

8. Did Kylie get what she deserved?

9. What do you think of David and his relationships with women?

ONE PLACE. MANY STORIES

Bold, innovative and
empowering publishing.

FOLLOW US ON:

@HQStories